PENGUIN BOOKS

Sonata for Miriam

LINDA OLSSON was born in Stockholm, Sweden. She graduated from the University of Stockholm with a bachelor of law degree, then pursued a career in banking and finance until she left Sweden in 1986. She has lived in Kenya, Singapore, Britain, and Japan and has been a permanent resident in New Zealand since 1990. In 1993 she completed a bachelor of arts in English and German literature at Victoria University of Wellington. In 2003 she won the *Sunday Star-Times* Short Story Competition. She currently lives in Auckland, and she is the author of the novel *Astrid & Veronika*.

Sonata for Miriam

LINDA OLSSON

PENGUIN BOOKS

PENGUIN BOOKS

Published by the Penguin Group

Penguin Group (USA) Inc., 375 Hudson Street, New York, New York 10014, U.S.A.
Penguin Group (Canada), 90 Eglinton Avenue East, Suite 700, Toronto,
Ontario, Canada M4P 2Y3 (a division of Pearson Penguin Canada Inc.)
Penguin Books Ltd, 80 Strand, London WC2R 0RL, England
Penguin Ireland, 25 St Stephen's Green, Dublin 2, Ireland (a division of Penguin Books Ltd)
Penguin Group (Australia), 250 Camberwell Road, Camberwell, Victoria 3124, Australia
(a division of Pearson Australia Group Pty Ltd)
Penguin Books India Pvt Ltd, 11 Community Centre, Panchsheel Park,
New Delhi - 110 017, India
Penguin Group (NZ), 67 Apollo Drive, Rosedale, North Shore 0632, New Zealand
(a division of Pearson New Zealand Ltd)
Penguin Books (South Africa) (Pty) Ltd, 24 Sturdee Avenue, Rosebank,
Johannesburg 2196, South Africa

Penguin Books Ltd, Registered Offices:
80 Strand, London WC2R 0RL, England

First published in Penguin Books (New Zealand) 2008
Published in Penguin Books (USA) 2009

1 3 5 7 9 10 8 6 4 2

Grateful acknowledgment is made for permission to reprint excerpts
from the following copyrighted works:
"A Lesson in Silence" by Tymoteusz Karpowicz, translated by Czeslaw Milosz.
Copyright © the Czeslaw Milosz Estate. By permission of the Czeslaw Milosz Estate.
"The Wall" and "A Voice" by Tadeusz Rozewicz, translated by Czeslaw Milosz.
Copyright © 1965 the Czeslaw Milosz Estate. By permission of Tadeusz Rozewicz
and the Czeslaw Milosz Estate.

Publisher's Note
This is a work of fiction. Names, characters, places, and incidents either are the
product of the author's imagination or are used fictitiously, and any resemblance
to actual persons, living or dead, business establishments, events,
or locales is entirely coincidental.

LIBRARY OF CONGRESS CATALOGING-IN-PUBLICATION DATA
Olsson, Linda.
Sonata for Miriam / Linda Olsson.
p. cm.
ISBN 978-0-14-311470-3
1. Fathers and daughters—Fiction. 2. Daughters—Death—Psychological aspects—
Fiction. 3. Bereavement—Fiction. 4. Psychological fiction. I. Title.
PR9639.4.O47S66 2009
823'.92—dc22   2008015624

Printed in the United States of America

For Max, Felix, and André

But words must be found,
for besides words there is almost nothing.

—SZYMON LAKS,
from the overture to *Music of Another World*

Sonata for Miriam

A Lesson of Silence

Whenever a butterfly
happened to fold
too violently its wings—
there was a call: silence, please!

As soon as one feather
of a startled bird
jostled against a ray—
there was a call: silence, please!

In that way were taught
how to walk without noise
the elephant on his drum,
man on his earth.

The trees were rising
mute above the fields
as rises the hair
of the horror-stricken.

—TYMOTEUSZ KARPOWICZ,
translated by CZESŁAW MIŁOSZ

I

1

Now I am here, in Kraków, where my life began. I stand on my small balcony looking out over the Vistula, ready for my morning walk.

It is spring, a mild and sunny day, with the gentle, filtered light of the Old World. It is kind, or perhaps just collaborating by throwing gauze over the memories, mine and those of this city. I can't see very far—there is a slight haze that consumes the river and the landscape beyond. On days like today, when the weather allows, I usually walk along Planty Park, sometimes stopping to sit on a bench for a while. In the morning I am often the only person there, watching the stream of people on their way to work and the crowded streetcars in the street beyond. In the afternoon the benches are filled with people: old men leaning on their canes, students reading, couples kissing, mothers with prams, people walking their dogs. But there are no joggers, no skateboarders. There is a serene, dignified quality about the park and about the people who occupy it.

I am here now, in this city where I was born. Kraków. And I am at peace. I think you can understand, Cecilia. You have found a place where you are at peace, haven't you? Here I am surrounded by life. By sounds. And I no longer feel outside. Although I have few friends here, I am filled with a sense of belonging. Yes, peace, I think.

After all these years, I have finally decided to separate my work from my home and have rented a studio in the old town, above one of the music stores. I share it with a group of younger musicians, but they have their own space and we get along well. I enjoy the thought of having young people nearby. It's interesting how quiet the process of making music has become. Not a sound escapes their studio, other than on Fridays when they have friends around for drinks before they leave in the evening. Our music is trapped inside our computers, our studios, and our heads.

Perhaps I am a trifle early today—the park is even quieter than usual. I don't sleep well, and I get up when I wake, sometimes very early. I no longer carry a watch—there is nothing that requires me to keep the exact time. I try to live with my body, allowing it to decide the pace. When I pass the church, I am surprised to see that it's only just after seven. The light is different from what I had expected, so I walk a bit longer than I usually do, down the eastern side, before I stop and sit on a bench to wait for the sun to reach above the trees. I watch the rays that thread through the new foliage, painting a flickered pattern on the ground. My eyes fall on the gravel by my feet. There is little litter in this city. Perhaps it is not yet prosperous enough to afford to discard much. But here on the ground, just by the toe of my shoe, there is a hair clip. I bend forward and pick up the small metal object. I put it on the palm of my hand and close my fingers around it.

And I remember another hair clip.

The memories come gushing back, competing for my attention. Strangely, I remember in reflection. Not the original event but the memory of it a year after it occurred. Perhaps this convoluted process allows some sort of understanding of the incomprehensible. I don't know. But it's my own earlier thoughts, triggered by another hair clip, that fill me. That, and the remembered sound of my daughter's voice. Our daughter's voice.

I remember the silence, too. The selective silence before and the total silence that came after. Silence was imposed on me from the very beginning, and I lived with it until it became my own. There were no answers, so there was no place for questions. Thinking about it now, it seems extraordinary that I was so accepting. That I lived for almost sixty years in such a deafening silence and eventually came to make it my own.

Sound is not always the opposite of silence. There can be sound over a gulf of silence, disguising it. Perhaps that is how it was with my music. I created it to hide the silence.

When did I begin to listen for the sounds? To hear the elusive voices whose absence had been at the center of my existence, like a blind spot in my eye?

I can take one individual note out of the music I am trying to write at the moment, and it could belong anywhere. Yet where it sits, where I have placed it, it follows what came before and leads to what comes after. Without it the whole would not be as it is. As the composer I must know each individual note in order to make the whole. Like the colors on an artist's palette, on their own the notes are absolute, yet when they are placed in a particular work, their individuality becomes one with the whole. They have to be chosen for what they are—red, yellow, blue—but with the effect of their combined potential in mind. It is necessary to know the parts in order to make up the whole. It applies to music, to art, and to life itself, I think. When you listen to the finished composition, or when you go about living your life, the individual components join to make a whole that can so easily be taken for granted. But it is not until you become aware of the parts that you can begin to understand the miracle. It took me almost a lifetime to start searching for the sounds, the notes that make my life's music. And it required a sacrifice so enormous that it did away with all that had made my life meaningful. But in the total silence that came afterward, I finally heard a first single note, and others slowly followed.

The individual note that began this music was the day I decided to take a walk in the Auckland Domain, although I didn't understand it at the time. As I parked my bike in the lot below the museum and stood to take in the bright February sun flooding a landscape without shadows, I had no idea of the terrible significance the day would come to hold.

No, that is not quite correct. I want to be precise. It was set in motion earlier that same morning. It began with the voice of my daughter.

Memories are unreliable. I carry memories that are now so worn I can't possibly tell if they are accurate. I'm sure they have been shaped by my handling. My obsessive dwelling on some of them. Added to those are memories that were kept for me by others and given to me after such a long time. I have no way of judging their accuracy but have to accept them as given and try to incorporate them with my own. Together they contribute to giving me a kind of past. A patchwork of pieces: some I have made myself, others I been given, yet others I have found by chance. There are holes where the missing pieces will never be found. At this point the overall pattern is emerging, yet the interpretation remains elusive.

I am here now, in this city that has been a silent backdrop to my life. In Kraków. Unlike Mr. Liebermann, with whom I play chess every Thursday, I am not hoping to meet anybody. That is not why I live here. No, perhaps it is the opposite. And if that is so . . . well, then perhaps this is not where I will stay forever. But for now it is the right place. I am working. I think. I allow myself to remember. I remember those I love, and in that sense they are here, too.

Get out, Dad. Have an adventure. It's Saturday!

If I had listened more carefully, would I have been able to hear more? Could I have heard it in the lingering sweetness of the final bars of the music that was playing in the background? Seen it in the light that washed over my daughter's face? In the graceful movement of her hand? Tasted it in the bitter flavors of the coffee?

Should I have known that this scene, in its everyday triviality, would become the shimmering crescendo of the memories on which I now sustain a sort of life?

2

That is where my brain wants to go, and I allow it. On this bench in a park on the other side of the earth. I close my hand around the small hair clip, and in an instant I am back on the deck of my home at Waiheke Island. In New Zealand. A year after that Saturday.

I had gone out onto the deck, as I had every morning since we'd had it built. But in the past year, the hauntingly beautiful view over the sea had lost its allure. I simply no longer noticed. I could no longer see beyond myself. Now I just went out onto the deck as a reflex, expecting nothing and therefore experiencing nothing.

Except on this particular morning my eyes fell on a small object, stuck between two boards of the decking. I bent down to pick it up, and I noticed that the slim hair clip was rusty. Had it been that long? I held it between my fingers, and the pain that had dulled over the preceding year emerged with a force that made me catch my breath in a gulp, as if I had dived into cold water. It brought with it everything, but first those words.

Get out, Dad. Have an adventure. It's Saturday!

I used to be surrounded with evidence of her existence. Fresh traces left along her path. Crumbs, socks, books, papers, pens, clips. I had sometimes ignored them, at other times been annoyed by them. But I had certainly not understood how valuable they would become. Then, afterward, when I knew that they were priceless, items to be treasured, there were so few. And I had gradually collected them, one after the other, until there were none left. This rusty hair clip must be one of the very last. Then what?

I lifted my gaze and let my eyes scan the sea in front of me. The morning was unusually cool for the peak of summer, still and quiet and with a feeling of looming showers. Curiously bland, anonymous. It had a date attached to it, February 10, but it had no personality yet, no character. Like each new day, it held potential, I suppose. Already the sea was dotted with cheerful sailboats, crisscrossing the wide expanse beyond my deck. There were sounds, too. The constant invisible cicadas. The rustling of the fern fronds below. The dull droning of the sea farther down beyond my house. Shrieks from seagulls high above. But, like the day itself, they were distant, impersonal, too ordinary to attract my attention. I absorbed them, but they generated no feelings, no energy.

I stuck the hair clip in my pocket and went inside to make a cup of coffee. I had stopped making proper coffee, just as I had dropped most elaborate routines. I filled the kettle, boiled the water, and poured it over three teaspoonfuls of instant coffee in a mug and then returned with it to the deck. My one remaining deck chair creaked as I sat down. It felt as if our relationship had developed into a kind of game, each of us waiting to see how long the other could last. Who would break first.

I turned the mug around in my hands. The coffee had no smell; it was just scalding liquid without taste. I placed it on the deck beside my chair and took out the hair clip from my pocket.

Smells and sounds and tastes are known to have the power to evoke memories. But I had never before understood the enormous power of tangible objects in this respect. I looked at the clip on my palm, and memories poured forth with almost unbearable intensity. Almost unbearable. No. Either things are bearable or they are not. There is no almost. And these memories were certainly bearable. I welcomed them. I reveled in their blinding intensity, the smarting pain of the sweet moments as they flooded back. The smells, the music.

Now it is as if I remember my grief rather than experience it. I remember the pain I suffered as the memories washed over me where I sat on the deck that day. Now I have only the memories of my own feelings, not the feelings themselves. That day the feelings were still alive, the pain real. Now I look back and I can see every detail, but I am not there, inside it. My own pain is now forever calcified. I carry it with me, but it is no longer alive.

Still, I follow the man I used to be, and abruptly I taste the flavor of another kind of coffee. The kind I used to have when I lived to savor such things. I can see Mimi where she stands in the door, struggling to heave her backpack up onto her back. Vladimir Martynov's *Come In!* is playing in the background. The air smells faintly of the sea and of the nail polish Mimi had used just before getting ready to leave. I hold my mug of coffee in my hands, slowly tapping the rhythm of the music against it with a finger.

Get out, Dad. Have an adventure. It's Saturday!

And she smiles and blows me a kiss, turns and leaves. My Miriam. Mimi, my daughter. Our beautiful daughter. Then she closes the door behind her, and all is silent.

On the deck that day a year later, I wondered if it had been within my power to change the course of life at that moment. Just before Mimi turned. I wondered if I could have stopped her then, delayed her. Say, for example, I had dropped my mug of coffee. A small accident, a slight burn as the hot coffee splashed my leg—would that have delayed her enough to change the future? What if I had acted then, rather than a couple of hours later? If I had said, "Hold on! Wait for me. I'll come with you!" Surely, in that moment I did have the power to change the sequence of events. I used to keep torturing myself with such thoughts back then. I no longer do. I look at myself as I was, and I pity that man. I watch him tormenting himself, and for a moment I feel relief at not being there. I suppose it must mean I have reached a kind of acceptance of the unacceptable.

What I actually did that day, when my daughter stood before me, was return the blown kiss with an exhalation, a light flick of my hand, and she was out the door, leaving behind those words.

Get out, Dad. Have an adventure. It's Saturday!

Like music they lingered at the back of my mind, out of my control and reemerging at their leisure. They must have registered, though, because a few hours later I did just what Mimi had suggested. With a feeling of light excitement, I hopped on my bike, rode down to the landing, and got on the midday ferry to Auckland. But unbeknownst to me, another drama had already been set in motion. One that would engulf everything and leave me with the ashes of my existence slowly settling.

3

We lived a simple life, Mimi and I.

But simplicity is underrated. It is possible to consciously create the complex, the contrived, but it is impossible to manufacture simplicity. It is given to you, and like innocence it disappears the moment you become aware of it. I lived blissfully ignorant of my fortune.

Now, from the perspective I have gained, I watch myself riding my bike along the winding roads with the smooth hills on either side. I can remember how I felt that day: light and a little excited. Alive. And so arrogantly sure of my right to happiness.

I think about that Saturday morning, here on a bench in a park on the other side of the earth, in another world. And I think about the rest of that day. The last day of my life.

What I have now is something very different. There is the irrevocable loss. I can still acknowledge what my life used to be, but I think I am honest when I say I no longer grieve. I am not sure how to describe the state of my existence. Lately I have begun to think that I have gained, that my loss has become an asset. My grief has become a positive: the core around which my life now evolves. I think I have reached a state of increased clarity, a new level of focus. The change of perspective colors everything I do, everything I experience. I have traveled far to reach this point, and I am not sure whether the journey is over.

I still remember what it felt like to be alive.

4

Mimi had left, and the house was silent.

I went out onto the deck and stood by the railing. One of the first things we did when we moved in was to have the deck built. In the summer we more or less lived out there, and the doors were always open. It was as if the distinction between indoors and outdoors ceased to exist. Waiheke Island is a place where houses are secondary to decks, I think. It is as if you have to live with nature here; human presence feels temporary and elaborate constructions out of place.

Your house on your island has no likeness to mine on Waiheke. My house is fleeting; it stays in the background. It was the setting that attracted me initially, and it was always what I noticed about our home. The view. The smells. The sounds. The house felt like a second skin. It lived with us, kept us warm when it was cold outside, cool when it was hot. It stretched to embrace our entire existence. But we took no particular notice of it. Compared with mine, your house is so old. It has a history that is always present. It needs care and company. It, too, embraces your life, I think, but more like a garment. I suspect that New Zealanders look at their homes differently. They love the outdoors, and they let it take precedence. They seem to have no need to hide from it. Gradually I came to view my home in that way, and it was a very liberating feeling. A little like swimming naked.

That day my eyes fell on Mimi's shorts lying on the floor

where she had dropped them when changing the day before. She left a trail wherever she went, and not just the tangible kind. She was rarely out of my thoughts. She was the warm center around which my life revolved. As I bent down to pick up her clothes, her words surfaced in my mind.

Get out, Dad. Have an adventure. It's Saturday!

When I still lectured at the School of Music at Auckland University, I used to catch the early-morning ferry, spend the hour on board preparing for class, get off in town, hop on my bicycle, and carry on uphill to the campus. After work I would make the same trip in reverse. The strict schedule that had been a necessity when Mimi was a small child had become a habit that stuck. I very rarely lingered in the city. And Mimi was right: I never took the time to explore. I would look forward to the weekend, yet when it arrived, I often neither worked nor relaxed. In my study I would look out at the sea and long to go sailing. When out on the sea, I would think about work. I certainly did not have adventures.

After I cut back my teaching hours the year before to spend more time composing, the days seemed to stretch before me without shape and form, some without any work done at all. Although logically weekends were no different from the rest of the week, they now felt particularly awkward. It was as if I no longer deserved to enjoy them.

But that Saturday morning, I left the house and hopped on my bike and rode down to the ferry. The sky was bright blue, the kind of hastily brush-painted blue that is Auckland's own, and there was a fresh salty tang on the light wind. Later, as I stood by the railing on the top deck of the ferry looking out over the sea, my fingers tapping the rhythm of the last movement of the score I was working on, I felt a sudden jolt of excitement. Maybe it was just the satisfaction of having managed to take myself out of the house. The feeling of doing something unusual, of having a little adventure, perhaps.

Now, watching myself standing there in the bright sunshine, it feels absurd. The extent of my arrogant lack of apprehension appalls me. My sense of cheerful anticipation seems grotesque. But at the time I lifted my face to the sun and felt the wind against my skin. And I do think I was happy.

Before I went to live in New Zealand, I believe I thought of the country as an island. Or rather two islands. If I had ever given it any thought at all. When I arrived, I realized how wrong I had been. There is no sense of being on an island. The sea is never far away, but New Zealanders don't think of the land as a couple of islands. It is a nation. Perhaps they love it with a particular passion because it seems precarious, a sliver of volcanic rock newly risen from an eternity of surrounding sea, so small and so far removed from all other land.

But when Mimi and I moved from Auckland to Waiheke, we really did move to an island. Although it was only an hour away, with Auckland visible across the Hauraki Gulf, we were never able to escape the feeling of being offshore. From our house we had a view that could make us believe we were the only people there. The only people in the world. All we could see was the steeply sloping bush with the green parasols of ferns, and beyond it the sea. I treasured the isolation, but I suspect that Mimi always longed for more company. More life, more sounds. For me the view without any traces of human intervention was a deeply satisfying backdrop to my life. I even came to consider it a necessity, something without which I could not function.

Those who come only for the summer have a brief and superficial relationship with Waiheke. They come for their holidays, and the island changes. It takes a deep breath and puts on a welcoming smile. It gracefully accommodates the invasion. I used to feel relief as the days grew cooler and the ferries returned to the winter timetable.

The first summer, when Mimi was four and we rented a small cottage on the other side of the island, I decided Waiheke was the perfect place for us. Peaceful, unassuming. Kind. Later, when we went back to visit that part of the island, even the coastline seemed changed, as if it had been smoothed by a giant hand. The quaint cottages had been replaced by smart town houses and major developments. It was no longer peaceful, definitely not unassuming, and probably not particularly kind. But where we came to live, on the other side, the urban sprawl had not yet penetrated. Although it was a long ride to the ferry landing, both Mimi and I would take our bicycles there. Like so many other aspects of our lives, it had become a habit.

That morning I watched the flow of sailboats passing by, the cluster of little dinghies anchored up to fish, and I realized I felt better than I had in a long time. When I consider my total lack of premonition, I am reminded of a holiday in Europe with Mimi. We had flown to London, where I had a few business meetings, and then we traveled through France and to Italy by train. It was Mimi's first holiday overseas. She was eight. Toward the end of the trip, we stopped in Naples for a couple of nights. On the first day, we took a tour of Pompeii, and the following day we went to the National Archaeological Museum in Naples. I remember Mimi's pinched face as we looked at some of the eerily lifelike plaster casts that had been molded in the pumice where the bodies of those who had perished in the ancient city had left their lasting imprints. She was particularly moved by a set of four: two adults, two children. We could see that the little girl's hair had been neatly braided, and I watched Mimi pull her own braid over her shoulder, running the soft tip across her lips as her eyes stayed on the exhibits in front of her. I read out the accompanying information, slightly censored, while I stroked her hair. What remained with me as we left the museum later was how unaware of the imminent disaster the people appeared to have been. Few seemed to have managed to take much with them when they tried to flee. The family of four had a box of jewelry and a small statuette, nothing else. I thought about how they would have woken up to a glorious August day and gone about their everyday life in the morning, while the cause of their death was already brewing in the crater of Vesuvius. The mother might have been combing her daughter's hair while the first traces of smoke rose.

We don't get warnings in life. Life-changing events seem to be preceded by the least advanced warning. You may be combing your child's hair or blowing her a kiss, and over your head destruction looms.

Getting off the ferry and cycling up Queen Street with no particular destination in mind, I was surrounded by people going somewhere, while I was cruising in leisurely fashion. I made my way up to K Road, crossed and continued down to Khyber Pass Road and then on to Newmarket, where the streets were summer quiet and business in the shops along Broadway seemed slow. I felt woozy, dazed, as if I had been thrown out into the bright light bereft of some sort of required protection. When I reached the domain, the vast, open grassy area lay almost empty and the museum sat on the knoll in dignified silence. I parked the bike and crossed the intensely green expanse, carried on uphill to the museum entrance, and sat down on the wide steps. Visitors were scattered in little groups on the wide stone slabs, and a few children chased each other at the bottom of the steps. I realized I hadn't set foot inside the building since Mimi was a small child. In those early days, when we had no social network and few friends, we had developed a range of activities that somehow seemed to fill the void. They were activities that required the two of us, together, to mirror each other's delight at new or familiar experiences. One of them had been regular visits to the museum, where we had both developed our own favorite spots. Mimi's had always been the dim rooms crammed with Pacific Island artifacts. She seemed particularly fascinated by the ceremonial masks. She would stand with her nose pressed against the glass, never tiring, always having to be pulled away. For me it was the Memorial Hall. The high-ceilinged space, with the walls covered by tablets bearing the names of lives lost in the wars, never ceased to move me.

Over time we had come less and less often, until we stopped altogether. Somewhere along the way, we had lost increments of each other as our respective social circles had widened and separated. I had to assume that this was a natural development, but I was never entirely certain. When Mimi had entered my life, she caught me ill prepared. When I think about it, the major events of my life have been single incidents, of the once-in-a-lifetime kind. My life has been a series of unrehearsed performances. As I sat there on the stone steps with the unforgiving light of the New Zealand sun washing over me, my carefree sense of adventure slowly vanished. Instead I felt exposed, revealed for who I was. An amateur, a dilettante. A man with a patchy past and little idea of the future. At the same time, I felt as if I had somehow been sent on a mission, as if Mimi were trying to make me see that there was some fundamental aspect of my life I had not yet grasped and was sending me on a hunt for clues.

I stood, walked up the steps, and entered through the revolving doors. The contrast with the bright air outside made the interior appear dark and still. Except for the staff in the entrance hall and the gift shop, the building seemed largely empty. At the turnstile I dropped a dollar in the box for voluntary contributions and walked through. I wandered aimlessly, my mind occupied by a process that wanted no conscious participation. Or perhaps I felt like switching off. When I focused again, I found myself on the top floor, in the Memorial Hall. My eyes scanned the lists of names on the tablets covering the walls, and I was suddenly overwhelmed by the thought of all the laborious work that had gone into inscribing these letters, all the names. It struck me that the technical work might have involved little thought of the person behind each name. It was possible—likely, perhaps even necessary—that the work had been reduced to a mere practical challenge, a matter of getting the right letters in the right order, an issue of inches and stone dust. I felt strangely affected by the idea that the names might have been inscribed simply as ornamental patterns.

I stood with my hands clasped behind my back and began painstakingly to read. As my lips soundlessly formed the names, the enormity of the loss swelled before me: the grief over all those young lives that had been cut short, over dreams and hopes that had come to nothing. I saw the names falling like drops into a vast black pool, where no rings spread on the surface, swallowed soundlessly with no ripples. The impact of the vision caught me unawares. For a moment I felt unable to move. Then I noticed an elderly man at the other end of the hall. He was standing with a straw hat in his hand and his eyes focused on one particular tablet. I could see that there was a measure of comfort to be had from this monument. The inscribed letters were tangible proof of someone's existence. There were family and friends to keep the memories alive. The names were not just marks in stone. Each name was still pregnant with life.

It took a conscious effort for me to leave the room. Disoriented, I couldn't find the stairs. Instead I turned a corner and found myself in the Holocaust Gallery. The small, dark space was filled with simple glazed cases holding family portraits, documents, and mementos supplied by Jewish refugees. I was the only visitor, slowly wandering through the narrow, twisting aisles. Eventually my eyes fell on a photograph in one of the cases along the wall. It was larger than a passport photo and seemed to be a professional studio portrait. The picture showed the young man's head and shoulders only, and the background was dark. He was formally dressed in a dark jacket, a white shirt, and a tie. I stopped for a moment, touched by the solemn face whose eyes met mine across time. The formal style of the picture made it difficult to assess the age of the subject, as if the man had been purposely made to look older than he was, but I thought he might have been in his early twenties. His dark hair was combed back, and he gazed straight into the camera with an expression of serious self-confidence, his eyebrows a little raised. Or perhaps the expression was just masking self-consciousness. It was only after I had inspected the face for quite a while that my eyes set on the small note to the left of the portrait. *"Adam Lipski, born 1920, Kraków, Poland."* I read the name silently first, then whispered it. Wiping my hand over my mouth and chin I fought a spell of dizziness. Then I read the brief text printed underneath the name.

"I saw my brother, Adam, for the last time in November 1939. I was told he fled to Lithuania together with a friend. The last time we had news of him was about a year later. Adam was a talented violinist with a bright international career ahead of him. But to me, more than anything else, he was my beloved older brother. I have never stopped thinking about him. I have never stopped searching. I have never stopped hoping."

The note was signed *"Clara Fried, Wellington."* I stood in front of the display, my eyes set on the photograph, whispering the name to myself.

"Adam Lipski."

When I finally left the room and walked downstairs and out onto the steps, I realized I had been inside for well over an hour. My eyes screwed up as I looked out over the city and the sea beyond, a shimmering surface fading into a slight haze in the distance. It felt odd to see the world unchanged and ordinary, when *I* felt as if I were suddenly on the brink of fundamental and irrevocable change. It was as if I had been magically set at the beginning of a path that I could not yet discern, while here in front of me the world lay blisteringly bright and unconcerned. I had walked into the museum un-thinkingly, and I had exited with a new way of looking at myself and the world.

My name is Adam Anker. But once it was Adam Lipski. I was born in Kraków, Poland. And when I had looked into a stranger's eyes, this man whose name I shared, for the first time in my life I began to hear the sound of questions never posed, and I was overcome by an acute sense of urgency.

5

I traveled back to Waiheke in the early evening, oblivious to the enormity of what had been unleashed.

I was pondering my day and its implications, standing on the ferry's upper deck with a can of cold beer in my hand. Coming back, there were more people on the ferry, but up-stairs only a few scattered groups. The warm, late-afternoon light fell in slanted rays over the sun-warmed seats and the passengers. A small child laughed on its mother's lap; a group of young girls giggled, the peaks of their caps touching as they bent forward. I felt myself relax, while the cool, bitter flavors of the beer filled my mouth. I looked out over the sea, where a number of boats of varying sizes and types navigated the glit-tering surface. The soft breeze was warm on the skin and the setting sun gentle on the eyes.

I got back to the house and opened the door to be greeted by stale, hot air. I crossed the living room and pulled back the folding doors to the deck. I took a shower, and then, instead of checking the fridge for something to cook for dinner, I grabbed another beer and sat down outside in one of the deck chairs. Early evening has always been my favorite time of day. As the day reaches its end, there is time to contemplate and let the brain change gears. I do most of my creative work at night. Possibly this habit also originated when Mimi was little, but I don't think so. Even as a child, I used to let my mind wander at night, wide awake as the fluorescent hands of my bedside

Donald Duck alarm clock met at midnight. Then, as now, I was overcome by a sense of anticipation in the early evening, hoping that the stillness of the night would help induce the kind of creative trance I need for my work.

Now, with the distance of two years, I look at myself in the canvas chair and the gradually fading light and I remember distinctly my sense of relieved resolve. I slowly finished the beer and went back inside, leaving the doors open to the night and the moths. I walked over to the small desk where I kept my laptop. I didn't bother to sit down but stood and watched as the screen lit up and the familiar jingle sounded while the computer booted and connected. A few clicks and I had the information. Clara Fried lived in Hataitai, in Wellington. I wrote down her address and phone number. Then I sat and put my fingers on the keyboard again. Somehow the afternoon filled with thoughts about my distant past seemed to have opened a door to my more recent past. One led to the other. I quickly found the second name I was looking for and added one more number to the note. Your number, Cecilia. I was looking at the name on the screen: Cecilia Hägg. I recognized the address, too. The island.

And then my phone rang.

It was just after eight, and I remember that my eyes moved from the screen to look out through the open doors at the setting sun on the other side of the sea. A mauve cloud hung over Sky Tower, as if it were attached to the spire.

I distinctly remember that I had no premonition. In fact, as my hand reached out to grasp the receiver, I felt excited: the aftermath of my day of adventure, mixed with something I can only describe as purpose, a renewed anticipation.

I was utterly unprepared.

Not that there is any kind of preparation to be had for calls like that one. Or that it would have made any difference.

I lifted the receiver and said my name, while I idly slid the paper with the scribbled phone numbers underneath the mouse pad. I listened while my life was sucked away, draining into emptiness with explosive force.

Afterward all that remained was silence.

6

It was February again, a full year later, when I picked up the mouse pad beside my laptop and took out the small piece of paper. It was another early evening, on another bright, sunny summer Saturday, yet it bore no other resemblance to the one a year earlier.

Why did I stay there for so long? The house, the island, and now I have come to think perhaps the entire country had died for me the evening the phone rang. It all looked the same as the moment before, yet it didn't resemble anything I knew or anything that had anything to do with me. Just as my own image looked more or less the same when eventually one day I raised my eyes to regard it in the bathroom mirror. But we were both irrevocably altered, I and the world around me. Or rather my perspective was fundamentally changed. From where I stood, nothing around me looked anything like before.

I think now that perhaps I had no choice initially. My world had petrified, and I was unable to move or shift even the smallest thing. I was embraced by a kind of paralysis that felt almost physical. It would be a year before some small measure of mobility would return. Perhaps a year is the organic time for grief to settle. It may be that we have to go through an entire year's cycle to begin to understand that life will never be as it was but that it can continue.

So the mouse pad had stayed where it was, as had the note that sat underneath it. I hadn't given it a thought. That evening, though, something had made me take out the small silver box that held the only tangible proof of my life beyond my own memories. For the first time in over a year, I flicked through the tattered pictures. I put them on my bedspread, then opened the album containing photos of Mimi that I kept on my table. Mimi as a bundle in my arms on a bleak January day in Stockholm. As a smiling toddler. In the hospital with a broken arm at four. First day of school. At the helm of the sailboat, tanned and grinning at the camera. Slowly I tore a selection of pictures off the pages and put them with the old ones on my bed. And I sat there and watched them for a while. Then I went to the living room and sat down in front of my laptop.

When my hand lifted the mouse pad enough to slide my fingers underneath and retrieve the paper, the act felt momentous. For the first time in a year, I was doing something beyond sustaining the barest minimum of existence. I felt guilty, but I felt a little alive.

Two weeks later I flew to Wellington to meet Clara Fried.

7

There are people who dread the approach into the capital's airport.

The gusts of wind rocking the aircraft, the wild sea below with irregular patches of white froth, the sharp black rocks rising out of the water, followed by the impossibly short landing strip. And occasionally, rather than a bumpy landing, an abrupt ascent and a wide circle above the bays, followed by a second wobbling attempt at touching down. But I have always felt excited, uplifted in every sense of the word. I usually ask for a window seat, because I like looking out over the sea and the city, an amphitheater framing the aquamarine water. I have always liked the capital the most from above.

In the end I didn't call Clara Fried but wrote her a note. Perhaps I felt that a letter would give her the option of ignoring my contact altogether. She would have time to consider whether she wanted to meet me, how to respond. I wasn't even sure I wanted a reply. A letter arrived in the mail only three days later.

> Dear Mr. Anker,
> Thank you for your letter. I am available to meet you when you come to Wellington. May I suggest Thursday next week? Kindly call me to make a time, when you have arrived.
> Yours sincerely,
> Clara Fried

The handwriting was young. In fact, I thought she must have had someone write the letter for her: the script didn't match the rather formal tone. I folded the paper and put it back in the envelope.

When I went to Wellington, which wasn't often, I always stayed at the same bed-and-breakfast in Mount Victoria. Over the years I had come to know the woman who ran it. Her name was Anna, and she was from one of the Baltic states—it was never quite clear to me which one. She was a small, wind-blown woman of an uncertain age and status who reminded me of an arctic birch: knotted and wiry, but dense. Hardened by the elements. She seemed enveloped in an aura of solitary determination, as if facing the world with her teeth clenched. She never smiled and never invited a conversation, and her responses were monosyllabic. But we got along very well. Without asking, I would usually get the room overlooking the harbor, and in the winter she would make sure to have it well heated. When Mimi was a child, I sometimes took her with me, and Anna would offer to look after her when I left for meetings. I could never quite understand why, but they seemed to have a special rapport. I once asked Mimi what they did together, and she said, "Anna says it's good to sit and think. She says people talk too much and think too little. So that's what we do." Then she smiled and shrugged her shoulders.

When I arrived that morning, Anna was at her desk in the corner. She had been reading, and when she looked up, her face was pinched and pale, as if cold in spite of the warm day. She pulled at the sleeves of her gray cardigan as her eyes briefly met mine.

"Usual room," she said, and handed me the key.

Her hands shifted papers around on the desk in front of her, and I knew she had words in mind, that there was something she wanted to say. But she remained silent, and when she looked up again, I thought she might have been shaking her head ever so slightly, and her pale blue eyes seemed to water. Without thinking, I shook my head in response as I took the keys and turned to walk across the room to the hall. I was relieved to turn my back to her. We believe that we are safe that way, I think. That our backs will protect us, hide our emotions. But it's a complete illusion, of course. Even the smallest child can read people by their posture. I once heard somewhere that it is possible to diagnose depression from people's gait, the level of energy with which they move their feet, how high above the ground they lift them. Our bodies are unreliable keepers of our secrets. Though it had been a year since I'd lost Mimi, I still was not able to face other people's reactions. Particularly those I had not seen since that February. In order to protect my feelings, I had to trust my back, hold myself erect, and put one foot in front of the other. My composure was thin as glass.

I phoned Clara Fried from my room. Her voice was strong and surprisingly dark, with a heavy European accent, and the message was delivered clearly and economically. She asked no questions, just gave her address and directions, suggested a time in the afternoon, and hung up.

As soon as I put down the receiver, I felt foolish. What business did I have with this old woman? What did I hope to achieve? I looked out the window, where I could see a glimpse of the sea, the surface whipped by the wind and sparkling in the sun. Was this woman holding the key to the void that was my background? Would she be able to shine some light into the darkness? Give me sounds where there had been silence all my life?

Could she tell me who I was?

8

Clara Fried lived in Hataitai, just around the bays.

On the way I stopped at a small café in Oriental Parade and had coffee, then wandered uphill, through Roseneath. The weather was clear, the air freshly cleansed by the constant wind, and the sky went on forever. I allowed myself time to take in the view. When I reached the peak, the outline of the tip of the South Island shimmered across the sea. I could see the backs of seagulls that hung in the air below the steep hill and a couple of windsurfers traversing the turquoise surface farther down. I felt as if I were standing at the helm of a large ship, with the sea and the sky open before me, the world trailing behind.

The house was one of many similar wooden cottages on the slopes of Mount Victoria, facing the airport. White, with pale blue trim, a small dry lawn, and along the white picket fence a row of agapanthus with yellowing leaves and parched flowers. I opened the gate and walked on the concrete slabs that crossed the lawn leading to the front steps. Before I even raised my hand to knock, the door opened.

Clara Fried was tall. For some reason I had imagined her short and plump, but the woman who faced me was almost as tall as I. She held herself very straight, further emphasizing her height. Although she was slim, there was nothing delicate or vulnerable about her. She looked confident and measured, dressed in well-pressed black slacks and a plain white blouse.

Her face was long and narrow, with pale and surprisingly smooth skin, strong dark eyebrows, a prominent nose, and a full mouth. It was not a beautiful face in a conventional sense, but striking. A pair of heavy gold earrings stretched the lobes of her ears. Her hair was white, and she wore it pulled into a tight bun. I held out my hand to greet her, but she ignored it and moved to let me inside. It wasn't until I turned to face her in the dimly lit hallway that I realized she was blind.

She walked ahead of me with certain steps, leading the way into a small living room. I stopped in my tracks, transported. I had entered another world, another time. The walls were covered with dark red floral wallpaper, which in turn was almost totally hidden behind paintings and framed photographs. The furniture was all dark polished wood and looked antique: a small sofa with a coffee table, a dining table and four chairs, a bookcase along the entire wall, and a grandfather clock in the corner. At the far end of the room was a piano, its lid closed. An Oriental carpet covered the floor almost from wall to wall, and dark red silk drapes framed the two windows, partly pulled closed and leaving the room in a red-tinged twilight. In spite of all its elaborate detail, the room looked oddly impersonal. It could have been a movie set, or a period display in a museum. Prompted by my hostess, I sank down into the sofa's soft velvet cushions. Clara Fried asked me if I would like a cup of coffee or tea, and when I declined, she pulled out one of the dining chairs and sat down opposite me on the other side of the table. The bright light and the sounds of the real world beyond the windows seemed distant.

"So," the old woman said, her unseeing eyes looking at

me, or perhaps through me. She kept her bony, rather large hands folded in her lap and sat with her spine straight but without leaning onto the back of her chair. Suddenly I felt ridiculous, even guilty, for having imposed on her. Mrs. Fried said nothing further but sat with her head cocked to the side.

"Thank you for agreeing to see me," I said, rubbing my palms.

The old woman nodded but said nothing.

"Everything began a year ago," I said. "At the War Memorial Museum. In Auckland."

Then I changed my mind and started again. "No, that's not right. I might as well say that it began when I was born. Or perhaps much earlier. In a sense, nothing has a beginning or an end, I suppose. But sometimes, in hindsight, we can see where the turning points in our lives have occurred. And it was there, at the museum, that I became aware of the void that I have lived with my entire life. I saw with absolute clarity how I had ambled through the years with no idea whatsoever of where I had come from."

I looked around the room again, searching for words.

"I first noticed the portrait of your brother and then your note. And finally his name. At that moment it was as if a closed door swung open." I cleared my throat and hesitated for a moment before continuing.

"Because of the name. As I explained in my letter."

I looked at the old woman's face, waiting for a response. She said nothing.

"But then . . ." I hesitated. "Something happened that made this newfound sense of direction meaningless. I lost my daughter."

Mrs. Fried's unseeing eyes stayed on my face, and she nodded slowly. I wondered if she had made her own investigation. If she knew who I was.

"I came to New Zealand almost nineteen years ago. It wasn't a considered immigration but a temporary arrangement. A flight. I don't think I ever thought I was coming to live here permanently. But the years went by so quickly. And we settled in, my daughter and I. Made a new life for ourselves, trying to erase our past. Just as my own mother did."

Again I waited, hoping for some response, but the old woman remained silent.

"In a sense I became a parasite, using my daughter as a life-sustaining vehicle. She developed roots here, and they came to nurture me as well. When I lost her, I lost my bearings completely. There was nothing for me here and nothing to return to. I look back now, and it seems as if there is no time at all between my arrival in this country and last year. Yet that time is all that I have to hold on to. The memory of that time is everything. Before, nothing. Now, nothing."

I felt as if I were making less and less sense, but still there was no visible reaction from the old woman, so I had to pick up the thread once more.

"When I came here with my daughter, it wasn't clear to me how long we would stay. If I thought about it, I certainly considered it a short-term arrangement. Time to consider how I should organize my life with her in it. A few years, perhaps. I was offered a job, I came, and I didn't think beyond the immediate future for the two of us."

"What is your profession, Mr. Anker?"

I looked up from my hands.

"I'm a musician. I teach. Compose." I hesitated again, then resumed where I'd left off.

"What I think I saw as an interlude, both privately and professionally, became the life I gave my daughter. I felt that the very decision to come here gave me some structure, something to pin my life on for the time being. Now I realize that I have lived my entire life like that: in the short term, one day at a time."

I cleared my throat.

"You see, I have never had any connection with my past. Twice my life has started anew, irrevocably leaving the past behind. First when I arrived in Sweden as a small child and then again when I came here. And each new beginning has been preceded by a kind of death. It has felt as if all I have ever had is the present, because the past has always been abruptly cut off forever, with no remaining ties, no connections. I now understand that it is impossible to create a vision of a future if you don't have a past. That perhaps in a sense the idea of the unknown can be conceived only with the building stones of our past. Good or bad, our past is the reference we need to enable the future. For eighteen years I was hoping I could slowly accumulate a sort of recent past that would suffice. Instead the present, too, was taken from me.

"As for the future, I have never known how to visualize it. Now less than ever."

I thought the old woman nodded, but she said nothing.

"Lately I have thought that perhaps for those who have grown up without knowing their beginnings, there will always be this lingering uncertainty. Happiness for them will always seem fleeting, volatile, because they lack the security that comes from knowing that even if happiness is lost, the memory of it will provide some comfort. It is easy to believe that grief and loss are permanent, if you lack the perspective that history allows."

I felt tangled in a web of words.

"The day I saw your display at the museum, I felt as if I had been guided there." I nodded to myself. "Yes, I think that is how it can be described. My daughter told me to take a trip into town and have an adventure. And so, breaking all my routines, that's what I did. It was as if the time were right, or so I thought. As if I had finally found a door to my past, and I was ready to open it."

I stopped, but there was no response.

"I don't know why I'm telling you all this," I continued. But Clara Fried only nodded again, or perhaps I just thought that she did. She said nothing.

"That Saturday, a year ago"—I paused for a moment—"I felt exposed, as if my limited life had been laid out for me to inspect. I could see my shortcomings as a father, as a musician, as a man, all revealed in the bright summer light. I also felt as though something was expected of me and that I had to try to understand what it was. Now I think that this chance, this chain of events, might have been given to me in order to save my life. It has taken me a year to learn to think of it this way," I said.

Mrs. Fried remained erect with her head a little tilted to the side. I sensed she was listening with her full attention but deliberately holding back her response.

The room was silent for a moment, with the ticking of the clock rising to fill the space.

"When I saw the name of your brother, I thought . . . I thought . . ." I made a gesture with my hands to indicate my difficulty in finding the right words. "I had intended to contact you then, a year ago. But before I had the opportunity, everything that was my life vanished in an instant."

I wanted the old woman to ask me a question and release me from my monologue. But she said nothing, and her face remained expressionless. So I picked up the thread yet again, hoping to arrive at the end. I stood and walked over to the window with my hands in my pockets. Through the narrow opening between the heavy curtains, I could see across to Miramar and beyond. The view was hauntingly beautiful, with the hills lit by the afternoon sun, layer upon layer of shifting hues of green and gray with glimpses of the intensely blue-green sea in between. I felt displaced, as if I were on a stage with the wrong set. The view was so completely mismatched with the interior of the house that it might as well have been a painted backdrop.

"At first, when I found your exhibit, my excitement was overwhelming. The connection. The name. I felt like running back home and contacting you immediately. There was my own curiosity, of course. My hope. But also I had my daughter in mind. Her right to my past. Her right to her own past." I searched my mind for the words to explain the spectrum of feelings.

"Now there is no longer any urgency. In fact, in an absurd sense, I don't mind if this search occupies the rest of my life." I could hear my own words, and it felt as if the explanation were as much directed to me as to the old woman. "At the same time, it seems even more important than before. Absolutely necessary. I need to try to find my past." It was becoming ever more difficult to choose the words, and to utter them. "It has become everything," I said.

In the silence that followed, the ticking of the grandfather clock took over the room. There were no sounds from outside. I felt as if the world had withdrawn, as if the dark room and the two of us were the only reality.

"But it may be just a folly, something I am stupidly clinging to. I may have wasted your time utterly."

There was again a moment of silence before the old woman turned to face me where I stood by the window. She finally spoke.

"Oh, no, Mr. Anker. Nothing is wasted, nothing at all. Quite the opposite, I think. As for my time, it means nothing. I exist, but time has no relevance. You may think that you have no future, but in my case it is a reality. My time is running out. So it's only the here and now that matters for me. And my connection with the past. I am glad you have come. You may not understand how glad."

Clara Fried looked straight at me, and it was hard to believe that her eyes could not see me.

"Let me tell you a story," she said. "Please sit down."

She waited until she heard me cross the room and take my place on the sofa before she began to talk.

9

"Once there was a little girl who loved to play the piano." The old woman seemed to hesitate, and she put the tips of her fingers to her mouth briefly before she continued.

That little girl was me, Clara Lipski.

I lived in a large apartment, where there were two pianos—one for me and one for my mother. I couldn't remember a day when I hadn't played music. The music came to hold my entire world: the apartment with its polished parquet that creaked as we walked across it, differently for each member of the family. Gently under the feet of my father, always in a hurry; softly as my mother sometimes danced on it. Loudly and with protest under the feet of Olga, our maid. It was only Adam who was able to cross the floors soundlessly, as if it cushioned his steps. Or as if he weren't quite there, as if his feet never quite touched the floor.

My little-girl's music rose from the keys of the piano, and it seemed to contain the sunshine that fell through the sheer lace curtains. To embrace the Sunday lunches when we all practiced French. It blended with the smell from the kitchen where Olga was frying placki. It caressed my mother's soft hair, my father's freshly starched shirt, the pink hyacinths on the dining table. It moved through the rooms and touched the dark wallpaper, the polished mahogany furniture, the rugs with their intricate patterns. It drifted outside through the open window, into the park where I walked on Sunday afternoons with my mother. It came to contain all the seasons: the winters with sleigh rides in the snow and ice-skating on the river, springtime with excursions beyond the city into the valleys that were covered in wildflowers, summers in the mountains with their smell of pine needles and resin. And my favorite season, autumn, with the leaves on the trees along the street below my window painting an extravagant fanfare of red and yellow, gold and orange, and the air filled with the smell of rain and wet soil.

My music captured everything about my life.

And so it was that when I lost the music, for a while I thought that I had lost all it contained. My very life. I lost the piano. My home. My father. Later my mother. And eventually my country. But it was the loss of Adam that silenced the music in my head. It was Adam's departure that opened the door and let the icy wind inside.

The old woman fell silent, apparently immersed in her memories. We sat in silence for a while. Then she inhaled and continued.

My brother was eight years older, a man while I was still a girl. He was tall—even taller than Father—but where Father was loud and intense, Adam was quiet and thoughtful. He played the violin, but he played it differently from the way I played the piano. You see, Adam was mute, and he expressed himself only in his music. To me that was all I needed to understand him completely. So I think he played because he had to, and he played with an almost frightening abandon. I listened with awe, but I was always a little frightened, too. There was no relief; every note Adam played was significant. The violin grew out of his hands—it was like a part of his body, and he simply had to use it. Just as his heart had to beat, his hands had to play in order for him to live. He played, and I would sit on the window seat in the music room and listen, my arms around my shins and my eyes on his face. For me the music carried my life; it wrote my history. For Adam it seemed to be life itself. When he put down the violin, he became that weightless body that could traverse the parquet soundlessly. Mysterious, but also vulnerable. And silent. It was as if when he stopped playing, he stopped living. And when the music was taken away from him, he had to leave and go somewhere where he could hope to retrieve it. His life depended on it.

Afterward, a very long time later, when I was no longer a little girl and when possibly I could have resumed my playing, I chose not to. There was no longer anything I wanted to capture. But deep inside, the old music began to play again, ever so softly. I could close my eyes and silently play the music, and slowly, slowly, I had them back—the memories.

Except Adam. I could never have him back, because he was not part of my music. He made his own, and I could no longer hear it.

The old woman paused for a moment.

"I know what this room looks like, though I can no longer see it. I prefer it that way, because what you see here is only a copy. A fake. Even the photographs. A folly, an attempt at re-creating something that did not need to be re-created. Because in here"—she indicated her head with a little knock on her forehead—"there it is, all of it. Except my Adam. He was taken from me, and I have been searching for him all my life."

She was silent, and then she lifted her hands and covered her face.

I felt awkward, racking my brain for something to say. But after a moment she lowered her hands and continued to talk, her voice just as strong as before.

"That display in the museum—it's a silly old woman's feeble gesture. I have thought of asking to have it removed. But then . . ." She left the sentence unfinished.

I said nothing.

"Come over here and give me your hand," Mrs. Fried said. I took my hands out of my pockets and walked across to where she sat.

"Not that one, the other," she said impatiently as I stretched out my right hand. I diligently gave her my left. "You are left-handed," she said, not as a question.

I nodded and then, realizing she could not see me, said, "Yes, I am."

"And you do play the violin, don't you?" she asked.

I nodded, but it was as if she already knew, so I didn't have to speak.

She put my hand between both of hers and stroked it softly, then ran her fingers along mine, one at a time until she got to the little finger, the crooked one. She paused for a moment, then abruptly dropped my hand.

"I will get you something," she said, and stood and left the room. I returned to the sofa and sank back into the cushions, unconsciously closing my right hand around the fingers of the left. Suddenly the room felt claustrophobic, hot and stuffy. I pulled at the collar of my shirt to loosen it. There were faint sounds from the room next door, followed by steps in the hallway, and the old woman reappeared, carrying a small cardboard box. She placed it on the dining table and reached inside.

"I have carried this for so very long," she said. "I never wanted them in the first place, but they were given to me." She straightened, and I could hear her inhale, still with her back to me. And again it struck me that there are moments when we can't bear to show our face to the world and have to turn our back on it. I could see that she held a small pile of what looked like letters, tied with a ribbon.

"There is another story I would like to tell if you can bear to listen," she said.

"Of course," I said. "It's my privilege to be here. To listen."

"Hope is so painful," the old woman said. "I take your hand in mine. I listen to your voice, and in the dead space of my heart the capillaries slowly fill with blood, the tissue softens. It hurts. You sit here in my room, and I can smell your body across the table. I know you are not a young man, yet to me you are. I have no way of knowing what you look like, but you are tall. Your steps are light—you are not heavy, I think. I listen to your voice, I hold your hands, and I can sense the magnitude of your sadness. Your new, bleeding grief, but also a very old, dark sadness. And yet I am overcome by my own hope."

Mrs. Fried sat down on one of the dining chairs and turned her unseeing eyes to me.

10

The day my Adam left, it rained.

He came back only to say good-bye, and his face was wet. His coat was wet, and his hands. He pressed his cold palms against my cheeks and crouched down, his eyes level with mine. He looked into my eyes and kissed my forehead. He put his finger first across his own lips, then across mine. in a gesture of silence, urging me to stop sobbing. He laid his hand on my head and stroked my hair, then stood and walked down the hallway without turning. Father was holding Mother in his arms, and the rain was beating hard against the windows in the living room. I watched Adam's feet cross the floor without a sound. After he had closed the front door behind him, I could see the wet prints on the parquet floor, and I knew that when they had dried, there would be no more live traces of my brother. I wished there were some way I could make them stay, but instead I watched them until they were soaked up by the wood and dried by the air.

Later that day I went into the music room to sit on the window seat. The rain streaked the glass, and the world outside was blurred, as if I were looking through tears. I saw the music stand by the piano, and I knew that Adam would never use it again. I would never hear him play. I think that was when I lost my music. I can't remember that we ever opened the lid of the piano after that day.

In the evening we had our first dinner without him. We ate in silence, and the sound of the rain filled the room. Our dining room, which had always seemed so warm, so full of light and happiness, was now barren and cold. The smells that had always blended into a familiar, appealing whole had splintered into separate layers, where some were intolerably sad, others alien, even revolting. The smell of grease and steam from the kitchen, the wilting flowers on the table, the burning coal in the stove—I could smell them all, individually, and they filled my nostrils with their disparate, unpleasant odors. I looked at the food on my plate, and the piece of meat in my mouth grew as I tried to swallow. When I lifted my eyes and saw my parents across the table, they were forever changed, too. In an instant we had become the same age, they no wiser than I. We were equally lost and bewildered. Months later our maid, Olga, left us, and with her she took the last traces of life in the house. But by then it seemed a small loss added to the others.

Wanda Maisky started coming sometime after Adam left, in late winter. I knew her, of course. I knew that she and her sister Marta used to play with Adam. But I didn't like her. I was a child, and she had never acknowledged me before. In the beginning, when she came to ask for her letters to be forwarded to Adam, she always asked to see Mother, but after a while, when Mother stopped seeing people altogether, she came to see me. She was always so very beautiful, but as everything around us changed, her beauty seemed more and more out of place. It didn't seem right. She was like a colorful migrating bird left behind in late autumn. And as soon as the thought had entered my mind, that is what she became. A bird. Later, with each visit, she seemed a little less colorful, as if she were shedding feathers, molting. More and more she came to resemble a pigeon, with her high bosom and pointed face with its large, cold eyes. Then, when she took to wearing her sister's dresses, which were so different, that added to my discomfort. Suddenly she appeared in somber gray and discreet pale purple: To me she became a pigeon altogether. She repulsed me, scared me, the way birds do. I don't like their jerky movements, their sharp beaks, their claws. Their unpredictable flight.

The first time she wore Marta's gray dress with the black bead embroidery around the neck something changed. I remembered Marta wearing it at one of the last house concerts. I remembered how beautiful she had been. Seeing Wanda wearing it somehow felt wrong. I sat helpless, a pawn in a game I didn't understand. There seemed to be a new kind of resolve in Wanda's manner. And as we all seemed to have lost ours, hers was especially disturbing.

She would leave her galoshes in the hallway but keep her coat on, walk into the living room, sit on the edge of the sofa, unbutton her coat, and pull the skirt smoothly over her knees. Then she would cross her slim ankles, and her cold eyes would set on my face. She always asked the same questions, told the same stories.

"How are your parents, Clara?" and "I hope your mother is feeling a little better," and "These are such difficult times," she would say with a sigh. Then she would look straight into my eyes. "People like us, Clara, we are survivors. And we need to be strong. Strong and practical. For all of us." She would stare into my face. "You and I, Clara." And then she would smile her conspiratorial smile with those small, even teeth flashing for the briefest moment, before pushing another letter toward me across the polished surface of the table. She never explicitly told me what to do with them. She'd just let the envelope sit there *between us while her pale, unblinking eyes kept watching me. I would sit stiffly on the chair opposite her at the table, my arms pressed against my sides, my eyes on my lap, refusing to be her collaborator. Then, with a quick intake of breath, she would stand up, pull her coat closed, and begin to button it. "Give my love to your parents, Clara," she would say, then give me a peck on the cheek, and her sweet perfume would linger as she crossed the parquet in quick steps, her high heels hard against the wood. I dreaded her visits.*

I put the letters in a box in my room. They have weighed on my conscience ever since. She never told me what to do with them, but we understood each other. There was a horrible sense of understanding. I was a child, but somehow I knew intuitively that she was playing a game with me. Giving me the envelope, and never a word of instruction. Except the last time. That letter was different in a way I didn't understand. She kept her hand on it as it sat on the table between us, holding me captive with her eyes. There was a new insistence in her look, and she talked slowly, emphasizing every word.

"This letter, Clara, is very important. Very important. I want you to do everything you can to make sure it reaches your brother." She paused, and then she said, with a little laugh, "But I am sure you always do everything you can. You are a clever girl, Clara. We understand each other, you and I." And again she smiled her conspiratorial smile. I felt my throat tightening, tears burning behind my eyelids, but there was no way I would give her the pleasure of seeing me cry. I bowed my head and took the letter out of her hand. When she had left, I added it to the others. I was never able to make myself destroy them. Nor did I want to read their contents. Collecting them and putting them

away made my part in the matter seem less significant somehow. I could almost convince myself that I had nothing to do with them at all. I would put them away, then go and wash my hands.

I became the caretaker of these unopened envelopes, and their weight increased over time. In the end, when I could carry only the barest necessities, I took them with me into my new existence. Perhaps because of my guilt: I needed them as tangible proof of my guilt. I have traveled to the ends of the earth with them. And as the years have passed, the weight of these unread messages has become more than I can carry. They intrude frequently, more often now that my life has slowed down and I can see the end. Sometimes I am overcome by a violent feeling of responsibility. I wonder if my actions, or lack of action, might have contributed to my own loss. If unwittingly I was my own destroyer.

Mrs. Fried held the stack of letters in one hand, tapping it against the palm of the other, hesitating. Then she slowly returned the pile to the box, reached inside, and removed a single envelope. She held it out to me.

"Take this with you when you leave," she said. "You are leaving, are you not?" I wasn't sure if she meant leaving her house, leaving Wellington, or going overseas. Then, from inside her left shirtsleeve, she pulled out a small business card.

"Here, take this, too. Szymon Liebermann is a dear friend of mine. You may wish to contact him. He will welcome you if you mention my name. He will understand."

She stretched out both hands with the palms turned up, and I placed mine on top of hers, palms against palms.

"It's not the loss. I think that with time we can learn to

accept our losses, even the hardest ones. It's not knowing. The exhausting pain of hope, even the slightest hope. That's how I have come to see it." The old woman's unseeing eyes looked straight into mine, and her lips twisted in a small grimace that I couldn't quite interpret. But I realized that she had no desire to ask me any questions. That our meeting was over.

"If you like, let me know what you learn."

I withdrew my hands, not knowing what to say or do. But she saved me from having to say anything at all by turning and leading the way out into the hallway.

She didn't offer her hand again, just opened the door and stood aside for me to pass. As I walked down the garden path, I heard her say something, and I stopped and turned.

"*Szczęśliwej podróży, Adamie. I wracaj szybko z powrotem!*" she said, and now she smiled, a fleeting quiver, lips closed.

I listened, and the foreign words reverberated in my mind.

11

I decided to walk back, uphill through Hataitai toward the peak of Mount Victoria. It was early afternoon, and the sun had moved around the point, leaving that side of the hill in the shade and illuminating the hills across the water. The wind had died down; it was one of those precious calm late-summer afternoons when the city took a brief pause. Or perhaps just stopped to inhale and prepare for the following day, which would almost certainly be windy again.

Once I reached the top, I sat down on the grassy slope overlooking the harbor. Again I was reminded of how much I liked Wellington from this perspective, from high above. During my visits I had often wandered up to the lookout, and I always felt as if I were at the very edge of the earth, getting a privileged glimpse of a place seldom viewed. Each time I returned home to Auckland, the one-hour flight was a step back into the real world after a brief visit to another, self-contained one. Wellington has a wild side to it, as if the tidy streets and picturesque harbor were just a front, masking underlying turmoil. The city is like a well-dressed woman whose feral eyes give her away.

I sat on the grass with the envelope Clara Fried had given me. I opened it and pulled out the business card first. The plain white card stated the name SZYMON LIEBERMANN, followed by a street address in Kraków and a telephone number. The envelope didn't seem to contain much else. I ran my fingers along the length of the paper several times without opening the flap, my eyes on the sea below, which lay flat, reflecting the sun that was setting beyond the hills of Khandallah. For some strange reason, I suddenly thought of my mother. Her last words.

"I have nothing to say." As if to emphasize her words, she closed her lips firmly. Her eyes, too. I knew she was in pain, though she never complained.

I sat by her bedside in the quiet room and listened to her labored breathing.

"Life is life; one has to be practical," she said after a moment, and opened her eyes. They had always been remarkable— large and very light blue. Now they seemed enormous: pools of still, opaque water. Cold, frozen. "I have tried . . ." She left the sentence unfinished and closed her eyes. I felt as if there must have been something I could do to help her, but I could think of no response. Then she spoke again.

"You could do with a bit more common sense, Adam," she said. "Be practical. Get on with your life. Don't look back. There is no help to be found in the shadows of the past. There is no help. We have to help ourselves as best we can."

And she awkwardly turned first her head, then her entire shrunken body. I stood, and for a moment I watched her narrow back. What had been a small but surprisingly voluptuous body was now just a will clinging to bones. I turned to leave the room, but before I had crossed the floor, I heard her voice again.

"There is no comfort anywhere, Adam. No forgiveness. We are alone with ourselves. With our memories. And better off without them."

The room went silent, and the questions I had wanted to ask burned inside my head. In the stillness, with her back to me, she uttered her last words.

"I have nothing to say."

She died during the night, and I never heard her voice again.

All she left me was a silver box and the photos it contained.

And the accounts. I was surprised when I was told that her estate contained such a large amount of money, distributed over a number of bank accounts in Sweden and Switzerland. Surprised and uncomfortable. They had nothing to do with me. *Mamma* was gone, and this inexplicable fortune was left behind. She died as she lived. Silent. And alone. It had taken less than six months from diagnosis to death, and she never once complained. Practical, ever practical. But also secretive, keeping even her illness to herself, leaving no will, no diary, no personal papers. And nobody to ask. She had closed the door behind her and left me with no key to the past. Just money.

As I sat on the hill above Wellington, my eyes fell on Clara's envelope in my hands. I opened it and took out two photographs. I looked at the smaller one first. It was a portion of a larger picture—someone must have cut it out of a group photo. I could see that the sides were trimmed a little unevenly. It showed a young woman, standing straight and looking into the camera. She wore a dark dress, perhaps a uniform of some kind, and flat shoes. Her dark hair was parted in the middle and braided. She looked very young and very vulnerable. I could see that she must have been in a picture with some other women—a few feet were visible behind hers, and on one side I could see part of a shoulder. I turned the picture over. On the back someone had written the name Marta and a number—not a date, perhaps a telephone number.

The other picture showed a young man in formal dress, holding a violin. It wasn't a studio portrait but seemed to have been taken at a function: there were people in the background. The man's large, dark eyes looked straight into the camera with an expression of mild impatience, as if he had just been asked to pose while on his way somewhere. He was tall and lanky, with dark hair combed firmly back.

The shirt seemed a little too big around the neck, and the jacket hung loosely on his body, as if the outfit had been acquired for the occasion and with growth in mind. There was no text on the back of the picture, but I recognized him, just as I recognized the woman. He was Adam Lipski, she the woman on the left in the photograph in my silver box. Marta. My mother's sister.

I sat holding the two pictures in my hand for a moment. Then, as I was sliding them back into the envelope, I noticed a small newspaper clipping inside. It was folded several times, and the yellow paper felt brittle as I carefully extracted it and unfolded it. I couldn't read the text but assumed it was Polish. In the top margin, someone had written a date in pencil, but it wasn't written in Polish. It was French: "*le 21ème février 1939.*" There was a picture and some text, approximately a quarter of a page.

I looked more closely at the picture. It was immediately obvious that it was Adam Lipski, probably taken at the same event as the photograph. He wore the same loose-fitting formal

suit. Beside him was a slightly older man whom I vaguely recognized: shorter, with thick, wavy hair and a marked dimple in
the chin, also in formal evening wear. The older man held his
right arm around Adam's shoulders. Both were smiling.

I didn't know what to make of it. I returned the clipping to
the envelope and stuck it in the breast pocket of my jacket.

I stood and began my descent.

12

"Leave a message."

Then, after a brief pause, "If you like." As if the clipped voice at the other end couldn't care less either way. Or wanted to make sure she was giving that impression. I held the receiver pressed against my ear as the short recording finished, followed by a signal and silence. I am not sure what I had been hoping to hear. The recorded message was intended for anyone and no one. I looked across the room and out the large window, my eyes focusing on the horizon beyond the bay, where I could see the lights of a ship moving like a cluster of fallen stars. I listened to the static silence for another moment, but I said nothing, left no message.

At least I had made the call.

I returned from Wellington with mixed feelings. When I walked through the door in the early evening, the house felt oppressively hot and stuffy. I opened the folding doors to the deck and went outside. As I stood resting my hands on the handrail, I realized how tired I was. Somehow the whole trip now felt awkward. An indulgence and a folly. But more than anything else, I was overcome by an acute sense of guilt, as if even the smallest emotional stirring, or feeling of excitement, were a betrayal.

I hadn't eaten since lunch, so I went into the kitchen and opened the fridge. I stood with the door open, again overcome by a pang of guilt. When had I last felt hunger? I couldn't remember.

There was nothing much in the fridge, but I fried two eggs and ate them on a slice of stale bread out on the deck. The sun was setting, and across the sea I could see the outline of Auckland city against a spectacular pink and orange sunset. I went back to the fridge and took out a beer. Standing on the deck with my eyes on the view, I thought about the one tangible remnant of my early life that my mother had left behind. The small silver box, and the photographs and documents it contained. And I remembered the first time I had seen them.

They were there, scattered over the gray linoleum that my mother would polish with angry energy every Thursday. Proof. She had arrived home earlier than expected and discovered me in the act. There was nothing I could say, and to my astonishment she said nothing. Instead, still wearing her coat, she crossed the floor, bent down, and gathered the papers that dropped from my hands, her own elegant, hard little hands moving as swiftly as when she dealt cards for her daily games of solitaire. The navy poplin of her coat rustled. Not a word was uttered, and I could hear her breathe as she awkwardly stood up again. She gathered the pictures, aligning the edges, then picked up the box and returned the pile into it. She waved me aside and walked up to her open wardrobe, where she paused with her back to me. She seemed to hesitate, and I could hear her inhale through her nose: a dry, angry sound. But she said nothing. I felt my heart race, and the room shrank until it seemed unbearably small, without enough air for the two of us.

Eventually she closed the wardrobe and walked to her small bedside table, placing the box in a drawer. Until the day she died, she never once referred to the incident. Nor did I.

And to me the silence was more frightening than any words could have been.

Later, when I felt I could articulate the questions, it was too late. The box and its contents became mine. I could take my time inspecting them, but they were silent.

I stayed up late. I sat on the sofa in front of the TV, but without watching. The volume was turned down, and the sound was just a wall of indistinct noise around my thoughts. I knew I should be working. I had recently accepted a new project, my first for a year, a score for a short film. The deadline was approaching rapidly, and there were still issues to overcome: sounds that eluded me, technical glitches that needed to be smoothed out.

Instead I stood and walked over to the large bay window. The wind that drifted in pulled with it a smell of the sea. Though that is such a natural thing to say, it's hard to explain. Does water smell? Or is it the meeting of the elements, the sea touching land? Does the sea smell in itself? That salty tang that is almost tangible—does it exist when you are out on the vast ocean and it surrounds you totally?

It was dark, and when I looked up at the sky, the stars hesitantly came into view, as if being lit one after another. I walked outside to my small studio, which is in a separate building below the house. There I sat on the front steps watching the sky. As I kept my eyes on the infinite darkness above, it slowly filled with stars until the Milky Way stretched like a wavering white band across the expanse.

And then I remembered the first time I had consciously studied the sky, lying on my back in the snow outside the apartment building where I lived in southern Stockholm.

Other children had been out making imprints of angels in the new snow. I had watched from the kitchen window, and when the children were called inside for dinner, I went out and lay down in one of the angels. I stared up into the black January sky, and I was totally unprepared for the sight. The longer my eyes focused, the more stars appeared, until the sky seemed to be alive with an explosion of white sparkles. The stars were so very close, or rather I felt as if I were being lifted up until my outstretched hand could touch them.

I stayed in the arms of the angel until the chill of the snow penetrated my jacket and hat. After that first revelation, all my life I have looked for spaces from which to observe the sky, places without distracting artificial light. Waiheke was accommodating in that regard, and Mimi and I used to turn off all the lights and sit on the deck trying to identify the constellations of the Southern sky. They were unfamiliar to me, and when she was little, she would get impatient with my lack of knowledge. But over the years, slowly, we explored that sky together.

Eventually I took my eyes off the sky, stood, and opened the door to my studio. I remained on the threshold, my hands in my pockets and my eyes resting on the desk that held the keyboard. The chair stood turned toward me, inviting me to sit. But instead I closed the door and walked away. The night was mild, and cicadas played loudly.

I finally went back inside, passed the door to Mimi's room, and let my hand touch the doorknob lightly, as I always did. I rarely went into her room anymore, but my hand reached for the door each time I walked past. I continued into my own bedroom and sat on the edge of the bed for quite a while, elbows on my knees and my hands clasped. It was even warmer in here, and after a bit I went over to the window and pushed it open. Taking a deep breath, I realized that I was aware of smells and colors. That I had watched the sky, heard the cicadas.

I pulled out the bottom drawer of the bedside table, stuck my hand into it, and felt around until I found the silver box. Before I opened it, I let my fingers run over the lid. When I had first seen it, as a child, I had been fascinated by the raised pattern on the lid and sides, which seemed to feature people involved in a mysterious sequence of violent, even erotic activities. Perhaps that had contributed to my sense of shame when I was discovered that first time, as if I'd been caught in the midst of an illicit act. Now I knew they were religious images—the Israelites fleeing Egypt. And I had come to wonder if the shame and guilt had perhaps been my mother's as much as mine.

I opened the lid and turned the box upside down so that the contents landed softly on the bedspread. There were two old black-and-white photographs, a more recent passport-size portrait, and one large glossy black-and-white picture. In addition there was a sheet of yellowed paper, folded in four, and a small two-leaf booklet. I took up one of the old photographs and looked closely at the familiar image. It was a picture of six young people, two women and four men. Three of the men were casually seated on the grass, their hands around their shins, their eyes looking straight ahead. Two were smiling, the third had a pipe in his mouth. Behind, and presumably on their knees in order to raise themselves above the seated men, were a man and two women. The woman to the left was petite, and her long dark hair was gathered at the back but had lifted in the wind and blew around her face. She seemed to be looking at something outside the picture to the left, where the wheel of a bicycle could just be seen lying on the grass. It was clear to me that she was Marta, Mother's sister, the woman in the photo Clara Fried had given me. The other woman had an attractively full figure, and she held one hand on her forehead, as if keeping her fair hair out of her eyes, while her other hand rested on the shoulder of the seated man in front of her. She was looking at the camera but bending forward a little as if just looking up momentarily, briefly interrupting an ongoing conversation. She was smiling. I knew she was my mother, but I had never quite been able to reconcile this image with my own perception of her. For me she never smiled.

Through some odd effect, the face of the man between the women was almost completely obscured, either by a fleeting shadow—perhaps from an object behind the photographer— or by some technical mishap. He was considerably taller than the two women and looked to be wearing a shirt and jacket, while the other men were in shirtsleeves. His hands rested on the shoulders of the two women, but there seemed to be a certain reserve in his posture, as if he were following the photographer's instructions rather than his own initiative. On the back of the photo, someone had drawn a rough outline of the group and in pencil jotted down the names of the kneeling three: Marta, Adam, and Wanda. The three men in the front were nameless, and no date or place was mentioned. My eyes focused on the blurred face in the center, and now my mind gave it the features of Adam Lipski. Clara Fried's brother. My father? If so, why had my mother never once mentioned him? And why was my name no longer Lipski but Anker?

I put the picture faceup on the bedspread and placed the other old photo beside it. This was a portrait of my mother and an older man. My mother wore a dark dress and had a string of pearls around her neck. The man was in a dark suit with a waistcoat that stretched over his portly stomach. They stood not touching and unsmiling. Beside my mother was a potted palm, and in one corner the name of the photo studio was printed in embossed gold: G&A, BERLIN. I had no idea who the man was but had always assumed he must be Mr. Anker. My mother's husband. The man whose surname I had carried all my life. If this was their wedding picture, it didn't seem like a happy occasion.

I put it down and picked up the glossy newer photo. This had been taken by a street photographer just outside the gates of Skansen, the outdoor museum in Stockholm. I remembered the day—a rare occasion. It showed the two of us, my mother and me, side by side. I looked closely at her now, trying to see her objectively. She was not yet forty, but she looked older. It wasn't her features so much as her pose. A conscious decision to be a middle-aged woman. I hadn't enjoyed the day—I was too old for seals and monkeys, too young for the historical villages and artifacts. And I was uncomfortable with the company. I looked at myself as a skinny fourteen-year-old, awkward and glum, dressed in shorts and a long-sleeved shirt, posing beside my *Mamma*. Wanda. She wore one of her usual floral-print dresses with a wide skirt, a light summer coat—unbuttoned—gloves, and a hat. Though her outfit was similar to those of the mothers of other children in my class, she somehow looked different. No other mother looked like her.

But then no other boy looked like me either. I remembered feeling, wherever I went, as if there were an invisible sign on my chest stating that I didn't belong. I felt it on my own and even more so in the company of my mother. Instinctively I knew that we enhanced each other's separateness. By ourselves we might have had a slim chance of blending in; together we were impossibly alien. It was as if we gave off a particular smell that was obvious to all. Here, in the picture, we stood beside each other, she clasping her handbag with both hands, I with my hands in my pockets, neither of us smiling. Side by side but not together. What was she thinking? Why had she taken me to the park? It was clear that she wasn't enjoying it. Nor was I. Did she do it for me? Or did she think it was something that normal people did? People who belonged? That our outing would allow us inside, if only for an afternoon?

I put the photo beside the other two and picked up the folded piece of paper. It was brittle and yellowed and had begun to break apart at the folds. I sat with it half open in my hands. I didn't need to read it to remember the text. It stated the place and date of my birth—January 16, 1941, Kraków—and my name, Adam Lipski, son of Wanda Lipski, née Maisky, and Adam Lipski. I placed the paper on the bed and picked up the small booklet, our passport, the entry document to a new life. The photograph stapled onto the document and partly covered with an official stamp showed my mother holding me in her arms. The infant was a bundle, impossible to identify. My mother looked pinched and serious. Or perhaps determined. But there was no hint of motherly pride, I thought. Or love. Perhaps such feelings were secondary to the immediate concern of survival. Her posture was stiff and awkward: I might as well have been a package that had been entrusted to her care.

I looked at this document to a new life, to the only life I knew, and felt nothing. The birth date was the same as on my birth certificate, but on the passport my name was Adam Anker, the name under which I had led my entire conscious life. The brief stretch of time that separated the documents was a void, my dead mother the irretrievably lost bridge between the two.

Finally I took up the last photo and placed it facedown on my palm, reading the words written diagonally across its back: *"Mig tyckes natten bära / ditt namn i svag musik / C."* It had been such a long time since I'd read or spoken Swedish. Now I whispered the line to myself: *To me it is as if the night carries your name in soft music.*

I turned the photo over to look at the image, though there was no need: the picture was just the tangible manifestation of the image of you that lives inside my body. I could picture every detail with my eyes closed. I could smell the fair hair that was pulled away from the solemn face, recall the texture of the skin that stretched over the forehead, re-create the exact intricate pattern of the ears, taste the lips, run my finger along the eyebrows. Remember the exact color of your dark eyes. I touched the photo with my fingertips and sat still for a moment. Here was the image of my daughter's lost past, just as the other photos represented mine. Here was the painful past that had been within my control. The past I could have given Mimi but chose not to. The mother I should have allowed her to know.

I slowly gathered together the photos and documents and returned them to the box. Then I held the box in my hands, the metal cold against my palms, and I thought about that first meeting. The first time I saw you, Cecilia.

It was December, and the annual concert had just finished. Students and teachers mixed with the audience on the floor, and I tried to make my way through the crowds toward the exit. I took a step backward to avoid someone, and instead I bumped into you. You turned, holding your glass high to stop the red wine from spilling onto your white blouse. Then you looked straight into my eyes and lowered the glass, but you said nothing, just nodded slightly.

"What do you play?" I asked, searching for something to make the moment last. At this you smiled and held up your hand, the palm facing me.

"This," you said, "this is my instrument. And these." You pointed to your eyes. In the dark room, they shone black. "I don't play music, I paint." You turned around, craned your neck, and your eyes searched the crowd surrounding us. "I am here with a friend. Or rather someone I know a little. She plays the viola." You turned back to face me, and there was a pause in our stilted conversation. And as in an irreversible chemical reaction, something was set in motion. Such a brief silence, yet as you opened your mouth to speak again, my life changed forever.

"But I think I have lost her," you said, and shrugged your shoulders.

I introduced myself and asked your name.

"Cecilia. Cecilia Hägg." You didn't offer your hand but lifted your glass and toasted me with a wry smile, as if mocking me a bit. Or challenging me. I couldn't think of anything to say that merited the effort of trying to override the noise, so I just lifted my glass in return. But then you bent forward, and I responded, meeting you halfway, and you spoke directly into my ear.

"My father was a musician," you said. "A pianist. You may have heard of him. Andreas Hägg."

I could smell your hair as it brushed against my cheek. I said nothing, just nodded. Of course I knew of him—a brilliant pianist who had died some fifteen years earlier. A tragic sudden death, I remembered. An accident on an icy winter road on the way home from a tour. A funeral service at Jacob's Church in Stockholm, attended by musicians from all corners of the country and many from overseas. Of course I had heard of Andreas Hägg.

I looked at you as you continued to scan the room, searching for your friend. Tall, almost as tall as me, and you held yourself very straight, with your shoulders pushed back, chin lifted. Your profile was clearly outlined in the backlight from the stage: a straight nose, a strong chin, and a high forehead. But the lips were soft, slightly parted. I never once considered how old you were—about twenty, half my age. The age of my students. Already at that first meeting, you seemed ageless to me. So young and so very beautiful, but with an aura of such fierce independence that age became irrelevant. Later, after I had lost you, the enigma of the two sides of your personality never ceased to intrigue me. The part of you that I knew loved me. And the other side that forced me away. The heartbreaking vulnerability. And the uncompromising severity.

When you turned to face me again, you focused those black eyes on my face, squinting and knitting your brow, and I felt as if I were under inspection, being appraised and evaluated.

After a moment you smiled that mocking smile once more and bent forward, this time putting your hand lightly on my arm.

"Let's go somewhere else. It's too noisy to talk here."

Stockholm lay asleep under a soft cover of new snow. It had snowed all day, but as we walked along Valhallavägen, only random snowflakes drifted in the dark air. The temperature had dropped, and the snow was light and dry and lifted with our steps. The city felt cleansed and silenced. The contrast with the noisy indoors could not have been more stark. For a while we remained enveloped in the lingering heat, but soon the cold, clear air penetrated and pushed us together. We walked slowly downhill toward the city center until we found an open restaurant. All the way I was acutely aware of your body next to mine.

It wasn't until I looked at the menu that I realized the restaurant specialized in Polish food. Hearty casseroles and stews. It was late, and we just wanted coffee, but the waitress was all smiles and showed no impatience or disappointment. It arrived swiftly, an elaborate affair with the strong brew served in individual copper pitchers with whipped cream and a small glass of brandy on the side. We talked about art. Music. Books, films. You looked at my hands, and I became conscious of them. You looked at me, and I felt a need to close my eyes, to stroke my chin while your gaze was fixed on me. Your eyes were extraordinary, your eyes. Glittering black pools of infinite depth and mystery, contrasting with the pale skin and blond hair that was pulled back from your face. Later I would discover that they were not black at all, your eyes, but the color of wild blueberries, yet there, across the table, they were as black as the December night sky outside.

You told me very little about yourself, but when you began

to talk about your work, I felt a short reprieve from the continuous scrutiny of my face. Suddenly your hands lifted from the table in swift movements, your eyes sparkled, and your speech became intense. Passionate.

"I paint because I have to. I can't describe it any other way," you said, stretching both hands across the table and looking at me as if to see whether I understood. "It is not always pleasant. In fact, it almost never is. No. It is frustrating. Hard. Dangerous."

"Dangerous?" I asked.

"Yes." You nodded, "Dangerous. Because it is all there. Exposed. Everything is laid bare for the world to see."

I nodded, though I wasn't sure I knew what you meant.

"It's like ripping open your chest," you added. "Or letting somebody—everybody, anybody—into your soul." You leaned back on your chair. "Of course, not everyone is able to interpret what is put in front of them. Or cares to. And that is a terrible risk, too."

Again you put your hands on the table that separated us, palms flat on the surface, and hung your head. I couldn't quite interpret your body language. Were you sad? Perhaps a little drunk? Tired? I could think of nothing to say.

But then you slowly raised your head, and I realized I had been wrong on all three counts.

"Will you come home with me?" you asked.

I sat in my bedroom on the other side of the world with a small photograph in my hand. The only tangible memento of our time together.

And for the first time since Mimi's death, I cried.

13

The silence had been disturbed.

The following week I tried to focus on my work, spending most days in the studio. But I found myself interrupted by thoughts of my meeting with Clara Fried. On Saturday I returned home in the late afternoon, my ears burning from exposure to the sun. The weekends were still harder than the weekdays. There was no logical reason for them to be: my life was not directed by the days of the week. But somehow it seemed easier to keep up the pretense of a kind of normality during the week. Earlier that day I had been sitting at the table on the deck with my morning coffee, and the prospect of another day alone in the house was suddenly unbearable. On the spur of the moment, I called Antony and Vanessa. Friends since we became neighbors when I first arrived in the country, they were sensitive and kind, asked no questions, expected no answers. During the past year, they had kept a thoughtful distance, but always making me feel that they were there for me, on my terms. They had no children—I had never known why—and Mimi had been theirs, too. Their grief had been double: sharing mine, while struggling with their own.

They had persisted with their invitations to lunches, dinners, and other occasions. Although I seldom accepted, I was always asked. Earlier that week they had called to suggest lunch Saturday with friends visiting from Sweden. The wife worked in film, and they thought I might enjoy meeting them. In my usual fashion, I had declined but then abruptly changed my mind on the day. The afternoon had slowly unfolded over food and drink and easy conversation. The Swedes were good company, and we discovered several professional connections. I realized I found it a relief to meet people who took me at face value. Who knew nothing about me. The hours passed quickly. Waiheke on late-summer weekends offers a kind of laid-back ambience it is hard to find anywhere else. I think the three of us who knew the island delighted in the obvious joy of the two guests.

I thought I had been careful with my drinking, but now I saw that perhaps I was feeling a little drunk. Still, when I came home, I went to the kitchen and took a can of beer out of the fridge.

I walked out onto the deck, placed the can on the handrail, and rested my hands on either side of it. The day had the comfortable warmth that follows weeks of consistent summery temperatures and sunshine. It was late February, schools had reopened, and true to form the weather had turned on its summery best. The sun was setting in a crescendo of gold beyond the outline of the distant city across the water. I stayed till I had finished the beer, then went inside and sat down on the sofa. Alone in the house, I was overwhelmed by my own presence. There were no distractions, no escape from my thoughts or my physical self. I clicked the CD player remote, and the sound of Glenn Gould playing the *Goldberg Variations* filled the room. It was the mature man playing, not the exuberant young genius, and I found it soothing and sad at the same time. As the music moved from the contemplative slow opening to the confident artistry of the faster movements, I rose and walked over to my desk. I lifted the mouse pad, pulled out the piece of paper, and held it in my hand, folding it and unfolding it several times while I stared blankly out the window. It would be well after eight there, not too early to call. I picked up the phone and dialed the number. And this time there was a reply.

"Cecilia?" I said.

14

"Adam," you said.

Instantly I was overcome by the same feeling as when you used to touch my face with your fingers each time we met. It was as if your hands had to touch my skin to make sure I was real. You said my name in the same way, as if reassuring yourself.

"Adam," you repeated slowly.

"Cecilia. How are you?" I said, cringing at the sound of the trivial words.

"Oh, Adam." There was a long pause, and for a moment I thought I had lost you.

"You might as well ask me who I am as how I am," you said quietly. "It's been so long. So very long."

"Yes," I said, my mouth dry. "Nineteen years. A very long time."

You didn't reply, so I started again.

"I will be in Europe next month, and I . . . I was wondering if you would allow me to see you when I come to Sweden."

When again you didn't respond, I repeated my question.

"Would you?"

I listened to the distant droning on the line, like the sound of muted rolling waves, and I could almost see the vast ocean that separated us.

"Yes," you said eventually. "Come here. To the island." Then, after a slight pause, "If you like."

I told you I would let you know the dates when my booking was confirmed.

I listened for your response, but there was nothing. The line went dead.

It was decided, but my journey to your island was not a straight line.

15

I was leaving.

Leaving the safety of Waiheke Island, my home for over fourteen years. Longer than I had lived anywhere else. My plans were not clear, but I instinctively knew that this departure was not like the ones I had made in the past. I wasn't fleeing; I was traveling toward a goal. I had contacted Mr. Liebermann, who had agreed to meet me in Kraków.

A year had passed since Mimi's death, yet my grief was still a physical, aching pain. It was still a conscious act to hold myself together, to move, to eat, to remember which day of the week it was, what time of day.

But the music was back. I worked again, though there was a fundamental difference in everything I did. It was as if my hearing had become sharper, as if a protective layer of skin had been shed. My newly awakened awareness was not like anything I had experienced before. My thoughts were clear, and often painful. Memories emerged without warning, and I was unable to protect myself against their impact. A week after my trip to Wellington, I had gone to town to see my travel agent. I had several reasons to fly to Europe; the trip was long overdue. I had avoided all commitments for almost a year, and I had developed a standard decline response that I habitually used. All the while I had known there would come a day when I would have to choose. Reenter the remnants of my life and try to build an existence from the fragments, or resign myself to mere physical survival. A kind of slow death. But I had deferred the decision, day by day, month by month. Now, finally, the moment had arrived. It hasn't been a conscious, active resolution but more like a chain of events, the beginning of an uncertain exploration; not so much my own initiative as destiny's. Minute steps that seemed to be taking me in a new direction.

There was the offer of a contract for a major film score. Ben Kaplan had phoned one day out of the blue and asked me to write the score for his new feature film. After a brief conversation, he had promised to e-mail background material. I didn't know Ben, though our paths had crossed a couple of times in life. However, I knew of his recent international success, and my dulled senses had registered surprise at the offer. Still, his e-mail had sat in my in-box for weeks before I printed and read the material. Then I e-mailed him to suggest a meeting. In Sweden. It was an exceptional opportunity, yet this was not what occupied my thoughts. What did was my own slowly gathering resolve to resume the thwarted quest into my past.

As with my trip to Wellington, the visit to the travel agent had triggered a multitude of emotions. It felt a little like learning how to walk anew. There was the distant memory of how these actions were once handled, but now I was using a different part of my brain to perform them. It was painful, difficult. Very slow. Yet, beneath the pain, I had to admit that I could sense a stirring of anticipation. I wanted to make this trip. I was ready for it.

And then, suddenly, caught unprepared, I was struck with the memory of the last time I had taken Mimi and her friend Charlotte out for dinner. It was just before the summer holidays, and for some reason I had chosen the revolving restaurant in the Sky Tower. But as soon as we sat down, I knew it had been a foolish choice. One look at the girls' faces and I saw that they were doing it for me, to please me, while I had thought I was doing it for them. We felt awkward, all three, but we worked our way through a three-course dinner, politely conversing and chewing while the city shifted below. At one stage, between the main course and dessert, the girls excused themselves, heading for the restroom, and I found myself alone at the table. I looked out over the sea, where the perfectly symmetrical cone of Rangitoto Island rose out of the water a little to the right, with sailboats drifting by in an infinite parade. Waiheke sat farther out to the right, merging with the contours of the other islands, all lightly shrouded in an early-evening mist. I looked down on the city, reflecting that it had been my home for almost eighteen years, and yet it seemed strangely unfamiliar from this perspective, high above. I suddenly realized I had never embraced it with my full consciousness as my permanent home.

When I turned my head, I saw the two girls approaching, crossing the floor while involved in an intense conversation. I followed them with my eyes, and as they sat down across the table, I felt that the seating was appropriate. The girls sat together on one side, I on the other, and I was aware that there was now a large part of my daughter's life that was becoming unknown to me. As they bent forward, laughing, I saw their hair blend together when it fell over their shoulders, Mimi's dark and Charlotte's blond.

After dinner I took them to Charlotte's home in Ponsonby. They waved to me, two slender, dark figures in the doorway, illuminated from behind, and I felt a mixture of sadness and relief. And guilt. Guilt because I was leaving, and guilt because I felt relieved to go. It feels absurd now, in retrospect. What did I know about guilt then?

On the ferry back, I sat on the top deck and watched the city gradually withdraw. It was clear and not yet completely dark, though the city lights were becoming more obvious as dusk settled. There were no other passengers on the upper deck, and I felt as if I were adrift on the sea, alone.

At home I wandered around the still space, suddenly aware of its every feature. It reminded me of the strange sensation of hearing Swedish spoken as a foreign language for the first time, no longer a physical part of me. The rhythms, the sounds, each individual word clear for me to hear, but I listened to it the way I listen to music that is not my own. On two different planes at the same time. The sheer enjoyment of the whole on the one hand and simultaneously a scientific evaluation, listening for each individual sound, separating and splintering, weighing.

I never made a serious effort to teach Mimi any Swedish, perhaps because I needed to embrace the English language myself. Or because I wanted to create a new context for my own life, and for my daughter's. Our shared new language was a barrier against the past.

My mother might have had the same reasons for never speaking Polish to me. I can see now that these abrupt and total abandonments of our native tongues severed the communication between the generations, causing misconceptions, half-truths; perhaps they even bred lies. My mother brought me up in silence, and I did the same thing to my daughter. Our lives had been built without history, like houses without foundations. We belonged nowhere. And here, my physical home, the only permanent home I ever created, seemed to be sliding away, withdrawing. At the same time, it became clearly visible, like a language learned as an adult: understandable, beautiful, yet not entirely mine.

I'm not sure why that day came to me with such clarity as I stood on my deck watching the sunset. It had not been exceptional; I often took Mimi and Charlotte for dinner in town. It was my small way of reciprocating the hospitality that Mimi enjoyed in her friend's home. Yet now, over a year later, it seemed charged with a kind of elusive significance.

A few weeks after that dinner, Mimi and I were sitting on the deck one night, and she told me how she'd felt when we had parted that evening.

"You never turned to wave a second time, Dad," she said. "You were relieved to go, weren't you?" She looked at me, searchingly, as if trying to read my thoughts. "You waved once, and then you turned quickly and disappeared around the corner. I felt relieved, too. I didn't want to, but I did. Charlotte kept pulling my arm, urging me back inside, but I wanted to stand there and watch you leave."

She turned her face toward me, a pale oval in the summer-evening dusk.

"I thought about what it used to be like when we said good-bye when I was little. I wondered if you knew how upset I got. That horrible sinking feeling when you released yourself from my arms. How you would stand and wave cheerfully before turning to go. I always waved back, smiling, but did you know it was all a fake? I knew yours was. I could tell from your back that the smile was just put on for me and gone the

moment you turned away. But it was all part of our silent understanding, wasn't it? To make it easier to say good-bye."

She looked at me with her painfully clear black eyes and
then said, "But I don't think it was a fair deal, Dad. I believed
we were equals, you and I, that we shared everything. But there
was always a part that was only yours. Because you had a life
before I existed. You had time that belonged somewhere else, in
some dim, distant past that I could never be a part of. When I
was little, I believed that our life only went as far back as I could
remember. Now I know that there was always a past where you
never took me. But I think it belongs to me, too. I really do."

She was so serious, it was as if she had rehearsed the entire
speech.

"I have always known that there were things I could never
ask, things I knew you would never tell me, that you would
never discuss. I accepted that. And it has been there all my
life, almost like . . . a handicap that will disappear if you never
talk about it."

Oh, my Mimi. How did I respond? What answers did I
give?

"But you see, Dad, for a long time I thought I knew anyway, somehow. I thought I knew all I needed to know. And if
we didn't talk about the past . . . well, that was because it was
too hard. We had a silent agreement, you and me. And for a
long time that was fine. For a long time it really was, Dad. But
the past was there all the while. We could pretend that nothing existed outside our small world, but we both knew that
was wrong. We carried all that had happened before without
ever talking about it. I told myself that I knew what had happened before I was born, before our life together. I couldn't

remember it, but I still owned it. That's what I thought. For a long time, I never felt I had to ask or explore. Because all that was yours seemed to be mine, too. And if there were things that were too hard to talk about . . . well, then that was something you carried for me. And I felt safe."

My wise, thoughtful Mimi. How could I have ignored your right to know?

"But, Dad, everything has changed. It feels as if one day I discovered a tiny crack in our perfect world, and now I'm watching it gradually open wider, day by day. It's not anything you've done or said. And it's not me either. I can see now that there will be parts of my life that you will never know. I know we love each other, but it doesn't mean we are the same. We don't see everything the same way. I need to make my own decisions, and I need to know enough to be able to do that. I need to know about my past so I can begin to live my own life, Dad. I need you to talk to me. About your life. About my life. About my mother. Talk to me."

I think about this, our last serious conversation. The most serious conversation we ever had. And all I hear is Mimi. Where is *my* voice? Where are *my* answers? I can hear her little-girl's voice earlier. The innocent questions that I, the adult, was always able to avoid. "Where is my mother?" "She can't be with us, not because she doesn't love us but because there are other things she needs to do." "What does my mother look like?" "She is so very beautiful. Just like you, my little Mimi." Disrespect was what I gave her. But how could I have done otherwise? How could I explain to my daughter what I couldn't explain to myself?

In the end all I gave my daughter was silence.

"It feels like everything we have carried around with us without ever talking about it is becoming real. It just won't stay in the background any longer, Dad. It's rising like a giant ghost out of the darkness, casting a shadow over everything. I can't pretend it's not there anymore. I can't make it invisible again. I'm not even sure I want to know, but I have to. Dad, I have to ask you. I really do. I need to know."

I thought of a moment in my life with my mother when perhaps, if I had been a little older, Mimi's age at least, I could have posed those same questions. I looked at my daughter in the gray light of the early evening out on the deck, and I was overcome by a longing for my mother. Not with love and affection, but because I needed her. I needed the opportunity to face her as my daughter faced me. I wanted to know how she would have handled the situation. She could have taught me how, or maybe she might have managed it so that it would have taught me how not to respond. But I had nothing, nobody to guide me.

In the end I remained mute.

What interrupted our conversation that night? I can't remember. A phone call? But the words had been uttered, and as Mimi said, we couldn't make them unsaid. They had taken on a physical presence.

Still, we kept them at bay; perhaps we both dreaded the moment when we would sit down and open the Pandora's box. I certainly did. But I think we were confident that the right moment would come if we gave it time. Arrogantly, we were sure of one thing.

Time.

16

My mother learned to speak Swedish, but she never really talked to me.

"*Mamma!*" I'd call out as I stepped inside the door.

And as usual the word would feel heavy and awkward, the syllables consciously formed, the sounds forced. I couldn't quite explain to myself why I'd call out for her. I could sense the moment I opened the door that the apartment was empty. Perhaps I just needed to make absolutely sure. Because if she had called back, "I am here, Adam. In the kitchen," well, then I would have had to drop the weight that I always carried with me and leap up the two flights of stairs in anticipation of meeting her inside. But in the silence, in the hallway, it would fall off my shoulders onto the floor, together with my school-bag. She had been baking. I could smell it as soon as I opened the front door to the building, and the smell intensified with each flight of stairs. Relieved, but with a lingering sense of guilt, I would walk into the small kitchen. The shiny linoleum was slippery under my feet. My mother didn't enjoy cooking, and I'm not sure that she enjoyed baking either. But she did bake, with a dogged persistence that was similar to that of her weekly cleaning and polishing of the apartment. It didn't seem to come naturally, and I never felt that she took any pleasure from it. I knew instinctively that the soft, warm buns that smelled of cinnamon and butter were an offering. A substitute for the love she was unable to give. I would come home from school and take in the cloying scent, but I'm not sure what feelings it inspired. A complex mix of emotions, never articulated or analyzed—a child's emotional response to a mother's vain attempts at reaching across the abyss of silence. I lifted the linen cloth covering the warm buns, took one, and dug my teeth into the dough, but I felt no satisfaction. Rather my heart sank, and I became acutely aware of some required response that I knew I was unable to deliver.

I would open the small fridge, take out the milk bottle, and pour myself a glass, then rinse my mouth with the cold liquid until the last remnants of the sweet cinnamon flavor had dissipated.

Some days she came home late. It didn't happen often, but she never explained why. I would already be in bed, my ears listening for the sound of the key in the lock. She would move quietly, whether out of consideration for me or because she wanted privacy, I didn't know. The soft rustling of her clothes, her stockinged feet on the floor—the sounds were barely audible. I saw them more than heard them. Then, finally, a deep sigh as she sat down at the kitchen table and picked up the worn deck of cards on the marble windowsill. I knew that her eyes would glaze over as her hands moved swiftly, first shuffling the cards, then splitting the deck in two, and finally the sharp prattle as the cards were flicked. Then the tapping of the cards against the hard Formica tabletop as she laid out a game of solitaire.

All the while I would lie in my bed, unable to wipe the image of her from my mind. However quietly she moved, from inside my dark room and with the door half closed I could still picture her, as if in a film. I could see her enter the hallway, turning and closing the door behind her and securing the safety chain. See her take off her hat and carefully put it on the rack before removing her coat and shoes, then running her hands over her breasts and stomach, straightening the fabric of her dress. She had dainty feet, narrow, with high arches. Often she would absentmindedly sit with them outstretched in front of her, turning and stretching them, pointing her toes where the stockings were darned, the patches like scabs. In the darkness I could see rather than hear her light her cigarette before the faint smell drifted into my room. Her quick fingers on the cards matched her feet, small and hard, with narrow tips and well-manicured nails. She wore a ring on her left ring finger, a plain band of gold, but I had always thought that fingers were made for other kinds of rings. Heavy and sparkling, with colorful stones.

She spoke Swedish with a heavy Polish accent, but she mastered the vocabulary perfectly. Every evening she would lie in bed, a hairnet protecting her firmly permed ash blond hair and her cat's-eye glasses sitting low on her narrow nose, and read from the dictionary for exactly fifteen minutes. "Ach, I read two pages of words every night. In a year I learn more words than most Swedish people know." It was probably true. But when she spoke, the words came out singularly, with no context, as if the effort of speaking in the new language did not stretch to giving the words a meaning. It sounded strangely incomprehensible, although absolutely correct. Empty, mechanical sounds.

I was ashamed of her. And I was ashamed of my feelings of shame. In school, at the end-of-year assembly, she sat like a foreign bird in the otherwise-homogeneous flock of sparrow parents. Her hat was wrong, her gloves, her shoes. Even the way she sat with her legs crossed at the ankles was grotesquely wrong. I dreaded her attempts at making conversation with the other parents—or, worse, her forced cheerful comments to my classmates. All the way home, I walked with my back rigid, my shoulders pulled up, and my head bent, putting one foot in front of the other with effort while I listened to her high heels *click-clack* against the pavement.

But sometimes, out of the corner of my eye, I would catch something else. A fleeting moment when the shadow of something drifted by. She could be standing by the window, pressing her hands against her lower back as if it hurt. Or she could pause by the kitchen sink, one foot resting on the other, and look out the window. And suddenly music would fill my mind. I would try to hold on to the image while I hurried to my room and took out my violin. And when I was able to stay inside that vision, the music would pour from my fingers.

She encouraged my music from the very start. Found me good teachers. When I practiced, she would sit in the green armchair in the living room, half turned away from me with her arms crossed over her chest. I was never able to see the expression on her face while I played, but she would sit immobile until I finished.

When I was nine, my teacher, Mr. Franzén, asked to see her and told her I was gifted, a serious talent. She came home visibly upset.

"I'm a practical person. I've tried to bring you up practical, too. Music is not practical. The School of Music!" she snorted, sucking hard on her cigarette and picking a tobacco flake from her lip as she sat down at the kitchen table. "Definitely not practical."

I said nothing, but in my mind the word "definitely" played

louder and louder and completely drowned all my thoughts. *Def-i-nite-ly. Def-i-nite-ly.* The syllables repeated themselves rhythmically in my head, rising higher and higher, jubilantly. She inhaled on her cigarette and looked at me with knitted brows, but I felt as if her pale eyes saw somebody else. She cocked her head, and at that moment, without words, we understood each other absolutely. Then she nodded slowly and stubbed out the cigarette in the ashtray. The fleeting shadows of the past had conquered the pragmatic reality she'd fought so hard to establish. The matter was never discussed again. I owned the music. But her defeat was terrifying, because until then I had considered her invincible. Later on, I sometimes had the impression that there were moments when she seemed to notice some other aspect about me. A half-forgotten memory. A ghost. All our time together after that day, the ghosts lived with us.

And between us.

II

A Voice

They mutilate they torment each other
with silences with words
as if they had another
life to live

they do so
as if they had forgotten
that their bodies
are inclined to death
that the insides of men
easily break down

ruthless with each other
they are weaker
than plants and animals
they can be killed by a word
by a smile by a look

—Tadeusz Różewicz,
translated by Czesław Miłosz

17

It was raining when I stepped off the train.

I had flown into Vienna the day before and spent a night there, hoping to adjust to European time. But I had slept little. Instead I lay in the anonymous hotel room wide awake and filled with a tangled multitude of feelings, while the city's hushed evening sounds drifted in with the mild spring air. I felt lonely—or alone, rather. It was over thirty years since I had last been in Vienna. A lifetime. I had no wish to explore the city this time; it was just a brief stop, and I was anxious to be on my way. I could hear the light rain tapping on the windowsill—all other sounds seemed distant.

My mother came to visit only once during the years I lived in Vienna. She arrived by train on a rainy night much like this one, except it was autumn, not spring. We had gone to meet her, Magda and I. I hadn't told my mother about Magda, thinking I would spring our relationship on her as a surprise. Magda looked beautiful in a new pale blue coat that had cost much more than she could afford. Her dark hair was gathered in a thick braid that ran down her back over the coat's soft wool. I knew she was nervous, and I pressed her hand while we stood waiting on the platform. For the first time in my life, I think I felt a slight anticipation at the thought of meeting my mother. It was as if Magda were a kind of offering. Innocently, against all reason, I thought she would be a catalyst to nor-mality. My first serious girlfriend. I can see us standing close together as the train approached, and I cannot for the life of me understand where my hope came from. My innocent, fragile Magda with the pale face and the vulnerable gray eyes. How could I have placed such trust in her powers?

My mother stepped off the train, and her eyes searched the platform until they landed on me. She smiled thinly. She looked almost happy, and my own senses responded. I smiled back and waved. She turned and placed her small suitcase on the platform beside her feet. As we approached, she looked up and slowly opened her arms, as if to embrace me. I took a step backward and put my arm around Magda's shoulders.

"Mother, this is Magda," I said, and Magda stretched out her hand in greeting.

The effect was so unexpected that I dropped my arm instantly, separating myself from Magda. My mother gasped, pressed her handbag against her chest with both hands like a shield, and stared at me. We stood as if paralyzed, all three.

Eventually I repeated my words.

"Mother, this is Magda. Magda and I are—"

Instead of responding, my mother picked up her suitcase and started toward the exit. I followed, trying to tear the suitcase out of her hand. At some point she stopped and turned to face me.

"I will take a taxi to my hotel," she said. "We will talk later."

And with that she walked off. Magda was crying and I stood feeling totally numb. My mother never talked to me about the incident. I saw her only over a short, awkward lunch. She stayed two days and never came to hear the concert that had been the reason for her visit. She died the following year. That winter Magda drifted deeper into her illness, and the following year she was hospitalized. In a sense I think I had always known that Magda would not be able to live in my world. Perhaps her vulnerability had been part of her attraction for me. Her elusiveness, the feeling that she would be mine for only a short time, and even then not totally mine. It had been that, the music, and her looks. Her solemn pale face and large gray eyes. Her rich dark hair, long enough to cover her when she curled up after we made love. And then there was the haunting beauty of her music. It would be many years before I could see in her what my mother saw that day as she stepped off the train here in Vienna.

You, Cecilia, she never met.

Now I lay in my hotel bed, dozing in short spells interrupted by fleeting, uneasy dreams, and I was relieved as night turned into morning and I could hear the first hurried steps on the pavement outside the window, echoing the sounds that I had always believed carried my very first conscious memory of my mother—her shoes clattering against the pavement, me trailing behind her in the light rain, holding on to her damp woolen coat, gulping for air that seemed to have been used again and again until all the oxygen had been taken out of it, listening to the tired shuffling of feet, coughs, a baby's thin wailing.

But I knew now that there were other, preceding images. I caught elusive glimpses of a time beyond the reach of a child's recollection. There had been a price to pay for the security of that grip on her woolen coat. A pact, incomprehensible and absolute. Life had started there and then. Her face had loomed over me, white and frighteningly distorted by the perspective.

"We are at home, Adam. Everything begins here. Always remember that. Don't look back."

I did throw a quick glance over my shoulder, but there was

nothing to see, just a mass of anonymous dark figures following us in the fine rain. In front of me, my mother's back was
the only known feature in a foreign world, my hand on the
fold of her coat a lifeline bought at a terrible price.

And here, outside the anonymous hotel window, there were
again those same sounds. Soles against cobblestones. Heel irons
going *click-clack, click-clack*. I stood and walked to the window, pulled aside the net curtain. I watched the street, shining
in the dull light that was neither night nor day. The glow from
the streetlamps was gradually dimming as day approached.
The city was about to resume its daily routines, and I felt relieved. I stepped into the shower.

After a quick breakfast, I made my way to the Südbahnhof.

From my seat on the train, I watched the passing landscape
through the dirty, rain-streaked window. I felt safe here—in
between places, in an anonymous no-man's-land—and I allowed myself to catch up on the sleep I had lost the night
before.

I woke with a start as the train pulled in to Kraków's
Główny station.

Once outside, I stood looking over the space in front of
me. Whatever picture I might have had of the city beforehand
was erased by what my eyes registered. Major construction
work was in progress—a redevelopment of the entire station
area, it seemed—but this Sunday evening all was still, while
wet tarpaulins flapped listlessly in the drizzle. The heavy ma-
chines looked like petrified giant insects.

I caught a taxi and tried to take in the view through the
grimy windows as the car drove through the city, but in the
gray light it had no distinct character. The taxi was old and

had lost whatever comfort it might once have offered. Although all the windows were rolled down an inch or two, it smelled of gasoline and cheap aftershave over a lingering base of stale food. But the ride was swift and short, and the driver spoke a little English. I had booked myself into a small pension in Kazimierz, a quick ride from the railway station. The taxi came to an abrupt stop, and the driver got out. I paid and retrieved my suitcase from the trunk, where it had been squeezed between tattered plastic bags and bundles of cloth. The driver banged the lid closed, lifted his hand in a friendly wave, and drove off, the car emitting a burst of oily fumes that were slowly absorbed by the humid air. I stood for a moment, looking up at the old building where muted yellow light seeped out from behind closed curtains in most of the windows. Rattan chairs and tables were piled high along the wall in a vain attempt at keeping them out of the rain. The street was divided by a median strip of land with grass and mature trees surrounded by a cast-iron fence in the shape of linked menorahs. The trees were coming into leaf, and a soft brush of fresh green hovered around the branches. Across the road I could see small groups of what looked like tourists in front of the Remuh Synagogue. I drew a deep breath.

"We don't talk about it. We don't even think about it. And you will see, it will go away." My mother stood in the doorframe, with the light from the hall making her a dark, featureless silhouette. "It will go away. We will forget." And she turned and left, pulling my bedroom door almost closed behind her.

But it didn't. It never went away. The questions that could never be posed took on a life of their own. And the silence nurtured them. After the day when I discovered the silver box, there were names, too. Kraków. Lipski. The lingering awareness of a *before* grew stronger over time. "Where were we before? Where did we come from?" The never-asked, never-answered questions grew like tumors, spreading through my body, coloring everything. Yet in a way they provided a strange kind of comfort. There was something beyond reality where I belonged. The memories themselves eluded me, drifted further and further into the shadows, but the awareness of their existence grew in intensity. Sometimes I would wake up in the morning knowing that in my dreams the shadows had cleared and allowed me a glimpse, but all that remained when I opened my eyes was the impact. Feelings of grief, excitement, joy related to something that had withdrawn and was once more out of my grasp.

What hopes did I have for this visit? What futile dream had brought me on this journey? Surely it was complete folly. An attempt to prove that there existed a retrievable past stretching beyond my conscious memory. A chase after dissolving shadows that might prove anyway to be figments of my imagination.

Later in the evening, after a walk around the city and dinner at a small restaurant nearby, I sat on the narrow bed in my bare room. I felt tired again. It was still raining, a fine spring rain. I got up, and through the streaked window I could see the street below, empty now in the evening. The trees were an intricate black filigree a shade darker than the sky beyond. Across the road I could see the outline of low buildings, with no lights in any of the windows. I could see no people; there were no sounds. I let the curtain fall back and left the window. My bathroom was not en suite but across the narrow corridor. I hadn't brought a robe, and the towel that lay on the bed was small. I felt self-conscious leaving my room in my underwear, towel and toiletry bag in my hands, but I met nobody.

Back in the room after my shower, I felt better. I pulled on a clean T-shirt and poured myself a generous whiskey in the glass on the bedside table. I'm in Kraków, I thought. Finally I am here. Where it all began.

The following morning I woke to a strange noise just outside my window. The room was still dark, but the light outside had a gray tinge to it, not the dense darkness of night. It took me a moment to understand what had awakened me. Pigeons. I got out of bed and stood quietly inside the net curtain. Three pigeons perched perilously on the sharp steel spikes intended to prevent exactly that. Downy feathers lay scattered on the ledge below, which was covered in droppings. Somehow the tenacity of the birds was inspiring. I listened to their monotonous cooing for a while.

I dressed and went downstairs to have breakfast. The space on the ground floor served as a breakfast room in the morning, a casual restaurant during the day, and a bar in the evening. It was painted a dark terra-cotta color and furnished with the same rattan chairs and tables as the area outside on the footpath. I ordered coffee, which was served swiftly. I was surprised to find it excellent, and instantly I knew that I had arrived not with an open mind but with all sorts of preconceived ideas. Breakfast came, a mound of homemade soft cheese with chopped chives, a few cucumber slices, a boiled egg and jam, and a small basket of fresh bread. Conspicuous speakers on either side of the front door emitted anonymous pop music. I was the only guest in the room. I ate slowly.

Afterward I stepped outside and was initially blinded by the glare. When I opened my eyes again, I felt as if I had been placed in front of a lost landscape suddenly revealed after a long time in darkness, as if the light had abruptly lit the stage especially for me.

I had decided to spend the morning walking the streets with no particular plan, just to try to get a feeling for the city. It was Monday morning, and I met people walking with purpose, on their way to work. Out on the main street, a streetcar passed by, filled with passengers. An old woman was selling pretzels from a blue mobile kiosk on the corner. I looked, I took it all in, and Kraków came alive before my eyes.

18

"But, Mr. Liebermann, how will I recognize you?" I asked on the phone.

"You will see," the old man responded. "I will be in Planty Park, on the bench opposite the Dominican Church. Do you know the city, Mr. Anker?"

I didn't think my one-day experience would count, so I answered no.

"No, not yet, of course. I understand," he said. "But you will find your way, I hope. At ten tomorrow. Yes?"

"Yes," I said.

The following morning I set out early and took a walk along the park that embraced the old town. Tulips flowered in abundance, and the grass was intensely green. I realized it had been a very long time since I'd experienced a European spring. The sense of marvel at the new growth after the long death of winter. It was still cool in the shade under the trees but warming quickly as the sun rose. I continued all the way up to the northern corner, where I could see the railway station across the now-busy street. The construction work was in full progress, and the narrow passages around it were filled with people. I turned and made my way back to our meeting point.

He was sitting on the bench, his legs crossed elegantly, one hand holding a pair of leather gloves. Somehow he reminded me of a character from an old black-and-white movie. It had been ages since I'd met someone dressed in a suit, a coat, and a hat. He stood up as he saw me approach, and when we shook hands, I noticed that he was short, so short that it made me conscious of my own height. But his handshake was firm, and he exuded a kind of confident energy that instantly made me comfortable. He suggested a café in the old town and we made our way up the street. We crossed Rynek Główny, the main market square, where the flower sellers were busy setting up their stands. Buckets filled with tulips, daffodils, and grape hyacinths covered the ground. Large flocks of pigeons wandered restlessly, awaiting their matching flocks of tourists. Mr. Liebermann led me across the square, walking briskly in rapid, short paces, gently nudging my arm as he pointed out buildings of interest and provided historical background and anecdotes. His English was excellent, though heavily accented. We continued up one of the narrow streets and entered a small café. It was warm and cozy inside, and the space smelled of freshly baked cakes and coffee.

"Let's sit over there, in the corner," Mr. Liebermann said, nodding toward a table by the window. The tables were covered with crocheted lace tablecloths, and each had a delicate vase holding a single cut tulip. I looked around the room. In the dim light from the wall chandeliers, it seemed timeless, a generic Central European café. As I had in Clara Fried's home, I felt transported.

"Mr. Liebermann, I am very grateful to you for agreeing to see me," I said as I sat down. The old man gestured dismissively with one hand and called the waitress.

"Everything in the right order," he said. "First we must have our coffee." He ordered coffee for two, but I declined his suggestion of cake. The order placed, the old man carefully removed his hat and coat, which the waitress quietly collected. I got the impression he was a regular. Underneath the coat he wore a gray business suit, a white shirt, and a burgundy silk tie. He sat down, panting a little. The coffee arrived, strong and served in gold-rimmed cups. Now that we were seated, our height difference was no longer an issue.

"So. Let us talk, Mr. Anker," he said, peering expectantly into my face, as if the excitement and curiosity were all his. The questions I had practiced in my mind now seemed ridiculous. I clenched my knees underneath the table and took a deep breath.

"I must apologize, Mr. Liebermann," I said. "I have come with nothing to give. I am here to see if I can find something. Something I believe I have been searching for all my life."

The old man's face retained its expectant expression, but he said nothing.

"Before I left New Zealand, I met Clara Fried, and she gave me your name and contact details."

The old man again waved his hand impatiently. "Yes, yes," he said.

"Let me show you this," I said. From the inner pocket of my jacket, I pulled out the envelope with my birth certificate and the photos—the two old ones of my own and the ones Mrs. Fried had given me.

"I grew up in Sweden," I began as I unfolded the passport. "But I always knew I came from somewhere else. My mother was determined to make a new life for us, and she never spoke to me of our existence before Sweden. Where we came from. To me it seemed as if we didn't quite belong anywhere. We had no relatives, no memories, no mementos. And we made no new friends, not even acquaintances. It was as if we were only half alive."

"Mr. Anker, may I ask what it is you do for a living?" the old man said, ignoring the papers on the table in front of him.

"I'm a violinist, but nowadays I compose, I don't perform," I replied.

The old man nodded.

"So, Mr. Anker, what is it that you are hoping to find here?" His amber eyes locked with mine, and I felt as if they saw more than I could ever tell.

"I was hoping to find the past. Glimpses of it. I want to know where I came from. I want to know who I am. There was such a long time when I convinced myself that it meant nothing. That I could live without knowing. Then . . ." I had to force myself to continue. "Mr. Liebermann, a year ago I lost my daughter, Miriam. And with her I lost my future. Gradually the past has come to take its place." I released the grip on my knees beneath the table. "It has become vital for me to trace it. It's the purpose of my existence now."

The waitress arrived with the coffee and a large slice of cake topped with whipped cream. Mr. Liebermann organized the cup and saucer and plate in front of him, then picked up the spoon and started on the cake. I sipped the hot coffee.

Eventually he put the spoon back on the plate and wiped his mouth discreetly with the paper napkin. He nodded again, but a few more moments passed before he began to talk.

"In good times delicate things can thrive. Music. Art. Beauty. All that makes life worth living. In bad times the vulnerable are forever lost." The old man looked out the window, where people strolled past in the stark spring sunshine. "And the good times are so very fleeting. Just interludes, I'm afraid. But the bad times last, and they cast their shadows over the good times. Even the brightest morning contains the memory of the night that was, and the one that is sure to come."

Mr. Liebermann rested his elbows on the table and clasped his hands. "I will begin with the name that has brought us together. Adam Lipski." He was silent a moment, as if choosing his words carefully. "Adam Lipski was my brother's friend. Or perhaps it is more correct to say that my brother was Adam's friend. I'm not sure if Adam had friends. He certainly had no enemies. Or so we thought. Wanted to believe, I suppose. Because it doesn't feel right that the innocent should have enemies." He hesitated, searching for words.

"You see, Adam was . . . not of this world." He looked up with an almost-pleading expression. "Otherworldly? Is that the word? He was the kind of person who cannot be measured or evaluated like the rest of us. Like beauty. It is not good or bad; it simply is. When Adam entered a room, the noise would die down, heads would turn toward him. I don't think he was aware of the effect he had on people. Especially women, but also men. Even children. But he knew the effect his music had. He must have. He was on the brink of a very distinguished career as a violinist. Invited to play with the very best already when he was a young man—a boy, really. This was before he finished at the conservatory and continued his studies in Warsaw. Music was all he cared about. It was his life. People say things like that lightly—'music was his life.' But I mean it literally. I don't think he had a life outside his music. People like him have no understanding of the world. Of the times."

I said nothing, and the old man continued. "You know, the girls called him Adonis." He chuckled, and his eyes glittered mischievously. "Adam was truly extraordinarily good-looking. Very tall, with thick dark hair and very large dark eyes. They would absentmindedly land on one of the girls, and she would blush and become speechless. But I don't think he understood. Or even noticed. The Lipskis took many things for granted. Don't misunderstand me. They were fine people. Good people. It was just that they thought the world was good, you see. Perhaps good people do. Felix Lipski, Adam's father, was a professor at the Jagiellonian University, a world expert on transcription of medieval sacral music. Mrs. Lipski, Sara, had been trained as a singer in Warsaw and Paris, I think, but she never sang professionally, though people said she had a very fine voice. And little Clara . . . Ah, my Clara."

He looked out the window again, then slowly went on, pulling forth the words one by one.

"This country. Our Poland. It is impossible to describe. Impossible to understand. There was a short time when there was hope. Optimism. My father had very limited education, but my mother was an only child and had studied French and music. She could play the piano, and she had dreams, I think. They worked so hard, my parents. They had a small grocery store here in Jana Street, not far from where we are now, just a bit farther up on the other side. The house is still there, but the shop is a smart art gallery now. When my little sister died of pneumonia—she was only three years old—my mother focused all her dreams on my brother and me. It was as if she stopped living herself and only lived through us. She pleaded with my father to send me to the new public school. And that was where I met Clara."

He straightened his posture with the help of a deep inhalation. Then he picked up his spoon again and began turning it with his fingers.

"It was to be such a brief time, just a term and a half, yet to me it was the most important period in my life. The only time of true optimism. Hope. And love. In my childish way, I fell in love with Clara on the first day of school. She was tall, and she had an air of sophistication about her, as if she knew things I could not even begin to imagine. And she was so very beautiful. Her dark hair fell down her back, shimmering in red when the sun touched it. Her eyes seemed to be able to look into my head and my heart. And she had the most contagious laughter, bright and confident, as if the world were filled with matters to laugh about. To my utter surprise, she chose me as her friend. There were moments when I thought that perhaps she loved me a little, too. We became inseparable. To me she seemed to have everything. She could play the piano, she could sing, she was bright—topped the class in all subjects, even physical education. She was fast, she was strong. Above all, fast. Effortlessly, she ran faster than any of the boys. I thought she was the most wonderful person in the world."

Mr. Liebermann fell silent for a moment. He twisted the spoon several times before finally returning it to his plate.

"It takes confidence to appreciate talent and ability. So many are unable to tolerate other people's success. For some time Clara seemed untouchable, and as her constant companion I was safe, too. But it only takes that first small stirring of evil, and nothing, nobody is safe anymore. Toward the middle of the second term, the situation at school started to deteriorate. At first it wasn't Clara and I who were the targets but a small boy called Józef. It began ever so slowly. The odd nasty word. A snowball thrown seemingly for fun. Books disappearing. The kind of childish behavior that is common everywhere. But then . . ." His words trailed off again.

"My father removed me from the school before the end of the second term after three boys had tried to throw me down an old well on the way home from school. I was transferred to the Jewish school. It felt like returning to the womb—that is how I would describe it, but there is no such thing as returning to the womb. The womb is before life. When you have lived, such a space is confinement. The womb is about preparing for life; it cannot be life itself. And I wanted to live. Oh, how I wanted to live. The teachers in the Jewish school, they could teach me nothing about the world I wanted to see. They spoke of the old world. The womb.

"After I left, I saw Clara only occasionally. During our time together at school, I had sometimes been invited to her home. Her parents regularly held musical soirées in their large apartment, and Clara invited me to come. They were magical evenings of unimaginable beauty. To lie on the soft carpet with the side of my body pressing against Clara's and her hair sometimes brushing my arm when she turned her head. To rest on my elbows and look up into the glittering prisms of the chandelier above. And to listen to the music that her brother and his friends performed. I could as well have been in heaven."

Mr. Liebermann seemed to be watching the scene in his mind, and his lips twitched in a fleeting smile.

"In the Lipskis' home, Adam's exceptional talent absorbed all the attention, not just because of its impact on the outside world but for who he was. What it was. He was the sun around which they moved, Clara and her parents. They seemed to be constantly on the alert for anything that might obscure the light emanating from him, the sounds. Not that Clara seemed to mind—quite the contrary. She was her brother's most ardent admirer and constant protector."

Mr. Liebermann bent forward as if he wanted to make sure I understood him properly.

"You see, Adam had only the one, truly exceptional talent. In every other respect, he was, ah . . . undeveloped, unformed. Helpless. And I think Clara knew it. Her parents certainly did. In a sense it was as if he was extraordinarily talented and utterly handicapped at the same time. Others saw just the one side. Because he was able to produce such wonderful music, they projected other qualities onto him as well, qualities he most certainly did not possess."

Mr. Liebermann sighed, picked up his spoon, and mashed the remnants of his cake.

"And when Adam and your mother . . ." He took an audible breath. "It was terrible to watch. Clara and I, we were only children, but even for us it was obvious. It was like watching two ships slowly sail toward an inevitable collision, knowing that they would both go under. Clara tried to steer Adam away. But what could we do? We were children. And there were other issues drastically impinging on our lives. Clouds towering on our horizon."

We sat in silence for a moment before I felt able to pose a question. "The Maisky family, did you know them, too?"

Mr. Liebermann, lost in his thoughts, seemed surprised to hear me speak.

"No, not well at all. We knew of each other, of course. But the Maiskys were prominent. Very wealthy. Very Polish. Mr. Maisky traded in heavy machinery. A brilliant businessman. Largely self-made. Well connected where it mattered. He had extensive business dealings overseas, traveled all over the world—to America, Germany, Sweden. It was said the family had property in France or Italy, too. They mixed in the highest circles. They were Polish first, Jewish second. Part of the nationalist movement. Very different from the rest of us. Not that it made any difference in the end. When the black night sets, the shades become indistinguishable. It swallowed us all. Polish, Jewish, Nationalist, Zionist."

He pulled out a neatly ironed white handkerchief and blew his nose discreetly before continuing. "The Maisky girls were beauties, each in her own way. They were icons to admire more than anything. They spoke French and German, dressed exquisitely. They were musical, too. Everybody knew of the Maisky girls. But no, I didn't know them personally. I remember Marta more than Wanda. She played the piano. I think she was good, but don't take my word for it. I am not musical, in spite of my mother's efforts. I know beauty, though," he said with an impish grin. "The beauty of women. Even then, as a little boy, I knew that Marta was a beauty. She was small and slim, but feminine. Vulnerable in a way that made you want to put your arm around her. You know. . . ." He shrugged his shoulders. "She was very pale, and her dark hair curled along her forehead. She looked fragile, like something lacking a protective layer. And her eyes, ah! Gray. But what gray! Like sparkling anthracite. Large and innocent, hidden under her lids as she kept them downcast when she played. But then, when she briefly looked up, it was as if the world became a little brighter. When she played, she had a way of biting her lower lip. Even then I found it . . . alluring." Mr. Liebermann waved to the waitress and ordered another coffee. I declined.

"And Wanda?" I asked.

"Oh, she was pretty, too," the old man replied. "Very pretty. But, you know, she was a couple of years older. She had almost crossed the line that made her an adult, no longer a girl. I suppose that influenced the way we looked at her. Marta, just like Adam, needed someone to look out for her. And for Marta, Wanda played that part. Wanda could do anything. She was brought up to be her father's heir, I think. Like a son. Very capable. She played the violin but somehow always in a secondary role, never the first violin, never solo. She was very competent. Capable and competent. She had a nice figure, delicate feet. Odd thing to remember, but I do. I remember that she used to take off her shoes at the house concerts, not as if she were tired from walking but rather consciously, as if she were proud of them. Showing them off. She would rub her feet, one against the other, slowly."

The old man looked at me and smiled again. "I must have found that alluring, too, but in a different way. With a slight sense of shame. But other than such observations, I did not know the Maiskys. And life has taught me how little we know about our neighbors. Later that ignorance would prove to be a good thing. There wasn't so much to tell."

Mr. Liebermann clasped his hands on the table, and I watched the spotted skin stretch over his knuckles.

"When my brother Pavel fled in 1939, he took Adam with him. There was a whole group of young men leaving from our part of town. I have carried with me always the sight of them in our hallway. Adam so tall beside Pavel, who was short and slight. My brother had a quick brain, but his body was not made for hardship. It was his dream to become a political cartoonist. He had a wonderful talent—there was nothing he couldn't draw. He could make you laugh with just a few pen strokes, then make you consider why you had. I often think of them standing there, each carrying an extraordinary talent that would be of no use. My mother cried silently into her hands while my father embraced first Pavel, then Adam. We never saw them again. Never. So this image is very important to me. I carry it with me wherever I go." He fell silent for a moment.

"I lost my parents the following year. My mother first, as we were separated when we arrived at Auschwitz. My father later, when he could no longer hold on to life. You would think that the last loss would be the hardest to bear. Being left alone. But that is not how it was. It was the loss of Pavel. The first. After that it was as if I were somehow prepared. The loss of my brother opened the door to darkness for me." Mr. Liebermann closed his eyes. When he opened them again, I thought he looked tired and drained. He pinched the bridge of his nose.

"After the war I ended up in New York. Alone. And even after many years, I would walk the streets and a part of me would scan the faces of the people I met. Searching, searching always for my lost brother. Sometimes the posture of a person turning around would make my heart skip a beat. A gesture, the shape of a head. It was like constant picking at the scab of a wound. Taking a perverse pleasure in the pain. I knew that my parents were dead, but I didn't know what had happened to Pavel. Or to Adam.

"In the beginning we had news from friends of friends. We heard that they had made it safely to Lithuania. That they were alive. Asking us not to worry about them. To look after each other, try to leave if we could. But the messages seemed tainted by the chain of people they had traveled through. Worn and faded. We never met anybody who had met them, only those who had met someone who had met someone who had met them. I suppose that, just like Clara, I have never been able to let it go. To let my brother go. Because the trail was never cut; it just dwindled. Faded into distant obscurity. I could never be certain. There was always a thin hope. And I nurtured it." He leaned back. "Perhaps I returned to live in Poland because of this. Perhaps I thought Poland would be the best place to wait. Wait till we meet again. Pavel and I."

He sighed and looked out the window for a moment, and when he turned back to me, it was as if he had closed one chapter and started on another.

"Do you know German, Mr. Anker? Do you know the word *hässlich*? Translated into English it means 'ugly.' But it means more than that, I think. It means worthy of hatred. Hateful. The house I live in is hateful. I think it was designed and constructed in hatred, and I think it survived the war because it had nothing to lose. It wasn't even worth demolishing—there was no beauty there to destroy. But I grow tomatoes on the balcony in the summer, and I take my walks in Planty Park. And I wait for my brother. Then, on the Sabbath, I go to the temple and I pray for my brother. I wait here in patience; I have all the time in the world.

"And this is all I have to tell you. I am sorry," the old man said.

"You have told me more than you can imagine," I said. "I am truly grateful."

"Mr. Anker, I know what it is you are searching for. You wish to know your father and your mother. I am sorry I have not been able to give you more. But I have a friend. He lives here in Kraków, and every Thursday I go and visit him to play a weekly game of chess." He looked up at me. "Do you play?"

"Not well, and it's been a long time," I answered.

Mr. Liebermann smiled and nodded. "My friend Moishe is very old, but his brain is as sharp as ever. There was nobody in Kraków who could beat him at chess when we were young. He won all the competitions—he was my hero. I am sure he could still match the best. When occasionally I win, I have long suspected that he just lets me, out of compassion. Or perhaps to give me some encouragement. I am his only partner these days, and he needs me." He smiled briefly.

"Moishe spent time in Lithuania with Pavel and Adam. Not a lot of time, but he is the only witness I have found who actually saw Pavel after he left here. He met them in April 1940. They were still alive then, surviving in the forests, constantly on the move. But alive. I can't for the life of me imagine either of them there. Pavel so soft and gentle, with a weak chest; Adam otherworldly, his delicate fingers good for one thing only. I still struggle with the images that occupy me. The two of them out in the cold. And the track ends there, leaving them in the forests. But Moishe will tell you. If you wish, we will visit him the day after tomorrow, Thursday. And then we will have dinner. I will cook the usual. Chopped herring. Not cooking, really, but this is what we always have, Moishe and I. And you will talk, the two of you. Moishe will tell you as Adam would never have been able to."

19

I walked Mr. Liebermann to his home.

It was, as he had said, *hässlich*. A drab apartment building with flaking plaster and rusting balconies. We said good-bye and agreed to meet at the same place in the park on Thursday, in the early evening.

I walked toward the river and then continued up to the Wawel, the old fortress looming high above. There were few visitors in the wide courtyard, and I wandered along the gravel paths virtually alone. Baroque music flowed from some invisible source: it was only when I came close to the eastern wall that I realized it housed a small music shop. I stepped inside and was greeted by a woman who was busy unpacking boxes. She smiled and returned to her work when I indicated I was there only to browse. It was a small shop with limited but eclectic stock, classical and jazz. When the recording that was playing came to an end, the woman inserted another CD. I didn't recognize the music but found myself stopping to listen attentively. A piece for cello and piano, it began softly yet with an underlying insistence in every note that slowly built toward a dramatic climax that was almost painful to listen to, followed by a heartbreaking lull, like the aftermath of violent tears. The woman behind the counter turned and looked up as I approached.

"What is that music?" I asked. She shrugged her shoulders apologetically. "No English," she said.

"This music," I repeated, pointing to the CD player behind her back.

"Ah," she said, and smiled. "Szymon Laks, *Passacaille*." She pressed the controls, and the music started again.

"Can I buy it?" I asked when the music came to an end.

The woman shook her head and patted herself on the chest. "My," she said. She paused and looked at me for a moment. Then she turned and removed the CD from the player, slipped it into a small plastic sleeve, and held it out for me, nodding. I fumbled in my pocket for my wallet, but again she shook her head and waved dismissively.

"Take," she said, holding out the CD. "Take. Please." I looked at her, noticing that she was pretty, though somehow too serious to make an effort to enhance her appearance. She gazed at me attentively.

"Thank you," I said, and accepted the gift. "You are very kind." I felt at a loss to say more. The woman turned and inserted another disc into the player, Chopin this time, and then she looked at me again.

"Listen," she said, pointing to the CD in my hand. "Come back. After."

I smiled and nodded. "Yes, certainly. Absolutely. I will come back. When I have listened. Thank you again."

I walked outside into the bright sunshine, crossed the courtyard, and stood by the wall looking out over the river. The wide, slowly moving waterway reflected the clear blue sky. It looked still, like an old painting, frozen in time, capturing the moment for eternity.

I spent the rest of the afternoon wandering the city. In a curious way, I felt taken back to my childhood in Stockholm.

Kraków had a serene, understated atmosphere that for some reason recalled my 1950s Sweden. The streets were clean, but it seemed to be not so much the result of efficient maintenance as an inherent lack of rubbish. The streetcars passed by unhurried, filled with passengers. Old women sold pretzels on street corners, and the vending carts looked as if their design had not changed over the years. Nothing looked new, but neither did it look neglected. To me it appeared like a city that had decided to stay as it was, doing the best with what it had. Like a person who refuses to interfere with the aging process, with the air of being well kept but old-fashioned. A little like Mr. Liebermann, perhaps.

I had lunch in a small restaurant on Jana Street, just down from the Florian Gate. It looked newly renovated yet retained its charm. The deep, carved wooden window niches created ambience. The room was lit only by candles, and at the end, where I was seated, there were two other single guests, which further added to my sense of comfort. I enjoyed the food, and I allowed myself two glasses of surprisingly good Bulgarian red wine to go with the wild mushroom pasta. I took my time, savoring the flavors, a little surprised over the fact that I was able to discern them.

Back on the street after lunch, I passed a small ticket office for events and concerts and decided to see what was available. There was not much on to be had, but a string quartet would be performing at St. Bernard Church that evening, and I bought a ticket. As I walked back to my hotel in the afternoon, I met people on their way home from work, many holding little bunches of tulips or daffodils. Just handfuls of flowers without wrapping, which reminded me of a time when my mother would send me to the small market to buy tulips on Fridays, and the old woman would pull out the stems from a large bucket, one by one. These days flowers seem to come off the fields in bunches wrapped in cellophane.

After a short rest in my hotel room and a few phone calls, I set off for the church. It was cool now that the sun had set, and I walked briskly. Without thinking, I had taken a left turn into Grzegórzecka, and somehow I knew instinctively that I was headed in the right direction.

It was cold inside the church. In fact, it felt colder inside the baroque building than outside, but the audience was surprisingly large, perhaps seventy people or so, of varying ages and seemingly both locals and tourists. They sat in the pews with their coats buttoned up, and veils of vapor rose from their mouths and dissolved into the darkness above. I realized that my limited association with churches, or temples of any kind, was always related to music, either as performer or as audience. I had never attended a church for any other reason. I closed my eyes and listened. The program was unadventurous—Handel, Mozart, Albinoni, Purcell—but professionally performed, with sincerity and emotion. I was surprised at how it affected me.

When I left and stepped out into the dark, chilly night, I felt cleansed. Peaceful. I ambled through the deserted city with my hands in my pockets, taking deep breaths of the crisp, dry air. I arrived back in the street of my hotel and realized that it was not too late for a light meal. There seemed to be several restaurants still open, and I decided to try the small place at the very end of the street, Arka Noego. The rooms were sparsely populated, and I was shown a table in the main dining area. I sat down and instantly felt at home. The décor was quaint, with a random collection of old furniture and paraphernalia. Taken individually, nothing was interesting or beautiful, but as a whole it was charming. I ordered barley soup and chopped herring, a beer and a shot of vodka.

In the outer room, three musicians played klezmer music: a young guitarist, an older man on the violin, and a young woman clarinetist.

Instantly I thought of Ben Kaplan. I had phoned him earlier in the evening to set up our meeting in Stockholm, but it had been a long while since I'd given any thought to that first time we met. Now, abruptly and very clearly, the klezmer music brought it all back.

I was fourteen, and I still had no real friends. Music occupied a large chunk of my after-school hours, which had left me even more of an outsider. Or that was how my mother explained my solitude. "My Adam has no time for games," she would say, as if she were proud of the fact that I had no social life. Or possibly relieved. I did well at school, which didn't particularly increase my social standing either. My one redeeming skill was running. I was tall and light and physically suited for it, I suppose. Perhaps I also had a reason to run. Without too much effort, and with little training, I ran fast enough to make it to the regional school championships that year.

I noticed Ben as soon as we were lining up for the first race, though I didn't know his name. I didn't know *who* he was, but I knew *what* he was. Perhaps there is something about outsiders that makes us spot each other. Perhaps, as Mimi once said about the two of us in New Zealand, we each carry a certain smell and subconsciously pick it up in others. Sniff it and recognize it. Those who belong know the ones who don't, and they wrinkle their noses, flare their nostrils, and inhale, accepting some and expelling others. I spotted Ben; he spotted me. Not with appreciation, or even interest. Just as a matter of fact.

In the finals we ran against each other. We were young, and we ran the eight hundred meters in an unsophisticated, straightforward fashion. I had no technique; until then I had gotten by on talent and stamina alone. Soon after we started, the rest of the runners quickly dropped behind, but Ben was by my side. If I tried to pull ahead, he followed; if I slowed down, he did the same. He was running on my left as if he were attached to me. His feet seemed to land on the tarmac exactly in pace with mine; his arms moved with mine. Even his breathing seemed to be synchronized with mine. Each time I resolved to shake him off, he seemed to know my intention before the actual act.

We broke the record jointly and shared first prize, but still we didn't say a word to each other. Then, as we were on our way to the locker rooms and just before rejoining our respective school teams, he stopped and looked at me and smiled a wide smile, showing off prominent front teeth with a gap in between them.

"I could have won, you know," he said, and punched me lightly in the chest. "As could you."

I didn't reply.

I didn't see Ben again for almost ten years. Then, one night at Costa Brava, the small restaurant that used to be the musicians' regular hangout after performances, I ran into him again. I can't remember that we talked much—there were quite a few of us, and he was with another group at another table. It was noisy and busy, but we did make the connection. He was working on a Ph.D. in physics, he told me. I had just signed my first orchestra contract. On his way out, he stopped by my table and invited me to join him and some friends the following week.

"A few of us get together once a month to play klezmer," he said. "Nothing special, just for fun." He looked at me with a slightly mocking expression. "I think you might like it." He smiled and added, "It might even be good for you."

I never took him up on the invitation, but I started to listen to klezmer music.

It would be another twenty years or more until I heard from him again. I knew he had directed a feature film, just released to good reviews. I had finished my first film score. He wrote me a nice note through my agent after reading a review in an American magazine that described the film as forgettable but the score as one of the best of the year. He was generous, and I made a note of that and continued to follow his career with interest, as apparently he followed mine. Both were patchy, but his seemed somehow more coherent. Happier. As if he were genuinely enjoying what he was doing.

And then I received an e-mail out of the blue suggesting a collaboration. The official reason for this trip. A chance to run side by side again.

I realized I was sipping my beer with a smile on my lips.

20

The following evening I met Mr. Liebermann again, as agreed. We strolled through the park, where the setting sun fell in extended strips of light on the gravel.

"Perhaps I should tell you a little about my friend," he said. "Moishe Spiewak is a . . . ah . . . an *unusual* man. But don't for a moment think that his . . . ah . . . eccentricity is a sign of old age." Mr. Liebermann smiled, and his eyes glittered. "No, he is just a very unusual person. Always was. He does things his own way. His thinking is different from other people's."

And as I looked at Mr. Liebermann, I couldn't help smiling, too. The expression on his face showed the depth of his love for his old friend.

Moishe Spiewak lived in Kazimierz, not far from my hotel, in an apartment building I would have assumed was uninhabited. There were no signs of life inside the house, one in a row of similar three-story apartment buildings along the street. The façade was dark, as if it had been exposed to decades of soot and pollution. The windows were black and dull; they had obviously not been cleaned for a very long time. I slowed down as I looked up at the uninviting building, but Mr. Liebermann pulled at my sleeve. "Don't worry. It looks deserted, but I can assure you it's not." He drew a key from his pocket and stuck it in the front door. It took him a while to get the key to turn, and then he pushed the door open, stepped inside, and gestured for me to follow.

The air inside the unlit stairwell was stale and cool. Mr. Liebermann fumbled for the light switch on the wall beside the front door, which slowly creaked closed. As it shut, we were left in darkness for a moment before a single lightbulb came on, giving off a dim glow that never reached the dark corners. I could discern a curved staircase across the cracked black-and-white marble tiles. Mr. Liebermann led the way, and I followed at his pace. At the first landing, two doors faced each other, neither with a name or a letterbox. Panting, Mr. Liebermann continued up the next flight of stairs, pulling himself along with a firm grip on the handrail. We reached the second landing, and he stopped with a hand on his chest, breathing heavily but with a smile on his lips. Again two matching doors faced each other. Nothing indicated that either led to an inhabited apartment, but Mr. Liebermann turned to one of the doors and knocked seven times, rapidly and rhythmically. I could hear no reaction from behind the door. We waited in silence.

Then, abruptly, the door swung open and warm light streamed out to where we were standing.

At first sight Moishe Spiewak seemed as short as Mr. Liebermann, but then I saw that he was afflicted by scoliosis and was virtually bent double. It was impossible to see his face when he stood in the doorway, but his voice was strong and clear.

"Welcome, please come in," he said in English, and stood aside for us to enter.

The apartment was simply exquisite.

The floors were polished parquet with a patchwork of fine old Oriental rugs. The furniture was sparse, but each piece was strikingly beautiful and displayed to luxurious effect. Overhead, two small antique crystal chandeliers spread soft light in the narrow hallway. And as I stepped over the threshold into the living room, I stopped in my tracks.

The room was not very big but seemed spacious because it was so sparingly furnished. The walls were covered with works of art that took my breath away. If they were genuine, which I had no reason to doubt, I was looking at a priceless collection—landscapes, hunting scenes, battles, a few still lifes, and paintings with religious motifs. But the piece that caught my eye was a portrait that seemed to be a pastel, perhaps a sketch for a painting. It was neither large nor striking in its colors, but when my eyes set on it, all the others seemed to fade away. The portrait was of a young woman seated by a piano, her left hand on the keys, but not as if she were playing; rather as if she had been caught in a moment of contemplation, preparing to play or having just finished. Her face was shown in half profile, and her eyes were downcast.

I averted my own eyes and caught Mr. Spiewak's gaze. He was watching me with a slight smile, peering at me from the contorted angle required by his handicap.

"You admire her, too, I can see," he said.

I nodded but said nothing.

"She is beautiful, isn't she?" he continued. "But that is not why I love her so much. It's her vulnerability, the fact that she seems to have been caught completely unawares. And she looks so sad. It gives me such pleasure to think that here in my room she is safe." He took a few steps toward the picture and turned his face to look at it. "She is not mine, of course," he said. "She never was. Nothing here is mine."

I looked around the room, at a loss as to what he meant.

"I consider myself their caretaker. They come here to re-
cover. To regain their dignity." The old man nodded to himself.
"Yes, I give them their dignity back. What I have here is like a
nursing home. I nurse them to strength again before they are
returned to their rightful owners. Some need a longer time
than others. This one has been with me for a long time. I just
don't seem to be able to let her go." Again he looked at the
portrait. "I will miss her."

I heard Mr. Liebermann clear his throat behind me as he
stepped onto the soft rug in the living room. I turned to face
him, and he looked more mischievous than ever. He chuckled
quietly when he saw the expression on my face, but he did not
speak.

Mr. Spiewak showed us to a small table with four chairs by
the window where the curtains were drawn, and we walked
over and sat down. Finally I saw his full face. He looked ancient, older than anyone I had ever seen. His dark brown eyes
under bushy white eyebrows looked at me and seemed to
know everything. Not just about me but about everything
human. He gazed at me for so long that I began to feel
self-conscious. Then he smiled and nodded slowly.

"Welcome, Mr. Anker," he said. "Or may I call you Adam?"

"Please, Mr. Spiewak, call me Adam. That is the part of
my name that was given to me when I was born. I'm not sure
how I acquired the other."

He nodded again. Then, without warning, a wide grin
spread over his face.

"Do you like my home, Adam?" he asked, awkwardly
glancing around the room.

"Your home is extraordinary, Mr. Spiewak," I answered.

"Moishe, please call me Moishe," he said. "How can we play chess if we are not on a first-name basis? But before we play, we shall eat. And talk a little." He slowly heaved himself up from the chair, leaning heavily on the table. Mr. Liebermann also stood, and I did the same. Instantly both men turned and motioned for me to sit down.

"You are our guest tonight. You stay here while we prepare dinner," Mr. Spiewak said. "And it will not take long—we have our practiced routines, don't we, Szymon?"

Mr. Liebermann nodded and smiled. "We certainly do," he said.

I watched the two men disappear down the hallway. Alone in the room, I breathed in the dry, comfortable smell. I looked around and felt curiously at home, as if a weight had been lifted from my shoulders. I stood and walked along the walls, studying the paintings and stopping in front of the portrait again. The young woman did not look like anyone I had ever known, yet she seemed familiar. Her pose, the way she was half turned away from me, lost in her own thoughts, echoed something I couldn't quite explain. My eyes stayed on the portrait until behind me I heard the parquet creak, and I turned to see the two old men entering the room with large plates, which they placed on the table. There was herring, surrounded by chopped eggs, apples, beets, onions, and mushrooms. A basket of dark rye bread. Then came the bottles—Polish beer and three varieties of vodka. Obviously they didn't know how minimal my knowledge of chess was. Or perhaps they did. Just one glass of vodka would flush away any vestige of skill.

With the cold food on the table, the two men sat down opposite me, and we slowly started to eat. I think it is a case of love or hate with Baltic herring. For me it's love. The salty fish and its accompaniments tasted wonderful. We toasted in beer and vodka and got pleasantly drunk. At least I did. I'm not so sure about the two old men, whose faces seemed to beam with anticipation rather than alcohol. "Mr. Spiewak, you live here all alone. Tell me about your life," I said.

The old man looked up at me. "Moishe, please call me Moishe."

I smiled sheepishly and nodded.

"Alone? Absolutely not. Do you not know that my entire family lives here?" he said. "And one very dear friend." I glanced quickly at Mr. Liebermann, whose eyes met mine, wide open, his right eyebrow a little raised.

"Let me tell you about them." And without waiting for a response, Mr. Spiewak began.

"On the ground floor are my parents. Judith and Michal Spiewak. They are both elderly, so I decided to put them on the ground floor. The steps would be too much for them. Judith is still beautiful, in spite of her age. My father, Michal, still plays the piano, and it pleases me that I have been able to give him a Steinway grand. He is practicing Chopin's Second Piano Concerto, and he is getting better and better, though it is said that no pianist should attempt this work after middle age. I often stop outside their door and listen. Better and better, each day a little different, as all live performances must be. It's a miracle.

"Opposite my parents there is Aunt Beatrice, my favorite aunt, the one with the thick coppery hair. She never married, though she was strikingly beautiful. Still is. Things being otherwise, she would have been an opera singer. And she would have married. I am so pleased that she is near her brother, my father, who can accompany her, musically and as a human being. They were always close.

"On the next floor up is my brother, Samuel, and his wife, whose name is also Judith, like my mother's, so we call her Dyta. Judyta with the dark, burning eyes, always so quick, as if there is never enough time. True enough. And all the children they should have had—six or seven, I think. If I listen carefully, I can hear the patter of their quick little feet, their voices lifting through the stairwell as they play.

"On the other side of the landing, there is my sister, Hanna. On her own, because I never found anyone good enough for her. I have given her paints and canvases, and I have planted so many pots. There is hoya and jasmine and gardenia—all the fragrances she likes. In the spring I bring her bouquets of lily of the valley. Her special furniture is there, including the canopy bed. I have bought it all back. It took time, and not everything is exactly as it was. Some is better, more beautiful."

I looked at the old man, not sure what to make of his story, but he looked back at me with the utmost sincerity. I nodded slowly.

"Ah, and then, here on the top floor, in the apartment on the other side of the landing, I have put Miss Maisky."

"Marta Maisky?" I asked, and the old man nodded.

"Yes, Marta Maisky. Because she needed somewhere to go. Somewhere to wait. She was so terribly alone, you see. There was nobody to look after her. Afterward. When her sister had left and her mother had died, she was so terribly vulnerable. Even if she had escaped the raid, I don't think she would have lived."

He stopped talking and looked at me as if he were expecting a response. When I found nothing to say, he continued.

"Now, tell me, Adam, about your life." He peered at me.

But before I had even begun to consider what to say, Mr. Liebermann interrupted. "How about a game of chess? Before we have exhausted our guest."

"Of course, of course. To the table!" Mr. Spiewak said.

And we began. I was rusty, and pleased to be watching the two old men play before it was my turn. Moishe Spiewak was in a league of his own, it was clear to see. It was also clear that he was underplaying in order to make his friend comfortable. While waiting for Mr. Liebermann to make his moves, he hummed softly. When the game was finished, Mr. Spiewak commented on the good aspects of Mr. Liebermann's game.

"Some good moves, Szymon," he said. "The strategy was fundamentally sound. A couple of minor mistakes. Not even mistakes, just little slipups. But for those, you would have won."

Mr. Liebermann smiled and winked at me. "Your turn," he said, and stood to offer me his seat.

Although I tried to apply whatever minimal skills I possessed, Mr. Spiewak won easily. Throughout the game he leaned back on his seat each time it was my turn, as if I had all the time in the world to plan my next move. And every now and then I almost felt his gaze guiding me, suggesting a particular move that I wasn't skilled enough to see.

Then the two friends played another game, which again Mr. Spiewak won.

"Let's take a rest and have some tea," Mr. Liebermann suggested.

Mr. Spiewak nodded in agreement. "Yes, let's have tea. It's time to talk."

21

"For me it's late," Mr. Liebermann said, and stood slowly. As I rose, too, he gestured for me to remain where I was.

"No," he said, "take a little time to get to know each other, you two." He put his hand lightly on my shoulder and bowed to his friend.

"Phone me tomorrow," he said to me. "Perhaps we can take a walk together." Then he turned and addressed his friend. "See you next week, Moishe. Good night. I'll see myself out." And he left.

"More tea?" Mr. Spiewak asked. I shook my head, and he took hold of the armrests on his chair to help him rise. "Let's go into my study. I prefer my chair in there."

The room across the hallway was lined with books, folders, piles of papers and boxes. A new, top-of-the-line laptop contrasted starkly with the rest of the room, which could have been from another century.

My host sat down in an old leather recliner and pressed a button on its arm to raise a footrest. With a gesture of his hand, he offered me the chair on the other side of a small table.

"Music?" he asked, and without waiting for my reply he picked up a remote control from the table. Chopin, the Second Piano Concerto, streamed out of invisible speakers at low volume. We both smiled in recognition.

"I think I owe you some background on myself," he said as he leaned back and folded his hands over his chest. "Or you may think I am mad."

I shook my head. "Remember, I have watched you play chess," I said.

"Ah, but lots of mad people play chess well," the old man said, smiling. "So let me explain a few things. Give you a little information about myself." He blinked slowly, and I noticed how his eyelids closed over his slightly bulging eyes. It seemed a conscious act, the very slow closing and opening of the thin, pale membrane. He said nothing, and the music took over the small room. Then, as there was a pause between movements, he spoke again.

"Chess is a remarkable game. Not just the game itself but also the way it connects people who have nothing else in common. Age, gender, language—it's all irrelevant. Even race. And religion.

"It's because of chess that I am here today. Before the German invasion, I was an aspiring chess master. A sort of low-level celebrity here in the city, and perhaps even the country. I was nineteen. It was my dream to travel, and I thought my talent would take me all over the world. And I suppose in a sense it did."

He paused, and again that slow closing of the eyelids, like a curtain going down, then up.

"I used to tutor a boy named Jan. His father was a well-known writer and philosopher. Poet. You may have heard of him."

He mentioned a name and paused for a moment, but when I shook my head, he shrugged and continued.

"The boy was an only child, and the father wanted to invest in his son all that he himself loved. A folly, of course, but a kindhearted and well-intentioned one. One of the things he wanted the boy to learn and to love was the game of chess. I welcomed the extra money, but I knew that the boy would never understand the essence of the game. He learned to play competently but not to love it the way his father did. The way I did."

He paused a little and seemed to listen to the music for a moment.

"I could no longer attend university, and it became diffi-cult to take myself to the part of the city where Jan lived. Without the arrangement being formally canceled, it just dwindled until it ceased completely. So I was very surprised when one day I had a message asking me to give another lesson. A car was being sent to pick me up. As I stood in the hallway, tying my scarf around my neck, my mother came out of the kitchen, drying her hands on her apron. She stopped on the threshold and stared at me, closing her hands as in prayer with the tips of her index fingers on her lips. And as I turned to open the front door, out of the corner of my eye I saw her stretch out one hand, as if wanting to hold me back. But I just said good-bye without facing her and walked out the door. I never saw her again."

Mr. Spiewak picked up the remote control and changed the music. We listened in silence while the first notes played—Mendelssohn's violin concerto in a recording with Heiftez. I looked up at the old man, for a second thinking he must know what the piece meant to me, but there was no indication that he was playing it for me, of course. Rather he seemed engrossed in his own memories and had closed his eyes. Then, slowly, the eyelids went up again, and he re-turned the remote control to the table and resumed his story.

"I never knew how Jan's father had discovered that our time was running out. He must have made some elaborate preparations after he heard about the imminent deportation of Jews. But he never discussed it with me—not then, not later. When I arrived at their apartment, they were ready to go, and we left the same afternoon. I was to travel with them to London, officially as Jan's tutor. And that was how I ended up as the only surviving member of my family. I survived. But I lost my life.

"Later, in Israel, I was surrounded by others in a similar position. The children of the lost ones. But unlike most of them, I was unable to embrace the newness, the hope. I felt ancient already, and it was impossible for me to live in that new world. Instead I settled in America. A new world, too, you might say." He peered at me. "But in a different way. The people there were more disparate. They had dreams, but they did not all share one dream. I felt I could live my old life there. I resumed my chess playing, but my passion was gone. Not just my passion for the game but passion generally. Still, it was through chess that I was introduced to people who were well established and eager to help me. And that is how I met Kalman Silber. Or rather first I met his Uncle David, who was an excellent chess player. He invited me to his home and introduced me to Kalman—or Cal, as he called himself—who was nine years older than me. Except for his uncle, Cal had no living relatives, and David had lost his wife and young son. Now the two men lived like father and son. I suppose I became a sort of in-between. Too old to be the son of David, too young to be the father of Cal."

Mr. Spiewak paused.

"In the kitchen there is some more beer in the fridge. Would you mind getting me one? And please help yourself, too."

I did as he asked and returned with two chilled bottles and two glasses. But the old man just took the bottle and lifted it to his lips.

"Ah, my throat was getting a little dry," he said. "It's been a long time since I've talked this much." He took another sip. "Now, where was I? Yes. My friend Cal. Let me describe him." He looked at me and cocked his head. "You may well wonder where this is leading. But there is a thread, as you will see. Just bear with me." He took one more sip of the beer.

"I told you I had lost my future. The war was over; it was the early fifties. So much seemed possible. Everything was geared toward an infinitely productive future. But I just could not get onto the bandwagon. Cal, on the other hand, would have nothing to do with the past. He lived in the future. Full of ideas, dreams, plans. Perhaps he pulled me into his business because we complemented each other. His uncle had made a small fortune in the fashion trade and had invested the funds for Cal to set up a modest art gallery—initially a humble place on the Lower East Side of Manhattan. He took me there one Sunday and showed me around. Art had never been my thing—I knew precious little about it. But Cal had studied art before the war, hoping to be an artist himself. Now he applied his talent when buying. He had a good eye and a generous personality. People trusted him, artists and clients. I couldn't understand what he needed me for. I looked at the works in the gallery, and they meant nothing to me. Cal said that didn't matter one bit. He needed me to be a counterweight to his exuberance, I think. A kind of devil's advocate. And also to manage the accounts and the finances.

"We worked well together. Though I did not come to gain any of Cal's ability to appreciate art, I did come to relate to specific works of art in my own way. I could stand in front of a painting and follow where it came from and where it was going, understand its nature. Just as with a good game of chess, a pattern would emerge. A kind of beauty. But it is a very private response that has nothing to do with how other people appreciate art, I think.

"Then one day we had a visit from an elderly client who had bought works from us before. She started talking to Cal about a painting she remembered from her childhood. An oil by the Hungarian artist László Mednyánszky, a landscape. She said she had dreamed about her grandparents' house the night before, and it had brought the painting to her mind. She wanted to find it. 'With your connections, Mr. Silber, perhaps you could make some discreet investigations? See if the work can be traced.' And that," said Mr. Spiewak, "was the beginning of my real interest in art."

He awkwardly pulled himself up by leaning on the armrests, pushed the button to lower the footrest, and stood up.

"Come," he said, and indicated for me to follow him into the living room again. He walked slowly ahead of me and stopped in the middle of the room.

"Everything you see here on my walls is looted art. As our official business thrived, our quiet sideline did, too. As it happened, I had a natural talent for discreet investigations. An inclination for delving into the past, perhaps. My international chess connections also served me well. And Cal had all the art knowledge, plus an extraordinary way with people. An instinctive understanding of their hidden motivations. You see, what we set out to do required a very specific combination of skills. We became part detectives, part researchers, part negotiators. And also, perhaps, an unlikely couple of avengers. Surprisingly, we proved to be very good at it. In a small way. We had to be careful not to become too well known. That would have lost us our advantage. But we managed to locate and return a number of significant works of art, mostly Polish but also Hungarian.

"Cal is dead now, and I am here, in Kraków. Our official gallery business is not so small anymore, and it's run by Cal's daughter, Barbara, and her two children, Dan and Rosa. Rosa has inherited her grandfather's charm and way with people, Dan his good eye for art. The gallery now has a branch in Los Angeles, one in Paris, and one in Tokyo. It makes a nice profit, increasing year by year. And our sideline is still just what it always was: a small nonprofit business on the side. When I retired to Kraków, I became the caretaker. Today the business is more interesting than ever. Small, but very interesting indeed. Here in my living room the works have a short reprieve, to gain back their strength and above all their dignity, before being reunited with their original owners. Except for this one. She has been here far too long. I just can't seem to give her up."

The old man stopped in front of the portrait.

"You know, I was in love with her," he said. "I have always loved her, and I always will." He stuck his hands into his pockets and lowered his gaze to the floor. Then he peered up at me.

"It's not her, of course, but I like to think that it could have been. The resemblance is very strong. This is a princess. Princess Renata Habsburg Radziwill. Not my princess. Not Marta Maisky. But I can pretend. I can do what I like here." He made a gesture with his arm, as if to take in the entire room, the apartment, and the building.

"I have built it again, my past. Better and more beautiful than it was. And I spend my days back there, in the past. In here."

We stood side by side, our eyes on the portrait. I felt a sudden urge to put my arm around the old man's shoulders, but he resumed talking and the moment passed.

"I have come to think that there are those of us who can love just once. For me that is certainly true."

I wasn't sure how to respond, but I sensed that he was waiting for a reply.

"I suppose I am one of those, too," I said slowly. "There has only ever been one woman in my life. Only one who mattered. And then there was my daughter."

"Ah, children," Mr. Spiewak said. "Another kind of love, I suppose. Absolute. Irrevocable."

He lifted his eyes to the portrait again.

"I used to hope that if I just waited patiently she would set her eyes on me and see me as I really was. Not the external me but my burning, passionate inner self. The real me. Somehow I thought that love would prove just. Fair. That the extent of my love would earn me hers, if I simply gave it time. If I was patient, she would see me and come to love me. That's what I believed."

I regarded him, engrossed in his thoughts. Then suddenly he turned around and looked at me again.

"If there had been time, then perhaps . . ." he said. "For patience to be meaningful, there must be time. It's obvious, no? What is patience if there is no time? Its very essence is time. And for me there wasn't any. No matter how patient I was prepared to be, no matter how willing to wait for love to develop. Without the time it was worth nothing."

He walked toward the hallway with cautious, uncertain steps, then into the kitchen, returning with a bottle and two shot glasses. I followed him back to the study, and we resumed our seats. Mr. Spiewak filled the glasses, lifted his, and toasted me.

"If I'd had the good fortune to have a son, I suppose he would be about your age," he said, and looked at me with his brows knitted and an odd expression on his face. Then he blinked twice and cleared his throat. "And I would have taught him to play chess better than you do." He smiled and raised his glass again. As he set the glass on the table, the smile faded and he seemed lost in his thoughts for a moment.

"You know what hurt the worst? What haunted me all those years afterward?"

I shook my head.

"The fact that I had abandoned her. I kept seeing her as she looked that last time. Outside her front door. She must have been exhausted from the long trip, and it was a very cold evening, though it was late April. We said good-bye, but she lingered, as if there were something else she wanted to say. She was so pale, and the soft skin around her nostrils had reddened in the cold air. When I lifted my hand to stroke her cheek, she held on to it and pressed the palm against her skin briefly. She looked at me with those clear gray eyes, but she said nothing. Later I would go through every minute of our time together, analyzing it, searching for lost opportunities. Things I could have done differently. And I always ended up there, outside her front door. I would see her eyes, and I convinced myself I could discern a desire to speak that could have been encouraged had I known what to say, what to do. Instead I let my hand drop, held open the heavy door for her to enter, and watched her disappear into the dim hallway. A week later I was in London. I never saw her again."

We sipped the spirit, which left a burning trail down my throat. "It's absurd that I was the one to escort her on that last journey. I who more than anything did not want her to go. Life deals us some strange cards."

The old man sat with his eyes closed.

"Her parents liked me, trusted me. And when she begged me to take her to Vilna, how could I refuse? I knew why she wanted to go, of course. I had no illusions. And I knew she would never be able to go by herself. My own parents only allowed me to go because they thought I was fleeing. That I was traveling one way to save my life, just as Adam and Pavel had a few months earlier. Perhaps Marta thought that she would be able to stay in Vilna. But Vilna was a strange kind of temporary haven for men only, not for women. There was no question of her staying. And when she had to return to Kraków, how could I let her do so by herself? My parents were devastated to have me come back. But in the end I abandoned them and Marta anyway. I survived. They didn't."

He picked up the remote control again. Another early recording—Chopin's Berceuse.

"Do you recognize the pianist?" he said.

I listened intently for a moment. "Rosenthal?" I suggested. The old man smiled smugly and shook his head.

"Friedman," he said. "Did you know he took an interest in Adam? He invited him to his last concert, here in Kraków in 1938. I think he would have been of enormous help to Adam while he developed as an artist. He was a very generous man. And a very proud Pole. He would have been delighted to help a fellow Polish musician on his path to an international career. He must have seen Adam's potential, I am sure. Adam's talent was for the world, not just for Kraków. Or Poland. I think we were both sure that our respective talents would carry us out into the world, Adam and I. So much we took for granted. As if talent itself were a guarantee. A ticket to the future."

We sat listening to the music. The old recording was technically terrible, yet for the same reason utterly moving. There was no smoothness; what we heard was totally unadorned and pure. Beautiful.

"Naïvely, I expected so much to come out of my passion for chess. Not just travel and wealth. No, foolishly, even love. I thought that with time it would deliver me the woman I loved. Like so many young people, I saw a connection between professional success and other good fortune. A total illusion, of course. And in the end I had neither." He smiled a little.

"Your turn," the old man said eventually. "Tell me about the woman you loved, Adam. The woman you love."

I had the distinct impression that he now closed his eyes for my benefit, as if to make it easier for me to talk.

"Her name is Cecilia," I began. "And I have not seen her for nearly twenty years."

I briefly closed my own eyes, and the images of our first meeting were as clear as when they happened. You stood before me, a young blond woman with dark eyes that looked at me with light mockery.

"I met her by chance, at a recital in Stockholm," I said hesitantly. "I suppose all first meetings are chance meetings, one way or another. I expected absolutely nothing of that evening. For me it was just an ordinary student recital, and I couldn't wait for it to be over and done with. It was a ridiculous first meeting, the kind you read about in silly romantic books. I bumped into her. Physically. And then it took me less than five minutes to fall hopelessly in love. If it had ended there and I had never seen her again, I think I would still have remembered. Always. But as it was, she gave me a year, and now she is forever living inside me. With reciprocated love you are lulled into a false sense of security. Arrogantly, you take for granted that it will last forever. I had no expectation of either my love's beginning or its end."

Mr. Spiewak stretched out a hand for his glass.

"Cecilia. She entered my life so suddenly, and I was . . . I don't know, I just never felt deserving. Her love was so absolutely pure. I was totally unprepared for a relationship like that. And then when she left me, I was equally unprepared. I don't know how to describe the kind of woman she was. The kind of love she gave. It was unlike anything I had experienced before. On the one hand utterly innocent. Unconditional. Yet always, for me, there seemed to be an aspect of it that I simply could not grasp. Consciously, I never understood, so it is impossible for me to describe." I looked at my companion and felt strangely sure that he could understand me.

"I loved her. To the extent that I am ever to love, I loved her. But she left me. She left me with our child. She gave me my daughter, Miriam."

Suddenly the old man's eyes were wide awake. He stared at me, as if in a state of shock. "She did what?" he said, almost choking on the words.

"She gave me our child."

He seemed to gasp for air while slowly shaking his head. "How could a woman ever do such a thing?" he exclaimed, and he kept shaking his head, incredulously, as if he could not begin to understand what I had told him.

"She gave me an ultimatum: I could have her or I could have the child. Never both." As I said the words, I heard how they sounded. "I knew she wanted me to understand. It was as if she were willing me to read her mind. But of course I couldn't. I was completely preoccupied with myself. My own grief. Yet it must have been there for me to see. I should have remembered that first evening, when she talked about her art. How painful it was for her to lay bare her soul in her work. How all our time together I had felt as if there were aspects of her that were there for me to see, if only I could apply the right sensitivity. That she wanted me to see something that escaped my inadequate ability. There was something for me to discover that she could never articulate. And when she told me about the child, I think that despite my feelings of utter despair, on some level I did understand. And this made the impossible choice not just possible but acceptable."

"So you accepted?"

The music had finished, and the old man's words hung in the air. I inhaled, but I couldn't fill my lungs.

"Did you never stop to reflect on why she gave you this choice in the first place? Why she did not make it herself?"

I found it difficult to breathe, to swallow. I reached out to take a sip of vodka but accidentally knocked over my glass. Mr. Spiewak waved his hand impatiently as I moved to rise, then pulled out a handkerchief from his pocket and soaked up the spilled liquor. He opened the bottle and refilled my glass, nodding encouragingly.

I felt my cheeks burn and my mouth go dry.

"All these years. No, never," I said. "I knew the extent of her love. And her own grief. So, for reasons that I can't fully explain, I accepted, because instinctively I knew she had no choice. I sensed that for her there were no alternatives to the two options she presented me. It was a very long time before I began to think it might have been within my power to change this. To introduce another alternative. That I might have been able to help her reach another decision. If I had talked to her. Asked the right questions. It is only recently that I have allowed myself to consider this."

The old man nodded.

"Some of us are given patience, others time. But we need both, don't we? And we need words. We need to talk to each other."

Suddenly I felt exhausted and my eyes stung. I leaned backward in my chair and closed my eyes.

"I have had the guest bed made up in Miss Maisky's apartment. I don't think she would mind if you slept there tonight," I heard the old man say. "She knows I love her and that any person allowed in there does, too. She trusts me."

And so I ended up spending my first night in Marta

Maisky's apartment. In a sense I felt a little like the artwork in Moishe Spiewak's living room. As if I had been given a reprieve, time to adjust to a new life. A new place.

I lay down in the narrow bed between the starched white sheets and watched the pattern made on the ceiling by the streetlights shining through the bare branches of the trees below. I thought about the woman whose shrine this was. My mother's sister. Moishe Spiewak's love. But when I finally closed my eyes, it wasn't Marta Maisky's face I saw.

It was yours, Cecilia.

III

The Wall

She turned her face to the wall
yet she loves me
why did she turn away from me

so with such a motion of one's head
one can turn away from the world
where sparrows are chirping
and young people are walking
in their garish neckties

She is now alone
in the presence of the dead wall
and she will remain so

she will remain against the wall
which will grow bigger and bigger
coiled up and small
with a clenched fist

and I am sitting
with stony feet
I do not carry her away from that place
I do not lift her
Who is lighter than a sigh

—Tadeusz Różewicz,
translated by Czesław Miłosz

22

"Will you come home with me?" you asked.

We walked back to your apartment in Gärdet.

It was close to midnight, and it was snowing again. Tiny dry flakes fell around us, and our steps made fresh imprints in the untouched white cover on the footpath. The odd car passed, gliding by almost soundlessly.

I didn't know what to expect, but your apartment was on the top floor of a 1930s three-story building, one of a block of four facing each other around a small park. I followed you up the stairs, and you opened the door for me. The space presented itself immediately: a narrow hallway opening onto a living room with a kitchenette. One large window and a door to a little balcony. The furniture was reduced to the essentials: a low double bed, virtually a mattress on the floor, and a large desk with a chair. A blank canvas stood propped on an easel. No curtains, no rugs, no plants—no softness. The walls were bare, although more canvases stood facing the wall in layers. That is how it looked to me the first time. Barren and a bit sad, utterly private, offering no clues as to your private life.

You threw your coat over the chair, opened the door to the balcony, and stood looking out, your back to me.

"Would you like a glass of wine?" you said without turning. I crossed the floor and stood behind you. The park below had a round centerpiece that might have been a pond but was now only a soft indentation in the snow. The benches around it looked as if they were made of cotton wool, their shapes blurred. The air was still and cool, and I took a deep breath, then lifted my hand and touched your hair.

You turned to face me, and with your eyes wide open you kissed me. You lifted your hands, and for a moment I thought you would embrace me, but instead you let your palms run along my arms as if drawing an outline of my body in the air. When I reached out to pull you closer, you took a step back, turned, and closed the balcony door. Then you walked past me and across the room and switched off the light. At first I could hardly make out your shape as you soundlessly moved to the middle of the room, where you stood and undressed with unhurried precision. Then my eyes adjusted, and I could see that your eyes were on my face while your clothes dropped to the floor around your feet. Now your pale skin seemed to glow in the room where the distant streetlamps and the re-flections on the snow provided the only sources of light. You released the clasp that held your hair together and shook your head. Your eyes never left mine. I slowly started to unbutton my shirt, but my fingers felt stiff and clumsy. You made no attempt to help me, just remained still, watching me intently.

Later, as I lay awake listening to your uneven breaths, watching your back, I tried to keep my mind blank. Yet as my eyes ran along your spine, from the slender neck that lay ex-posed on the pillow, the vulnerable shoulder blades, the smooth line down to the half-covered roundness of your but-tocks, I realized that it was already too late. In a matter of a few hours, you had entered my life irrevocably.

We had not exchanged a word since you turned off the light. I'd opened my mouth to speak while you undressed, but you stretched out your hand and put your palm lightly over my mouth, silencing me. We lay down, and you sat astride my body, your hands running over my skin. Before kissing me again, you traced my lips with your fingers. It was as if you were creating something. Creating me. But you said nothing. And throughout our lovemaking I had a feeling of being an object, not a partner. It wasn't that you ignored my pleasure, quite the opposite, but I felt left outside. You offered your entire physical self with such passion but gave me nothing of your soul. Your eyes locked with mine, but they were like glass—you could look through from the inside out, but they allowed no insight.

Afterward you curled up with your arms crossed over your chest as if embracing yourself, turned your back toward me, and went to sleep. And I thought you looked so unbearably alone that it brought tears to my eyes.

Self-contained and mysterious, you lay on your side, turned away from me, holding on to your own arms. After some time, sounds escaped your lips. Muted, sad, incomprehensible. And so utterly private.

I slipped out from under the sheet and dressed in silence. It was snowing more intensely now, and the view through the window was a white swirl. The world outside looked as safe and contained as the scene within a snow globe. I pulled on my coat without turning on the light, then felt in my pocket for a pen.

In the dusk I scribbled a short note on a business card, asking you to phone, and put it on the ledge of the easel before leaving.

23

I still find it impossible to believe that we had such a short time.

For me those nine months made everything that came before totally insignificant. For the first time in my life, I felt that I belonged absolutely. I was alive, finally. Do you remember those Sunday walks out toward Djurgården? It was a cold winter, with lots of snow that kept being replenished, offering us pristine white planes that seemed to go on forever. Sometimes you would turn your face and look at me, as if to reassure yourself that I was still there. I had the same need, and I held on to your hand or your shoulders, just to make sure. And every now and then we seemed to stop at the same time, simply to look at each other.

For Christmas, I bought you a potted hyacinth. I stood on the threshold of your apartment for the second time, and I felt like an idiot as I held out the wrapped plant. But you smiled and took it, and when I saw you unwrap it with such gentle care, I knew it was right. I never gave you flowers again. Just that once. We both knew the significance of the small, fragrant white bloom. When it wilted, you put the pot in the kitchen cupboard and said you would keep it for next year. Did it ever flower again?

Do you remember the first concert we went to? The young violinist, Mintz, still only twenty-six but already a star. You told me you knew nothing about music, that the experience had died for you with your father. So I felt all the more grateful when you agreed to come. I sat beside you in the packed Konserthuset in Stockholm, and it was as if I were hearing the music for the first time, too. When the soloist began to play, you turned your head to me briefly and smiled, then searched for my hand. Now and then during the performance, I cast a quick look at you, but your eyes remained fixed on the violinist with the utmost concentration, and you never returned my glance, just held my hand.

Whenever I later heard Tchaikovsky's Violin Concerto, it was always your serene profile that came to my mind. Eventually the image became too painful, and I avoided the music altogether. It is only recently that I have listened to it again.

I listen with closed eyes, and I still see your face.

It still hurts. Because it is not those first scenes I see.

It's the one when it all ended.

24

When we left your island that morning, I thought I would never see it again.

"You decide," you had said.

We had sought shelter in the old boat shed, and the door stood wide open to the rain that hung like a curtain in the doorframe.

"It is your choice."

You turned and looked at me, and your face seemed strangely pale, ashen. The only daylight seeped in through the water below our feet and flickered over your skin, and it was all shades of white and gray. Yet I knew that you had been burned by the intense summer sun during the week. I searched for words, the right words. Words that would change what I sensed you were intending to say. Stop you from saying what I knew was coming. Or, if they had been uttered, retract the words, make them unsaid. I knew there must be other words that would suffice. They had to exist. But words were never my medium. It was silence that I had been taught. I was an expert on silence. And then, when I needed words more than ever in my life, they completely eluded me.

I said nothing.

Instead I reached forward and put my arm around you, gently twisting your body toward me. You didn't resist, but neither did you accommodate me. And after a brief moment, I had to let you go.

There was the soft hiss of the constant, windless rain, and the uncertain, wavering light gave the space a sad, surreal pallor.

"It's impossible. It's impossible now. And it always will be."

You kept your eyes on the water, where tiny fish darted back and forth in spasmodic movements. Then you straightened yourself and looked at me again.

"I wish I could make you understand," you said slowly, your eyes fixed on my face. I should have heard the enormous weight of each word. I should have known what to do.

I listen to those words now and I can hear that they sounded like a plea, but I didn't hear it then, when it mattered, did I? I didn't understand. And I allowed the moment to pass. I said nothing, occupied with my own chilling dread. You returned your eyes to the water underneath our feet, and your voice became a whisper, as if you didn't trust it to speak.

"I love you, Adam. I have never loved anybody else. I have loved you since the moment you bent forward to listen to me after apologizing. No, from the first moment I saw you up there onstage. Before I knew who you were. Ever since that first evening, I have loved you. Everything about you. Your body lives inside me. The way you move. Your eyes. Your hands. Your smell."

As if to confirm what you said, you lifted your hands and almost touched me; then you let them fall and clasped them in your lap. Helplessly, I watched as you lowered your head and covered your face with your hands. I knew you were not crying. It was as if your grief were beyond that. As if it could find no expression. A long time later, when I was able to watch these scenes again, to think about you, I realized I had never seen you cry.

You remained sitting exactly where you were, with your thigh touching mine and your feet dangling over the surface of the water, but I felt as if the distance between us were growing in minute increments—too small to see, yet absolute and irrevocable. And despite my resolution not to, I was the one who began to cry. My hands gripped the edge of the coarse wooden planks until the knuckles whitened, but I was unable to stop the flow of tears.

I could hear you inhale deeply.

"You must choose, Adam."

But how could I? You had given me an impossible choice. How could I choose between this new life and you? There was no room for compromise in your clear eyes as they glistened black. And before I opened my mouth, I was aware of the enormity of what I was about to say. How with a few simple words the door to all that had made my life worth living would silently close, never to open again. But my lips parted, and the words were there. The insignificant few words that instantly changed my existence.

"I accept, Cecilia," I whispered. "I will care for it." I looked down into the water below. "I will be the father of our child."

You said nothing. I swung my legs up onto the landing and rose clumsily, stretched out a hand and helped you up, and we stood face-to-face. You looked into my eyes, then nodded slowly.

"You must promise me you will go away. Never try to contact me. That is how it has to be," you said.

Now I nodded, and I could feel the tears running down my face.

"I will bear your child, Adam, but you must never expect me to be its mother."

I am sure there were words I could have said. Questions I could have asked. Pleas I could have made. But my stiff lips remained closed. I held on to your wrists, as if wanting my feelings to be absorbed through your skin. Wanting you to understand the depth of my grief. Wanting you to know that I had made the one choice I could, but that the sacrifice was impossible to endure. I thought about me, not you. I wanted you to take pity on me and change your mind. I never even tried to consider you. And so I allowed the moment, when perhaps there was still a possibility of reaching you, to pass.

You tore yourself free, turned abruptly, and walked across the room, out into the rain. I sank to my knees and curled up with my hands between my thighs. Finally I released my despair and cried loudly, sobbed wildly in the falling rain.

We left the following morning. Overnight the rain had stopped, and as we untied the moorings and reversed off the landing, the sun filtered through dissolving clouds. The dark rocks along the waterfront steamed as they warmed, and the smell of the rain lingered in the air. I watched the two swans that lived on the little islet across the bay as they slowly glided on the calm sea, side by side. You had told me they returned every year to the same nest to produce just one egg that never hatched.

We traveled slowly, too, as if we both wanted to make this journey last as long as possible. I watched the coastline of the island as we passed. It looked different from this perspective—more contained, less inviting. I knew I would never see it

again. And I was grateful for this first loss. For its insignifi-
cance. For the opportunity to learn to accept the unacceptable in small steps. I was hoping that gradually I would build
the strength, the resilience I would need. Because soon I would
have to make the one unbearable sacrifice.

You, Cecilia.

25

The morning after that first night, Moishe said I could stay on in Marta's apartment. And so I came to move into the home that the old man had created for the woman he loved.

We soon established a daily routine. Because of his handicap, Moishe rarely ventured outside. There was no elevator in the building, and only with enormous effort could he navigate the stairs. A woman came three mornings a week to clean and do errands, but the rest of the time the old man lived his solitary shadow life with his imaginary family. He seemed to have no friends or visitors other than Mr. Liebermann, but he was often busy on the laptop or on the phone.

Each evening we played two games of chess, never more. I did improve, but often when I looked up after a move, I would meet Moishe's amused gaze, and he would gently shake his head. We listened to music, and I discovered that he had an impressive collection of CDs.

The following Wednesday we sat as usual in the study sipping vodka and listening to the CD that the woman at the music shop in Wawel had given me. *Passacaille* by Szymon Laks. After the music finished, Moishe turned to me.

"I met him, you know. In Paris. A remarkable man. Do you know about his book? *Music from Another World* was published in France, but it took many years before it was finally published here, in Polish. The Communist regime found Laks's descriptions of the camp life too . . . positive. The fact that he'd been allowed to live because of the music he was able to create somehow made the Germans look too human, apparently. His fundamental humanity was held against him and his book. But it's so wonderful. More than anything, it describes the irrepressible, positive power of music, of any art form. And of those who create it.

"I talked to Szymon today," he said. "I mean our Szymon, of course. He has received a letter, or rather a small pile of letters. From his friend Clara. Clara Fried. He wanted me to ask you if you would like to have them. Mrs. Fried sent them to Szymon because she wasn't sure if you would want them. She wanted to give you the choice of not reading them. But she told Szymon they are yours."

I opened my mouth to reply, but the old man raised his hand to stop me.

"Think about it overnight," he said. "Sometimes it is best not to know. Sometimes fate filters information for us."

He took up the remote control, and Laks's Passacaille began to play again.

"But who am I to give advice?" he added, smiling a little as the music finished. "I have re-created my own past because the present proved too hard for me to live with. I am living a coward's life. If you can call it a life."

I couldn't think of anything to say.

"But you are here to find out about the past, aren't you? The real one."

"Yes, I suppose I am. Perhaps because, like you, I have lived in a self-made world. Not because I chose to but because it was imposed on me. And unlike you, I had nothing on which to base a version of the past. For years music was my refuge. My own music and that of others. The music I played and the music I composed came to make up the history I never had. I convinced myself that the music I loved the most held some mysterious connection with my past. But then when I met Cecilia, everything changed. It was as if I had woken up from a lifelong slumber. Everything around me took on a new color, a new texture, a new smell. I brought her to concerts, and every piece sounded new. We went to hear Shlomo Mintz play Tchaikovsky that spring, and it was like hearing it for the first time. I had searched for memories, for a connection with the past each time before, but now I was listening with the future in mind. The change of perspective had an extraordinary effect."

I looked at the old man, wondering what he might make of my rambling, but he only nodded for me to continue.

"It lasted less than a year. From December to August. Nine months. Yet when I visualize my life, it looks like a thin gray pencil line until the December night when I met her. Then an explosion of colors and flavors opened into a bright, all-encompassing world of light. And then again, just as abruptly, a thin trail again. Afterward I had the memory of light. And I had Mimi, my daughter Miriam. I was forced to adjust my perspective. It was not as it had been before Cecilia. It is difficult to describe the tumultuous emotional journey of that short time, followed by that painful autumn and early winter before Mimi was born and we left Sweden. I went as far away as it is possible to go. Perhaps because I was afraid I would not be able to keep my promise otherwise. I had to be physically far removed. It was pure luck that I was offered a position at the School of Music in Auckland at just that time. And it was there that I had to face death and birth simultaneously. Every jolt of joy at the thought of my daughter held an element of grief over the loss of her mother. And as soon as I felt a stab of grief, I was overcome by a feeling of guilt, because I had every reason to be so very happy for having my daughter.

"It was impossible to reconcile."

26

I decided to defer my departure from Kraków by a week.

I wrote to you, explaining that unforeseen developments had delayed my arrival. I couldn't quite understand myself why I wrote instead of phoning. Perhaps I needed a little more time to choose how to explain what was happening.

When I crossed the landing and rang the bell on Moishe's door the following evening, I had made a decision about the letters.

He kept the door unlocked for me, and I entered without waiting for him to open it. I could hear music coming from the study, but when I looked inside, he wasn't there. Once again he was playing my CD, the Passacaille. I continued along the hallway and found him in the living room. The space where the portrait had hung was empty, and the picture was on the floor leaning against the wall.

"It's time," he said with his back to me. "She should go to her home." He turned, and I saw him quickly wipe his eyes with his fingers, then pinch the bridge of his nose. I averted my own eyes.

"I have made arrangements for her to be picked up tomorrow. Would you mind taking her with you into the study?" The old man bent over with enormous effort and lifted the picture from the floor with the utmost care. He held it tilted a little and seemed to be looking at it before holding it out to me. I nodded and walked over and took it from his hands.

It weighed almost nothing. As we entered the study, Moishe asked me to remove the large framed map that hung over the desk and to put the portrait in its place.

"And I have made a decision about the letters," I said. Now it was Moishe's turn to nod.

We sat down in our usual chairs.

"Mendelssohn?" the old man said. I smiled, and he turned on the music.

We listened for a while, and Moishe poured us a shot of vodka each, which we sipped.

"I knew you would want them," he said quietly. "I just thought you should think about it carefully. Prepare yourself. They are over there." He pointed to his desk, and I rose and walked over. The small pile of letters sat on the polished wood, tied with a blue ribbon. I stood looking at them.

"Go on," Moishe said. "My study is yours, but you may wish to read them in the other apartment."

I hesitated.

"I'll go and prepare our dinner." Without waiting for a response, he rose from his chair and turned to leave. I still could not make myself touch the letters. I looked up at the painting. Then I heard the old man speak from the doorway.

"Why don't you make yourself comfortable in my chair?" He walked to the CD player and inserted another disc, clicked on the remote control, and left me alone. It was a piece for piano and violin, but I didn't recognize it.

I picked up the letters and sat down in the soft leather chair. I felt empty, devoid of feeling, as if I were floating above and beyond everything around me. My hands were stiff and clumsy as I slowly untied the ribbon. The top letter was sealed and addressed, but it had no stamp. I flicked through the pile and noticed that none of them had. These letters had never been mailed. Just written. They were all addressed to Adam Lipski, at an address that looked like the name of an institution, perhaps a school, in Vilna. I put down the letters, stood, and walked over to the desk, looking for a knife. It felt wrong to tear open the envelopes with my fingers.

I found a letter opener among the pens on Moishe's desk. Carefully I slid the blade along the edge of the envelope and opened it. But instead of taking out the letter, I returned the opened envelope to the pile and put them on the table beside me. I went out to the kitchen and stood in the doorway watching Moishe for a moment before he sensed my eyes on his back and turned around.

"I think I'll go into the other apartment, if you don't mind," I said.

He smiled a little and nodded.

"Do you know what's in the letters?" I said.

"How could I?" he replied. "They have never been opened."

"But you have some idea?" I insisted.

He cocked his head and looked at me.

"That's neither here nor there," he said. "They are yours now. Go and read."

As I walked down the hallway, he called after me, "I'll be here when you need me."

I took the letters from the study and let myself out.

The other apartment lay in darkness as I entered. I walked into the small parlor and sat in a chair by the window. It was a clear spring evening and not entirely dark. Still, there wasn't enough light for reading, so I turned on the floor lamp. It was silent inside, but through the slightly open window I could hear a blackbird sing.

I took out the first letter and began to read.

It was dated April 1940. The handwriting was graceful and soft and somehow youthful.

Kraków
April 1940

My dearest,
I have arrived home safely. Safely. Safe. Home. They are
words that have lost all meaning. There is no safety to be
had for us, and our home is no longer a home.

Moishe escorted me to the border, and we spent the night
in a safe house. That word again. The truth is that nobody
feels safe anymore. Nobody seems to sleep anymore. It is as
if we go through the familiar routines but they have lost
their original purpose. At night we lie down, close our eyes,
pull our blankets over us. But in the silence we don't sleep.
We listen and we stare into the solid darkness. In the
silence we become more alert, more awake. The sounds
that used to be comforting have taken on a sinister quality.
The click-clack of heels on the paving stones that used to
signal the arrival of a loved one now indicates approaching
danger as it echoes against our stretched eardrums. Doors
opening in the night are admitting not a lover inside but
evil. The creaking of the hinges tenses our muscles, as if
preparing us for flight. Even in the morning, the sound of
birds lifting into the clear air, wings flapping, shrill

shrieks—it is no longer the sound of a new day breaking; it is the sound of desperation, fright. And nowhere is there any safety.

But my Wanda is here, and she looks after me. You know how clever she is, how strong. Father has not returned since his last journey abroad, and Mother worries. Often she stays in her room all day. Wanda takes her food and sits by her bed, but even Wanda cannot make Mother eat. There is no music. We don't play anymore. We hardly speak. It is as if we walk on tiptoe, careful not to disturb the fragile stillness in here. I sometimes sit down by the piano and let my fingers run over the keys, remembering how we used to play together. But there is nobody here to tune the piano, and I can't find strings for my bow. Our dear Sofia has left, and dust is settling on the piano and everywhere else. I walk around the apartment and know I should be grateful. Grateful for being here. For being alive, for being with my dear mother and Wanda, here in our home. But all I can see is that which is no longer here. Father. Moishe. But most of all I see you, my love.

We don't walk in the park anymore, and we don't receive any visitors. Wanda tells me the Lipskis are leaving and that your parents and Clara will follow. I do hope so. I hope they will be safe.

Wanda tells me she knows how to get this letter to you, and I trust her. My dearest, I can picture your hands as you unfold this paper. Your beautiful, beautiful hands. And I long to hold them again, to warm them with my breath.

your

Marta

There were two other similar letters, both dated in May. And then the one dated in June:

Kraków

June 1940

My dearest,

It is summer. I gaze out through the window, and I can see that the chestnut trees are dropping their flowers. The petals ride on the wind and look like snowflakes. It feels strange that such things are still happening. Such summery, lovely, ordinary things. That it can be summer at all.

I don't go out these days. Wanda sets out in the morning, and sometimes she is not back till after dark. I don't ask where she has been or what she has been doing, and she never volunteers any information. She just quietly hangs her coat in the hallway and sits on the sofa by the fireplace, where she takes off her shoes and rubs her feet, one against the other. She has lost weight. The first day I noticed she was wearing one of my dresses it felt so comforting. It is as if Wanda is doing the living for all of us. Often I don't bother to dress at all but wander in my dressing gown around the still space of the apartment where nothing is alive anymore. I have not been well, and I can't keep my food down.

Mother doesn't leave her bed, and we can't get Dr. Katz to come here. In fact, we can't get a doctor at all. Wanda looks after Mother, but I have come to think that there is nothing that can be done for her. I think she is willing herself to die.

My darling, here I am complaining when I really should be grateful!

Last Sunday was my birthday, I turned twenty-one, and you know what my dear Wanda made for me? A cake! She had found fresh eggs, white flour, and sugar. Even some fresh cream! She tried to make a napoleon cake. She is a terrible cook, but she tried. Just to make me happy. We sat in the parlor and lit a candle, and I tried so hard to show how grateful I was, but my eyes kept filling with tears and I couldn't swallow. Wanda pushed her plate away, too, and beckoned for me to come and sit beside her on the sofa. I lay down with my head in her lap. She didn't move, although my tears wet her skirt. She just stroked my hair and said, "Hush, hush, my little Marta, don't cry. All will be well."

But it won't, will it? Nothing will be well again.

At night I lie in my bed, and sometimes I can see myself from above. I can see the entire room: the bed, the small bedside table, and the little rug that Father bought for me in Italy when I turned twelve. Do you remember the pattern? The lifelike beautiful deer and the delicate flowers?

I am being silly, I know. How could you? I should have thought you saw me when you came to my room, not some old rug! But I lie in my bed with my eyes closed, and I can see it with frightening clarity, because I know I will lose it soon. The music stand by the window and the piles of sheet music on the writing desk. And, you know, it is as if I am not here any longer. This room, this house, and the city are no longer of any concern to me. The body underneath the

red blanket is no longer mine. But I feel as if I am closer to
you than I am in the daytime. And that is all that matters.
   My love, be safe,
   Marta

And then the next-to-last letter:

Kraków
July 1940

My dearest,
It is very hot. And there are no sounds. We are all holding
our breath. I keep the window open, but there is no relief
from the heat. All is so terribly still. There are no birds, no
people, it seems. Sometimes, when Wanda is away and
Mother is asleep, I feel as if I am the only person here. Here
in Kraków, and the world.
   I wouldn't mind at all, if only I could feel your presence.
But you are no longer here, here in the world. I know that
now with an awful certainty.
   I used to be sad when I sat down to write to you, but at
the same time I also felt the happiest as the pen ran over
the paper. The words flowed easily, and all the while I felt
that they would reach you. That they would bring us
together. It was with happy sadness that I thought of how
you would hold the paper and read my words. Now I feel
nothing. I can't imagine your hands touching this sheet,
and the words no longer flow. They are painfully difficult
to find. And I feel as if I am writing them for nobody.
   But this is the last letter, and I have to write it.
   I am with child, Adam. Our child grows in me. When

Wanda told me, I could not make myself believe what she said. But in the weeks since, I have accepted it. Yet it is not joy that fills me. No, it is dread. I love our unborn child. I love its unknown features. I dream of its voice. But it is the kind of love one has for a lost loved one. It is tinged with such sadness that it is a torment to be filled by it. The sense of foreboding is overwhelming, and I feel so alone.

It is not right. Nothing should be born here. Not here, not now.

Wanda tells me I have to try to eat, and she says I must sit by the window with my face to the sun when the weather is good. She buys food for me, and I know I should be grateful. Yet as I put it in my mouth, I am revolted, and the harsh sunlight hurts my eyes. I long for the shadows inside my room.

Mother is very weak, and I think we will lose her soon. When I talk to her, she doesn't open her eyes, and I can't be sure she hears me. I sit by her bed and watch her face, where no life is present. It is a mask, and I think my mother has left it behind. I think she may already have gone. I wish I could follow.

I have no more words.

If the child lives, I will name him Adam. I am certain it is a boy. I will give him your name because I know I can, now. I know you are not with me anymore.

Marta

There was one more letter, but the handwriting was different, more confident, the stems and the downstrokes sharp.

Kraków

January 1941

Dear Adam,

*I have no way of knowing if this letter will ever reach you,
but I feel it is my duty to try one last time to contact you.*

*You have a son. We have named him Adam. I tried to
convince my sister that it was not appropriate, but she was
insistent. In fact, it was as if all her energies were focused
on that one aspect of his birth. It drained her utterly, and
she was not strong beforehand. She is very weak, and I fear
for her life.*

*When this letter reaches you, if it does, I will have left
Poland and your son will be with me. I have used my
father's contacts, and I am confident that we will be safe. As
for Marta, I will have no way of knowing her fate. I have
had to make some practical choices. It is not possible to save
us all. Life deals us challenges, and we have to face them
with courage and pragmatism. We have to make sacrifices
and then accept the outcome without regret. My personal
sacrifices have been considerable, but they were necessary in
order to save my life and that of my sister's child. Your child.*

*If one day you are in a position to contact us, please
write to my father's lawyer in Vienna. I have enclosed the
address. Please refer to me as Mrs. Anker and the child as
Adam Anker.*

*Unlike my sister, I am not a person inclined to unrealis-
tic dreams and hopes. I live in the present. However—
[illegible, the words crossed out]—everybody has
dreams. It is just that some indulge and let the dreams take
the place of reality.*

Others have to be realistic. For the sake of all of us.
Fondly,
Wanda Anker, née Maisky

Blindly, I stretched out my hand and switched off the light. I sat in the gray pallor with the letters on my lap. The blackbird was still singing outside the window.

Marta. Beautiful, vulnerable Marta.

My mother.

The mother I felt I had glimpsed throughout my life. The fleeting image of something, someone else. The fragile woman with the anthracite eyes. My mother.

I was struggling to breathe.

After a while I collected the envelopes, walked into the bedroom, and opened my suitcase. I took out the folder with the photographs, then sat down on the bed and flicked through them until I found the two pictures of Marta. The one where she stood beside Adam, her hair blowing around her face and her eyes on something just outside the picture. And the one where she stood with her long braids hanging down her chest, her feet close together, so serious. The slim young girl's dark eyes stared back at me as before, but for the first time she had a voice. And she said that she loved me. That she was my mother.

Suddenly I understood what Wanda had seen as she stepped off the train in Vienna. Not me and Magda, but the man she loved and the woman he loved. Adam and Marta. My parents.

I lay down on the bed clasping the pictures and buried my face in the pillow in a vain attempt at silencing my sobs. But it was as if all my life's accumulated grief had finally found an outlet and was allowed to take its course. I screamed, I cried, until the grief became bearable. Afterward I lay staring into the air above the bed.

And eventually I fell into a dreamless sleep.

28

I woke, disoriented, to a knock on the front door. I was still dressed and felt exhausted, in spite of a long night's uninterrupted sleep. It was ten past eight. I got up to open the door.

"You missed dinner, so I have prepared a proper breakfast," Moishe said. "Come over when you are ready." He turned and crossed the landing back to his own apartment.

He had set the table in the living room for two. There were boiled eggs and sliced tomatoes and cucumbers. Tuna in mayonnaise, pickles. Two kinds of fresh bread. Cheese. Jam and butter. A bowl of fruit. Moishe came in carrying a teapot, asking if I preferred tea or coffee.

"I have made both, just to be sure," he said, and smiled.

We sat down opposite each other. I studied the old man's face and tried to imagine what he would have looked like as a young man, escorting my mother safely back from Vilna that cold April evening. Hopelessly loving her.

"Do you have any photographs at all from before the war?" I asked. He shook his head.

I pulled the two pictures of Marta from my breast pocket. He slowly put down his napkin and took them. He said nothing while inspecting both photos for a long time.

"She . . ." he began, but stopped. He put the pictures on the table, took out a handkerchief from his pocket, and blew his nose.

"I will make copies for you," I said.

"You know, that young man there," he said, "that's me." I retrieved the group picture and looked at it closely. The young man seated to the left, in front of Marta, smiling into the camera, was the old man in front of me. It was easy to see the likeness now. The eyes—those large, slightly bulging, intelligent eyes.

"We all belonged to a bicycle club. Except for Adam—I don't know why he happened to be there that day," Moishe said, his eyes fixed on the picture. "Such a nice day it was. Everything still seemed possible. A year later, nothing at all." He put the picture on the table.

"I'll make a copy for you," I repeated. But Moishe shook his head.

"No, I don't need it. Thank you; it's all in here." He pointed to his forehead. "Over the years I have made my own photo album in here, and the pictures are entirely mine. That is all I need."

We sat in silence. I peeled an egg, and Moishe poured coffee for me, tea for himself.

"Why did she do it?" I asked.

"Who? Marta?" he said.

I shook my head. "No, Wanda."

"Ah, Adam, that we will never know, will we? She loved him, of course. She was in love with Adam. But what made her take you with her? And leave Marta? Perhaps a sense of responsibility. Family loyalty? Love? Jealousy? We will never know. Sometimes there is more than one reason behind our decisions. Often the reasons are complex and contradictory. And often we are unaware of them."

"You knew?" I asked. "Did you know what happened?"

The old man looked up at me, twisting his napkin between his fingers.

"When I was still in London, I tried my best to find out whether my parents were still alive. Where they were. And I tried to find out what had happened to Marta. I soon discovered that my parents had been taken to Auschwitz, and eventually I was told my father was dead. It wasn't until after the war that I found out my mother had also perished. But I had no reliable information about what had happened to Marta. Many years later I met a Dr. Katz in New York. I had started playing chess with the residents of an old-people's home every Sunday. It began when an elderly friend of mine ended up there, and it continued after he died. One day I was introduced to a new resident. He told me his name was Josef Katz—Dr. Katz—and we quickly established that we were both from Kraków. And, as you do, we started trying to find points of connection. It wasn't long before we reached the Maisky family. And he told me."

We both busied ourselves with bread and butter, and Moishe poured more coffee and tea.

"Dr. Katz had been stripped of his license to work as a general practitioner in Poland early after the German invasion and had moved back with his parents, who ran a small orchard just outside Kraków. Late one evening in January 1941, he received a message from one of his old patients, a Miss Maisky, that she desperately needed his services. She was prepared to reward him very generously indeed if he agreed to be taken to her home. The message said that a car was waiting outside on the street. Returning to the city was, if not impossible, associated with considerable personal risk, but the message assured him that all such risks had been eliminated. So he decided to go."

I felt my fingers begin to tingle, and my mouth went dry. I took another mouthful of coffee.

"He told me that during that black January night he delivered a healthy baby boy in the Maiskys' apartment on Bernardynska Street."

The old man looked at me.

"The baby was fine, but the mother was very weak. Dr. Katz left them in the early morning. In the hallway he talked to the other woman. Wanda Maisky. He told her that her sister was in need of care. Normally, he said, he would have arranged to have her hospitalized. But as things were, all he could do was to leave her in her sister's care. Wanda told him she feared that her sister would not survive long, that she had no will to live. And she asked Dr. Katz to issue a birth certificate that declared herself to be the mother of the child. She assured Dr. Katz that she would take full responsibility for the boy and that her chances of saving his life would be much better if she could present him as her own."

Moishe took a sip of tea.

"You must remember that these were desperate times. A life seemed to have little value from one perspective, while being priceless when seen from another. Dr. Katz would have felt that, I think. He must have considered that on the one hand the child he'd just delivered could be lost the following day; on the other hand, he must also have been filled with all the feelings that accompany—or should accompany—a birth. The sense of having witnessed a miracle, the start of a new life. He told me he didn't hesitate for long before doing what

Wanda asked. His reward for the night's work was safe passage out of Poland. He left the following week and managed to save himself and his parents. Wanda Maisky had extraordinary resources, he said. Connections."

"Did you ever find out what happened to Marta?" I asked.

The old man closed his eyes, as if seeking a moment's privacy before answering my question. Finally he nodded.

"Yes, I did. I did."

He looked at me almost pleadingly, I thought. As if what he was about to say was too difficult to utter. But then he spoke.

"Marta never made it out of the apartment. In March the city was 'cleansed' of the few remaining Jewish citizens. Whatever protection Wanda had been able to maintain had disappeared with her and the child. When she left for Germany. We'll never know exactly how it happened. Perhaps it was entirely lacking in drama. Or perhaps Wanda took the child for a walk and came back to discover the house being searched. We don't know. But when the apartment was raided, Mrs. Maisky was found dead in her bed. And when Marta refused to leave her bedroom, she was shot."

The old man rose slowly and awkwardly and walked over to the window, where he stood with his back to me.

"Wanda had married a business associate of her father's in December 1940. Karl Anker. He was a prominent German businessman with considerable influence. He was much older than Wanda, closer to her father in age. He had proposed to Wanda years earlier, but, as you know now, she loved someone else. Like mine, her love was hopeless. And Karl Anker became her ticket out of Poland. Her ticket to survival. She made a choice. Who are we to judge her?"

Suddenly I felt physically sick. Bile was rising in my throat. I stood and hurried out to the bathroom, where I bent over the toilet, retching, while tears welled up again in my eyes.

After a while I splashed cold water on my face and returned to the living room. Moishe was still by the window, looking out. I joined him and followed his gaze through the rather grimy glass. We looked out over the Jewish cemetery, where trails of tourists wandered between the headstones. The grass was a bright spring green, and weeds grew high along the wall.

"Why did she never talk to me?" I said.

"Also impossible to know, of course. We will never know. And in the absence of knowledge, we must believe that her reasons were good. That she did what she could. What she thought was best. You must believe that."

He turned and peered up at me for a moment. Then he stretched out his arms and took hold of my shoulders.

"There it is. The knowledge. Now you have to live with it. You have to adjust your existence to embrace the truth. And I do think that the most important part, the only important part, is that you now know that there was so much love. There was love around Marta. And there was love around you. Keep that in mind always, Adam."

29

The following day I was again woken by Moishe's soft knocking on the door.

"Breakfast is ready," he said.

When I joined him a little later, he handed me a large envelope.

"I think that you, like the portrait, are ready to move to your real home," he said, and looked at me with a hint of a smile. "Sometimes extraordinary coincidences occur in life. The other day I heard about an apartment that is for sale." He nodded toward the envelope. "I have made some inquiries, and I think that we could negotiate a very reasonable price. That is, if you're interested."

I opened the envelope and took out some papers. They were all in Polish—a description of an apartment, also a plan and a couple of photographs. One showed a remarkable view over the Vistula.

"Do you know whose apartment it is?" he said with his head cocked and the smile broadening. When I didn't respond right away, he continued. "It's the top-floor apartment on the corner of Bernardynska and Smocza. It's the Maiskys' old apartment."

I was stunned.

"If you're not interested, that is absolutely fine," Moishe said. "But if you would like to have a look, I am happy to arrange for us to see it."

I smiled back and nodded. "I would like that," I said. "I have lived in my house in New Zealand for almost fifteen years. But when . . . when Mimi died, I came to realize that the house means very little to me. At least that's how it feels now. My feelings may change, of course. And it is there—I can return. I will return. It is an extraordinary place. If I were to describe it, you would think I am mad to consider giving it up. But there is nothing tying me to the land there now. I want to come home, I think. So yes, I would very much like to go and have a look."

"It's decided, then. I will phone the agent immediately."

Moishe ordered a taxi to take us to the address. It was a sunny day and warmer than previously. The kind of day when the closed pale green buds on the trees seemed to decide it was time to open. A miracle, equally extraordinary each year. We stood on the pavement looking up at the façade. It was an elegant four-story building with a turret on the corner. A little dilapidated but with retained dignity. Each corner apartment had a bay window, except for the top one, which had a small balcony instead, overlooking the river.

"This is where I said good-bye to Marta that very different April day. So cold, with so little promise." The old man struggled to turn his head and look up into the sky. "And today, so very full of promise," he said. He took my offered arm, and we walked inside.

The real-estate agent was standing by the open door when we finally reached the fourth-floor landing. She waved for us to enter the empty apartment. The parquet creaked loudly as we strolled through the rooms accompanied by the middle-aged woman, who spoke good English.

"Naturally, you may wish to renovate. The bathroom and the kitchen need doing up," she said. "But I must stress that it is a unique opportunity. We don't often see this kind of property come on the market. You are lucky to know Mr. Spiewak," she said to me, and smiled widely, showing teeth with two prominent gold fillings. "Mr. Spiewak is a good friend. When he showed interest, I wanted to give him first look." She turned to Moishe and continued the conversation in Polish before smiling at me again and telling me to take my time exploring the rooms.

The hallway opened onto a generous parlor, which in turn led into a dining room. Down a corridor were three bedrooms and a spacious study. As I stopped and stood on the threshold, looking into the smallest bedroom, Moishe softly touched my shoulder.

"This is Marta's room. I think this is where you were born," he said.

I tried to analyze my feelings, but it was futile. It felt as if I were no longer touching the floor. I was removed from the present and drifting toward the past. I walked inside and let my hand run along the wall as I approached the window and looked out. The room faced the Wawel, and I could see a glimpse of the river to the left. When I turned my back to the window and let my eyes run over the bare floor, I thought I could discern marks in the parquet along the wall, as though made by a heavy piece of furniture. A piano, perhaps. I tried to imagine the room furnished, like the apartment that Moishe had created and where I was staying. A canopy bed. An Italian rug with a hunting pattern. Pictures on the walls. Music. Books. Voices. Footsteps across the floor. Smells of food, perfume, flowers. Life. And the young woman who had occupied the room. My mother. She had given birth to me here. And she had died here. I kept wiping my mouth and stroking my chin while taking deep breaths of the slightly stale, dry air. I walked the length and width of the room several times before again stopping by the window.

Then I felt Moishe's light tap on my shoulder, and I slowly followed him back into the parlor, where the agent stood waiting.

"As you can see, the apartment was divided into two at some stage, but it is now being sold as one unit. I really do think it is a very special opportunity."

We shook hands and agreed to get in touch the following day. I asked her to call us a taxi.

Outdoors, we stood side by side waiting for the car. At the same time, we both turned to each other, and I lifted my arms and embraced the old man. "Thank you," I whispered over his shoulder.

I couldn't hear him say anything, and I let go. He turned and pulled a handkerchief from his pocket and blew his nose loudly.

"I believe I'll take a walk," I said. "I need to think."

Moishe still said nothing, just nodded and busied himself with folding the handkerchief. When the car drove up, I helped him get inside.

I walked across the street and up the grassy slope to the Wawel. The small music shop was open, and I went inside. The woman was there and smiled as she recognized me.

"Thank you for letting me listen to your CD," I said, pulling it from my pocket. "It has given me a lot of pleasure." She kept smiling but didn't respond.

"I would like to give you this," I said, and pulled out a

second CD. She took it and looked at it. It was an unlabeled CD in a white paper sleeve.

"It's a piece of music I have written," I said, pointing to myself. "I wrote it last year. For my daughter. Please accept it as a gift."

"You?" she asked with raised eyebrows. I nodded, and she drew the CD from its cover. She turned and inserted it into the player behind her. When it began to play, I sank into the chair beside the counter. It was the first time I had listened to it since it had been recorded, just before I left New Zealand. I had never heard it outside my studio. I hadn't played myself— one of the bright postgraduate students at the School of Music was playing the violin and my Russian friend the piano. Now it felt strange, as if the music had moved into its own space and taken on a life of its own. I closed my eyes. I expected tears, but instead I was overcome by a sense of calm. As the music played, my muscles seemed to relax and I could feel my face soften.

The first movement finished, and I looked up.

The woman behind the counter stood with her back to me. Her head was bent, and her hands seemed to cover her face. Before I could say anything, the door opened and another customer entered. I watched her straighten and turn, and I realized she had been crying.

"Thank you," she said. I nodded slowly.

"I am leaving," I said. "But I will be back."

She looked at me, and I wasn't sure if she understood. Then she turned and removed the CD from the player and slid it back into its cover.

"My?" she asked with a thin smile and a hand on her

chest. I indicated that it was, and she lifted her purse from the floor and put the CD inside. Then she stretched her hand across the counter, and I took it in mine.

"Come back," she said.

I nodded, and we both smiled before she turned her attention to the other customer.

In the evening Moishe and I played chess with Mr. Liebermann, as usual.

"I think Adam will be leaving us soon," Moishe said after we had finished our meal. I looked at him, startled. I certainly had not indicated that my departure was imminent. I hadn't even been aware of thinking about it. He smiled broadly.

"Tell me if I'm wrong, Adam," he said.

I shook my head slowly and smiled back. I realized that the time had come for me to go to Stockholm.

"You are right, of course. I'm beginning to worry about this ability you have of reading my mind," I said, still smiling.

"Logic, just logic," the old man said. "Like chess. Pure logic. The work is done here. You finally have a home. And you have important things to do in Sweden. You have to leave. But you will be back, no?"

I nodded. And I was aware of how comfortable it made me feel to think of my return. The possibility of the apartment. My two friends.

"Gentlemen, time for some serious chess. Let's show Szymon how your game has developed," Moishe said.

We played our games. And Moishe won all his, as usual.

30

The following Monday, I flew to Stockholm.

From my window seat, I watched the land below as we approached Arlanda Airport. It was still a monochrome landscape, shades of gray. I thought I could discern patches of snow in shady areas and ice on the lakes.

Ben Kaplan stood waiting as I came through the gate. He smiled with those familiar front teeth, and although I had met him only twice in my life, he somehow looked like an old friend. His smile felt very comforting. He had insisted on picking me up and had offered his home as a place to stay.

"I have far too much space since my wife left me, but I'm too lazy or too busy to look for something else. Plenty of space for guests, for sure," he had said when I phoned him from Kraków. I had considered the offer but decided to stay in a small hotel by Slussen, just a short walk from his apartment. There was no way to get out of his offer to pick me up, though. And here he was.

"I haven't made any plans for tonight," he said as we were driving south toward Stockholm. "I wasn't sure if you would rather have a quiet evening to yourself or if you have other plans. If you feel like it, you are most welcome to come over for a glass of wine. I could outline what I have in mind for this new film. And you could tell me a little of your projects."

I hesitated, trying to search out my feelings. Did I want to spend my first evening back in Sweden with this man? A stranger, really. But before I had consciously decided how to respond, the words came forth.

"That sounds really good. I would like that."

Ben smiled and nodded.

He dropped me off at my hotel and gave me instructions on how to get to his apartment, a five-minute walk.

In my room I unpacked a few things, then sat down on the bed and picked up the phone.

You answered on the second signal, as if you'd been expecting the call. Our conversation was brief and light, a simple exchange of practical information. We agreed on a time for my arrival two days later. I asked if you wanted me to bring anything. And it was over. I sat for a moment, oddly upset. Had I expected you to say something more? Should I have expressed myself differently? Should I call you again?

I stood and went to have a quick shower before leaving my hotel.

Later I sat in Ben Kaplan's kitchen. The apartment was near the Katarina Church, and we had just heard the bells chime. The window stood slightly open, despite the chill outside, and the air smelled fresh.

"My daughter died last year," I said in response to his question. I had no idea why these words emerged. Apart from a brief statement of the fact that she had died, I hadn't talked about her with anybody. Certainly not volunteered any information. But here it was. And all he had asked was what I'd been doing the last year or so.

He stood by the kitchen bench arranging cheese on a wooden board. For quite a while, he was silent, and his back expressed nothing. Then he walked toward me and sat down at the table. He took a small sip of red wine.

"My son died when he was four. Lukas."

He was quiet for a while again.

"His name was Lukas. For a long time I never talked about him. But, you know, sometimes not talking about what absorbs you totally is not such a good idea."

He put the glass on the table and clasped his hands.

"For a time we never talked about Lukas's death. Never. We resumed our social life but never talked about our son, who was never out of our thoughts. It was surreal. On the surface our lives resumed, but underneath there was total chaos. But then my wife started to talk about it. And she talked of nothing else. In death Lukas came to occupy more of her than he ever had in life. Before, she would drop him off at nursery school. Have baby-sitters around. Have him stay with her parents and mine. But in death she wouldn't leave him for a second. She carried him with her everywhere she went. Even at night. Gradually the rest of the world disappeared for her, till there was just Lukas. And his death."

He took another mouthful of wine and encouraged me to try the cheese.

"Our guilt was all-encompassing. She was on the upstairs balcony playing with Lukas when I called for her to come down and help me put the kitchen window back on its hinges. The room smelled of the paint and thinners I'd been using to repaint the window frame. She came down the stairs, and we lifted the window and tried to align the hinges. It was heavy, and we were balancing it with difficulty, focused on our task, when he fell. He seemed to slow down in midair in front of our eyes while Lena screamed and the window crashed to the floor. 'Noooo!' she screamed, begging for it to stop. It felt as if the glass broke with a crash that covered the sound of his small body landing on the pavement. But I don't think that is true. I think we heard him land first. He died instantly."

I said nothing: there seemed to be no appropriate response.

"We never talked afterward. We never mentioned the stool that had been left on the balcony. Lena never said it was my fault for distracting her. But I knew. And while Lena survived by holding on to our son, I survived by burying him. I threw myself into the film project I was working on. That was the year I made *Let Your Longing Rest*, which was nominated for an Oscar for Best Foreign Film. I existed in the vortex of a raging storm, and I didn't have to think. When I finally reentered my life, it was like a desert landscape. There were no shapes, no colors. Nothing. I couldn't understand what to do with it. But slowly I started talking to him. To my son. I picked him up again and held him to my chest. And the journey began. Today he is always with me, in everything I do. But it is not with feelings of guilt and grief that I think of him. Now I am able to rejoice in the fact that I had a son. That I *have* a son. I no longer lament the fact that he was taken from me, because he wasn't. He can never be. He is mine, and I can love him. And I can accept myself now."

He smiled a sad smile, showing the gap between his two front teeth.

"Did you know?" I asked, and he nodded. I shook my head. "I used to dread that. The look in people's eyes. The sympathy.

Their feeble attempts at comforting me. Or pretending every-thing was normal. But I dreaded their words most of all. I never listened. And I never talked."

"Tell me," Ben said. "I will listen."

And for the first time, I tried to talk about the death of my daughter. My Mimi.

31

"I look back at this past year, and it is a void. Now that I can see it, it fills me with a bizarre kind of longing to be back in there. To rest in that emptiness. Because there are times when the real world overwhelms me.

"But there is never any going back in time. In life. And that time is now out of reach. I have to try to cope outside. While it lasted, I did nothing. I thought nothing, because thinking would have meant remembering, and that was simply unbearable. Yet what I thought was a constant was really a process. I drifted toward life again, incrementally. But I was helpless: the process had its own timing, and I wasn't even aware of it until abruptly one day I realized it was over. I was alive.

"As soon as I began to remember, I heard the sound of music again. There was an earth-shattering silence the first time I went into her room. But day by day, week by week, it softened, and gentle sounds appeared.

"It is still impossible for me to recollect the time between the phone call and the day when I was able to sit on her bed and fill my nose with the smell of her room. There are days that I will never remember, I think. Not even in my dreams does that time return.

"But I used to dream about my bicycle trip to the ferry. The pedals were leaden, utterly heavy to push, and there was a strange light, like the last golden light before a thunderstorm.

Eerie and still. I stood heavily on the pedals, applying all my weight, and the effort was enormous. The light made me nauseous. It was totally silent. Then I heard her voice. Not as she sounded when she said good-bye that day but her voice when she was little. And she called for me.

"*'Help me. Help me, Daddy.'*"

I felt my voice break. Ben stood and walked over to a CD player that sat on a shelf by the table. He flicked through a small stack of CDs and inserted one. He remained standing for a moment, with his back to me, listening to the music as it started. Bach, a toccata and fugue, I noticed distractedly.

Then he sat down, and I continued, with the music a soothing background.

"Mimi was meeting her friend Charlotte at the ferry landing in town that day. When she didn't arrive as agreed, Charlotte waited for another two ferries, while phoning our home repeatedly, terribly worried. My cell kept receiving her messages where it sat on my desk in the empty house. Meanwhile I was strolling through the War Memorial Museum, unaware of the gathering storm that would sweep away my life.

"Mimi was found by two German backpackers. She was dead, but the autopsy indicated that she might have been alive for quite some time after being hit by a car. She hadn't accidentally landed where she was found—someone had dragged her off the road and hidden her bicycle.

"In my dreams she kept calling for me. I will never know if she did in real life. Whether she was still alive as I came bicycling past, my face lifted to the sky, whistling. Did my daughter call for me? I have not been able to erase that picture, never will. Mimi taking her last breaths completely alone, with no comfort. Me running past, arrogantly ignorant. Whistling.

"They never caught the person who hit her. In my numbing emptiness, I kept traversing the island, looking for suspicious cars. Asking people for information. Posting notices. As if it mattered.

"It was only when I ended my feverish activities that I first heard those soft sounds. I ignored them for some time, but in their gentle way they persisted. And eventually they linked and joined until they began to sound like music. And that," I said, looking up at Ben, "is the only work I have done this last year. I have written down that music. *Sonata for Miriam*."

The music in the background was now Eugène Ysaÿe, and we listened for a while in silence.

"My daughter . . ." I said, searching for the words. "My daughter never had a mother."

I closed my eyes and inhaled the green air that drifted in through the open window.

"You see, I had my daughter at an enormous price. Her mother asked me to choose between her and our child. I'm not sure I made the right choice. There *was* no right choice. I only know that the moment I was told I had created a child, I could never give it up. Mimi came to be the center of my world. She stood for everything that was good in my life. I loved her more than it is possible to express in any form. Yet all these years I have grieved over the loss of her mother, Cecilia. Over the irreconcilable fact that losing the woman I loved led to my gaining the child that made my life worth living."

Ben looked at me. "Cecilia Hägg," he said.

I stared at him. "Did you know?" I asked.

He shook his head. "I knew *of* you then. People talked. She was, what . . . twenty? Half your age. Very beautiful. Very talented. Up-and-coming artist. And you were well known. One of the top violinists in the country. Today you would have been in those gossipy magazines, you two," he said with a smile.

I shook my head, returning his smile. "I was so totally absorbed in her that it would never have occurred to me to imagine how it might have looked to others. And it seemed to be such a short time. Not even a full year before it was over. She made me promise never to contact her again."

Ben filled our glasses and took a sip of his.

"And I haven't," I said. "I thought about her. I dreamed about her. But to me the conditions she set were irrevocable. And being far removed in New Zealand, it became easier. Gradually Cecilia became just a bittersweet dream. A fleeting image that enveloped both me and my daughter, constant but invisible. It wasn't until right before her death that Mimi even mentioned her mother. Began to ask questions. I let the matter rest, thinking there would be time. Time for me to prepare, time for Mimi to grow to understand. But she was never to know. I never told her anything about her mother."

I felt tears rising in my eyes and lifted my glass.

"I did to my daughter what was done to me. I made her motherless. It wasn't Cecilia who did that, it was me. It was in my power to give my daughter her mother. I could have made it understandable. I could have told her of my love for Cecilia. And her love for me. But I chose not to. I have to face that, take the responsibility. I also have to face the underlying reasons. Reflect on my true motive.

"In the end I'm no better than Wanda, the woman I called

Mother, who was actually my mother's sister. I now know have no right to judge her. What difference do the reasons make? It's the effect of our actions—or our inaction—that matters. For all I know, my 'mother' may have had as valid a reason for her behavior as I claim to have for mine."

"Unlike film, real life rarely provides an opportunity for a retake," Ben said. "Perhaps that is why I like film so much. But I do think we have to give ourselves the same amount of leeway that we give others. Forgive ourselves. Have pity on ourselves. And perhaps even love ourselves a little."

It was late. I offered to help clear the table, but Ben shook his head.

"I'll walk you back to your hotel," he said. "Let's stop and look at the city from Mosebacke on the way."

As we opened the door, we were instantly caught up in the cold night air, as piercing as I remembered it from the early-April weeks of my childhood, when the light indicated spring but the weather felt colder than winter. In spite of the chill, we did stop and take in the view from Mosebacke. The old town lay like a glittering giant ship on the dark water.

"Would you consider moving back here?" Ben asked, his eyes on the city below.

I followed his gaze, inhaling the cold, dry air.

"I have just bought an apartment," I said. And as I said the words, it became reality. I had made the decision to buy the apartment in Kraków.

"Here?" he said, looking at me in wonder.

"No, in Poland," I said. "Kraków. I have . . . I have friends there."

He nodded and returned his gaze to the view.

"It's important to have friends around you. Your friends. And your family," he said.

"Yes," I said, "it is. It's the only thing that matters."

We carried on down toward Slussen, and when we parted outside my hotel, we agreed to meet for lunch the following day to discuss business.

I had agreed with Cecilia to drive down to the island on Wednesday, and I planned to pick up a rental car and do some shopping after my meeting with Ben the following day.

In my room I opened the window and leaned on the sill, looking up into the clear night sky.

The stars were all familiar.

IV

32

"Cecilia?" you said, and I listened.

I listened to you saying my name, and time stopped. Or stopped being relevant. I was catapulted through time, losing my bearings. Then I listened to the silence between us. After that first word, it was as if I could hear the distance, see it. An eternity. I said nothing.

The first morning when the phone rang, I was in the shower. The muted sound surprised me. It was early, just after seven. Nobody phones me in the morning. Although barely audible through the sound of the running water, it felt like an intrusion in the permanent peace of my house. Knowing that I would not make it downstairs in time before the answering machine kicked in, I stood still under the shower until the beeps ended, leaving an intensified silence behind. When I came downstairs, I saw the flashing red indicator light and lifted the receiver to hear the message. But there was none, just a faint drone. Wrong number, I thought, and deleted the blank message.

The second call came a week later. Not quite as early this time, but early enough to catch me in the kitchen, finishing my breakfast. The unexpected sound gave me a start, and I set my coffee mug on the table. My mother calls occasionally, but always between five and six in the afternoon, after her first drink and before her second. It still happens that Anders phones, always late, sometimes after midnight. Other than those calls, which have a pattern of sorts, there are infrequent business calls, but they are predictable, related to a specific exhibition or project, and they always occur during business hours. This was different.

Afterward I felt as if I had known it would be you even before I heard the sound of your voice. As if ever since that first, unanswered call, I had known.

I lifted the receiver and heard you say my name, and nineteen years of silence were instantly erased.

"Cecilia?" you repeated. You said nothing, leaving me with the initiative. But I just listened to the charged air between us until you spoke again.

"It's Adam," you said finally. Did you think I could have forgotten your voice? I pressed the receiver hard against my ear. Waited. And then I said your name.

"Adam." And I knew how hard it had been to keep it inside me all these years.

"Would you meet me if I came to Sweden?"

All at once the carefully nurtured, protective layers of time were ripped away, and I was again by the window watching you cross the parking lot far below, your footsteps a straight line of small dark spots in the wet snow, leading away from me. Carrying our child. And I knew I would never find you again. The snow would melt, and there would be no trace.

"I will be in Stockholm in April for some business meetings. Would you let me see you?"

I listened but didn't trust my voice to speak.

"Cecilia?"

I looked toward the window, where a muted sun edged over the horizon, casting a slanted weak light through the glass.

You talked, but we both knew that the words were super-fluous. I allowed myself the luxury of the sound of your voice, but the words themselves meant nothing.

I couldn't be sure why you had called. But I knew you could be calling only if your promise not to contact me no longer had any relevance. There had been an instant glimmer of hope at the first sound of your voice, but the awareness now froze my entire body. My hand on the receiver felt cold, my fingers stiff.

"Come here," I said finally. "To the island. If you like."

After I had returned the receiver to its cradle, my lips formed your name again.

"Adam," I whispered to the silent kitchen. "Adam."

I knew it wasn't a matter of whether you wanted to come or not. I knew you had called because it was necessary. That you needed to come. Because you had nowhere else to go. And I regretted how my words had fallen.

Afterward I pulled on my jacket and knitted hat and wan-dered up to the lookout. I climbed the side of the rock, where I know each small crevice like the lines of my hand. With time wild violets would fill every crack, but now the gray gran-ite lay bare. When I stepped onto the summit, I was panting. There was no wind, and I could hear the beating of my heart in my ears. I scanned the sky where the sun had now pene-trated the purple haze that lingered along the horizon to the east. The day would be clear, but there was no warmth in the air. I looked down at the house where it sat in solid silence, as it has for a century and a half. In the summer it is hardly visi-ble from up there, embedded in lush greenery. Now it was fully exposed, the bare branches of the trees offering no protection.

I suddenly realized that you'd never seen my island in the winter. I had forgotten how short our life together was. For me it was forever.

I returned my eyes to the sea. The smell of the cold water filled the air; the ice had never set properly this winter. It was colder with the open sea, something I learned only after living here through my first full year. I pulled my hat tight over my ears and breathed into my mittens. There were no waves; the sea was just undulating softly, as if rustling from beneath, the dark surface dully reflecting the sky that gradually paled as the sun rose.

Instead of retracing my footsteps back down the side of the rock, I crossed the summit and walked down the other side, where it slopes gently toward the settlement. I passed the scattering of old houses down there, silently hunched together, abandoned now in winter. A couple of motorboats slept under tarpaulins between the houses and the sea, and water lapped slowly against the foundations of the empty landing. I continued along the path where the grass lay smooth and dry. The months ahead would be its short period of uninhibited growth—after the snow and before the invasion of the feet of the summer guests.

Do you remember how small my island is, and how you still can't glimpse the sea when you walk down toward my boat landing? That's how they wanted it in the old days. Shelter: it was all about shelter. Perhaps that is why I like it so much. I feel safe here.

I passed my house to the left, with the open fields to the right. Here, too, the grass would have a limited time of unhampered regeneration before the herd of young heifers arrived by barge from the mainland. I turned right by the old oak tree, the one you photographed so beautifully, and the bay lay open in front of me. During those first years, I often imagined you there, naked, your arms outstretched, your face turned toward the sun, declaring this to be the most beautiful place you had ever seen.

I thought you were the most beautiful sight I had ever seen.

I continued down to the water and onto what remained of the wooden landing. The entire far end had broken off during the winter storms and drifted across the bay, and now it sat awkwardly on the opposite shore. I looked down into the dark water, which had no color yet. It seemed as dead as the vegetation along the shore, where last year's dried seaweed constituted a black barrier between land and water. I stepped on board my small boat and opened the stiff blue canvas that covered the cabin. The zipper yielded reluctantly to my clumsy, mitten-clad fingers. Inside, the cold air was saturated with the smell of gasoline. I unfastened all the wing nuts and pulled back the entire cover. It had been well over two weeks since I'd run the engine, but it started on the first try. I untied the moorings and slowly maneuvered the boat over the shallow water, standing by the helm, my eyes scanning the flat surface ahead. I needed the open sea.

Because the sea absorbs everything.

33

When I didn't hear from you again, and the weeks passed, I began to doubt my own memory. Perhaps it was all in my mind, I thought. Had I made up the phone call because somehow, subconsciously, I wanted to see you again? All these years, and I had never once tried to find you. I believe that I am honest when I say that I have never, not once, even toyed with the idea. I allowed you to walk across that parking lot, and I knew I could never ask to see you again.

But then I got your letter. It was real. You had found me, here on the island. And I was allowing you to come. I wasn't quite sure what my feelings were. A combination of anticipation and dread. You said you might be delayed. Something unexpected had come up during your stay in Poland that might delay you. You would let me know. You said you would phone from Stockholm. I wondered why you had written. Why didn't you just call me? But oddly, the letter seemed more reliable proof of your arrival. I kept it on my bedside table.

Later that day, when I came back to the house, I went out to the studio and began wrapping some finished paintings for my next exhibition. I looked at them critically and thought that perhaps you might have liked them—you always liked my abstract work the best. The exhibition is called Aspects of a Void. It is not my title: the agent came up with it. It sounds pretentious, I think. Perhaps it shouldn't have a title at all. It would be more fitting, for I have tried to paint nothingness. A soothing emptiness. But it doesn't matter—you won't see them. Not here anyway. I had to meet the mail boat and make sure they got safely on board later that day. And somehow it felt appropriate, as if I were cleaning up. Tying up the loose ends of my existence so that when you arrived, I would be able to let you see only what I wanted to show you. And watch you without distractions. Listen to you.

I had not been conscious of any intention to make changes in my life, but as I looked around the studio, I was overcome by a feeling of unease, as if for the first time I could see it objectively. See it as it would look to others. To you. During the time I have lived here, almost fifteen years now, my studio has become part of my physical self. And like my own body, the dusty space, where the canvases sit on the floor and sketches and notes line the walls, has become just a vehicle for my work.

I carried the three wrapped canvases outside one by one as they were done, stacking them by the door. Over the years I have become proficient at making crates, and they stood ready for the canvases to slip into. I was grateful for the weather. I can manage large crates only one at a time, since I have to carry them over the cliff to get them down to the main boat landing. A hassle if it rains. But otherwise I don't mind. It takes a while, but I cherish the labor. They are not heavy, just unwieldy. That day I had plenty of time. It was early, and the mail boat was not due until noon.

The work finished, I sat on the smooth, flat rock by the landing, waiting. There was still no warmth in the air, despite the sun, but all it would take was that first spell of warm weather and the grass and the wild orchids would respond. I have learned that it is impossible to say when this will happen. It may still have been weeks away, or it could begin the following day. I felt the cold rock underneath me and remembered that day down here, on these rocks, making love with our hats on. I thought about it for the first time in many years as I sat there watching the vast, empty sea in front of me. I let my hands run over the smooth rock, and it was cold to the touch. The dark granite soaks in the heat from the sun, but in the early spring it never penetrates deeply. It takes the sun to warm it anew each morning. That day in March, the sun had no warmth to give.

There have been years when it has snowed in June, and years when the trees have been fully open mid-May, but March is still winter in the archipelago. You have to be observant to notice the subtle signs of the approaching spring. Watch the sky. Be sensitive to the gradually lighter mornings. Watch the birds return, the eider ducks first. Each year it gives me the same jolt as I see the first small flock land on the islet across from the landing. It takes a trained eye to spot them once they are out of the sky. The gray rocks and the gray sea absorb the gray birds. Keep them safe as they prepare for spring. It seems as if it's the birds that bring the spring, not the other way around. And once I know they are back, the weather is of no consequence. Cold weather delays the invasion of the summer people. The long weekend at the end of May inevitably brings the first lot, but not until midsummer are they all here. And my peace of mind will be disturbed for two months.

As always, I could hear the boat long before it appeared from behind the point, and I stood and waved.

Later, back by the house, I stopped and looked up into the sky. I have come to know the sky here on the island. I live with it in a way I never had before, particularly the night sky. The soft black August sky that sparkles with stars that seem to burn in layer upon layer, the depths revealed only to the very patient observer. The misty gray November sky that touches the smoking sea and blends with it. The sharp January sky, brittle like black glass. And the early-summer sky, just a paler version of the day, the night that never is. But the March sky that day was of a noncommittal kind, colorless and empty.

I opened the front door and went upstairs to my bedroom. I stood on the threshold looking inside with a critical squint. I realized that it still looked like the girl's room it once was. The narrow bed was unmade, the sheets mismatched. The small chest beside it had lost all but two of its handles. The old cast-iron woodstove was still there, though I never use it, and the storage space beside it was concealed by the sun-bleached flower-patterned cotton curtain. I was sure it hung there gingerly on its string that summer, too. The wallpaper was the same—the one I was allowed to choose when my father first bought the house. Little steamships on bright blue waves, the once-cheerful pattern now faded into a fleet of ghost ships forever adrift in a white nothingness. My father was not a practical man, but he insisted on doing the work himself, pipe in his mouth, his shirtsleeves rolled up. He cut several lengths too short, and the last one, half hidden behind the curtain, was a patchwork of leftover pieces.

I don't think I ever told you anything much about my father.

There was always too much silence around us, Adam. So much unsaid.

Running my hand over the dry paper that had come loose from the wall, allowing the mice free run at night, I remembered tracing the waves with my finger, telling stories of journeys that we would make across the seas, my father and I. Away across the seas, far, far away.

Always just the two of us.

Right then I met my own eyes in the mirror above the small chest of drawers at the foot of the bed. I lifted my hand and brushed the hair away from my face and took a step closer. I could instantly see every detail, and I assessed them all objectively, from a technical point of view. If I were a painting, I would store it, I thought. I would put it where I keep the other ones I don't want to share with the world, the ones I don't need to see. The ones that stand facing the wall in silence. They threaten to invade my life again, and I can't allow them to look back at me. With their backs toward me I can ignore them.

But here was my own face, and it was doing just what I don't allow my paintings to do. It was staring at me, disturbing my peace. My dark eyes, with their slightly hooded lids and the constant critical squint that has planted permanent creases on my brow, stared at me. I took in my pale skin, my wide mouth with the corners pointing a little downward. My light hair, with the ends bleached blond by last summer's sun but the roots darker. I loosened the clasp that held it together and shook my head. How long had it been since I had a haircut? I couldn't remember.

I looked at my hands. I used to like my hands. Do you remember that they were the first part of my body I showed you? How I held them up to you and said something like, "These are my instruments." Such a stupid thing to say, but I was struggling for words. For something to say that would make you stay a little longer. I had been looking at you while you played. There was something about the way you held your violin. About *your* hands. Do you remember what it was that you played? I do. That Bach partita that you played again here on the island, just for me. And then when the music finished, I watched you cross the room. I couldn't make you bump into me, but I willed it to happen. And when it did, I was stunned. Silenced. Hence those awkward words.

I still like my hands, though, and they are as important to me as my eyes. I held them up in front of me, and another memory surfaced, like a scene on one of those discs that came with the little toy camera I had as a child, my ViewMaster. Just the one deceptively lifelike image, bright and three-dimensional. I saw myself on the granite slab outside the front door of this house. My mother was sitting in one of the garden chairs, a magazine in her hands. I wasn't looking at her, but I knew she was there. The sun was setting after a hot day, and it made the shadows fall strangely extended over the grass. The warmth of the day still lingered in the air, but under my feet the grass already felt cool and a somewhat damp.

"It's bad luck to compare hands," my mother said. My hands were resting on my knees, palms up. We were not comparing, we were delighting in the symmetry, the visible sign of belonging. Me and my other me. My Angela. The two soft little-girl's palms were almost identical, one mirroring the other. At my mother's words, I lifted one hand, and slowly the other one followed, the palms softly touching in the air. There was no need to say anything. But I smiled where I sat there in the shade. We smiled. And the sun disappeared behind the trees.

In front of the mirror in my bedroom, I lifted first one hand and then the other and stroked my cheeks. The palms were rough, and they smelled of turpentine. I lowered them and turned them over. Normally I never give them a thought. They are just tools for my work, no more a part of me than my brushes and my knives. As important, and taken for granted. But here they were on display, and I could see that they were good, strong hands, the fingers long and straight, the nails short and not too clean.

I walked back to the bed and started stripping off the sheets.

And so I began preparing myself and my house for your arrival. What did I expect? I simply don't know. But for the first time in many years, I went downstairs and turned on the old tape deck in the kitchen. I played the Mendelssohn. The one you said was only the first. The beginning of our journey. But it became the last. The only one. I had kept the tape there all these years, but I had never played it again.

I sat down at the table. And as the second movement began, I closed my eyes and cried.

34

Your call affected all my routines.

I found myself pausing, brush in hand, and staring out the window, with no clear thoughts in my mind, yet strangely preoccupied. Then I had to concede and invite my consciousness. It was like being born a second time, becoming aware of the world. Of myself. Allowing feelings.

I took to wandering up to the lookout daily and sat there staring out over the sea until I could hear the mail boat. The weekends felt like an eternity.

It seemed impossible that it would ever be summer again. There were no signs of life anywhere. It was mid-March, and in places on the mainland there would be days of warm sunlight. But here the icy water greedily swallowed the sun's warmth. The landscape was shades of gray. The granite rock, the bare trees, the sea. Even the sky seemed to be a pale gray. The wind was light yet numbed the skin.

I began ordering groceries from the shop on the mainland more often, to justify my walks down to the landing. But it wasn't the arrival of the grocery box that caused the stirring anticipation I was hesitant to acknowledge. Normally I would have left the pickup until a convenient time, not bothering to try to meet the boat. But now I was keeping this lonely vigil on the crest of the cliff, where I could hear the boat long before I could see it. Then I'd have time to walk down as it came around the point and hove to. I had no reason to think that you would write again, and there was no justification for the disappointment I felt each time there was no mail.

On the days when I didn't expect groceries, I would return to the lookout after checking the mailbox.

When I was a child, I took for granted that the island was always as it presented itself when we arrived in June. And that it remained as it looked when I watched it recede from the stern of the boat in August. It belonged to me; it would be there, suspended, until I returned next year.

Now I know the remarkable metamorphosis it goes through. And how painfully short the summer is. Just an interlude. As a child I knew it only in its summer finery, and I always left it before the party was over. And that was how you saw it, Adam. You knew my island only in the summer. And you knew only that part of me, too. The summer part. And perhaps a little of the spring. But never the long, dark, silent winter. I never invited you there. Did you know it existed? Did you ever think there must be another me, too? Or did you not want to know? There were moments when I came so very close to talking to you. But it never seemed to be quite the right time. And I never felt I had quite the right words. Not until much later, long after I had lost you. After that day on the ice. When finally I was on my own. Truly myself.

Too late.

One day as I sat watching the sea and listening for the boat, I realized I had more time than usual, and I felt a little cold. The boat wasn't likely to arrive before noon—half an hour away. I decided to walk to keep warm. I rarely walk along that side of the island anymore, other than to get the mail. But when I was a child, it was my territory. I would climb up the steep granite cliff and then down to a small ledge in the rock, a shallow cove in the sheer wall. The rock was very dark there, and always warm, and there was just enough space to sit side by side, feet dangling over the water below. Nobody could see me, or so I thought. And it was here that I learned to dive. It was here that my other me took the plunge for the first time. Sometimes I brought my fishing rod, but the fish I caught were tiny, and I always threw them back. I watched from above as the silvery bodies landed with a splash, then recovered and with a swift whip of tail disappeared into the depths.

To get there I always took the same route. Over time my bare feet created a narrow path across the paddock where the cows grazed. Usually I climbed over the fence, not bothering to open the wide gate, then dashed across the grass, carefully avoiding the cowpats. When the cows were near, it was always my other me, my Angela, who had to climb first and beckon me to follow. Telling me the animals were friendly. Later there were no longer summer-grazing cows on the island, and nobody looked after the fence. Only recently has it become viable to keep cows here again, thanks to the intricate funding resources provided by EU membership. But the young heifers are kept on the other side of the island.

Nobody comes here anymore.

Nobody uses the path either.

I stopped and stood looking out over the area where the paddock once was. Aspens had invaded, always the first to take advantage of land that is left to itself, and their bare, straight trunks stood in dense groves, interspersed with junipers and tangles of wild rosebushes. It was impossible to see where the path once ran. I stepped over the remaining half-rotted fence posts and began walking toward the high cliff. I zigzagged between the trees and bushes and then climbed the granite wall. Back then it had seemed enormous—steep and rough and a little dangerous. Now it was a quick climb to the top and down the other side, where I slid into the small cove and sat on the ledge with my legs against the side of the rock. I looked down onto the dark surface below and noted the smooth, rounded top of the rock rising out of the water a short distance from the shore. It had been my safe haven, my goal as I emerged breathless after each dive into the cool water. No, that's not quite right. It was only I, never Angela, who needed it. My stiff hands used to stretch forward fervently through the water until finally my fingers touched the stone and I was able to heave myself up. But Angela loved the water. In the sea she was brave. Graceful.

It happened that Angela left me in the water. And at once it felt as if I could see myself, all alone in the chilly sea. My breathing became rapid, and suddenly swimming was no longer swift and easy. "Come back, Angela!" I cried as I struggled to stay afloat. "Please, come back to me!" I cried again, my teeth chattering, while I trod water and turned around in circles, my arms splashing frantically. But there was no sound, no movement. I was alone. "Angela, *pleeeease!*" By now my salty tears were mixing with the brackish water. "Please come back!"

Then the water parted and her head appeared, the hair dark and pasted over her head. For a moment she was something alien: an animal, a sea creature. Her pale hand wiped the hair from her face and she swam the other way, toward the shore, her little white feet cutting through the surface as she made the swift turn, the water silk against her skin. And we were safe.

I looked at the dark sea below and watched it lap against the granite. Seaweed undulated just below the surface, as if it were longing to leave the rock it was attached to, and I felt the taste of the salt water on my tongue. My fingers were cold. I stuck my hands in my pockets and looked out over the sea again.

Even as I heard the motor of the mail boat, I stayed where I was. When I finally heaved myself out of the ledge and climbed back up on top of the rock, I could see the boat down below, across the small bay, a toy boat with a toy figure moving along the landing. By the time I got there, the boat had been and gone, and my cardboard box of groceries sat underneath the jutting roof of the old shed.

My mailbox held only the paper.

35

I began to wait.

Though my days evolved at their usual calm pace, it was as if I could hear a distant sound, a hesitant whisper that lingered when I went to bed and flowed into my dreams. I wanted to be left in peace to listen to it.

There were few disturbances, but those that occurred took on a new sharpness. I started resenting my mother's evening calls. My customary mild annoyance at the sound of the phone was replaced by dismay, and I left it to ring while I tried to control myself. I'd hear her voice and try to contain my impatience.

I listened in silence while she talked.

"I do care," I said as she paused briefly, trying to keep my voice down. "You know I do." I held the receiver a little away from my ear as she spoke again.

"It's normal for children to phone their parents. That's what *normal* children do. They care enough to at least give them a call occasionally. *Occasionally.*" She repeated the word, struggling with the consonants. I braced myself for the inevitable drawn-out finish.

Afterward I opened the front door and stood on the front step. The granite was cold under my soles. The air was fresh and chilly and smelled of evening, but it was still light. It was spring, the dead spring of the islands. No visible signs of growth, just the gradual extension of daylight. I had laid the perch net the night before and caught seven fish. I had cleaned them and put them in the freezer, saving two for dinner. Now I walked back inside and took the plate with the two small fish from the fridge. I slipped them into a plastic bag and placed them in the freezer, too. I had lost my appetite.

I had not heard from you again, and your silence was affecting me more than my mother's persistent presence. I carried it with me throughout the days. I listened to it and began to look forward to my nights more than my days. In my dreams you became real: I could see you, hear you. I caught myself keeping an ear out as I tried to work in the studio, and I took to leaving the door to the main house open so I would hear the phone. Subconsciously, I kept track of the time of day. Too late for you to call. Or too early. But I made no attempt to call you. No, at least that.

I had sent off the paintings for the exhibition, and there was no pressing work waiting, so I took out the portrait again. I put it up on the easel and spent hours looking at it.

"Come, I'll hold you," I whispered.

And I remembered how I had sat on the front step, my bare feet close together. It was summer, but the evening was damp and cool. My hands twisted the small rag that I always carried with me, and I kept my eyes on my feet. My hair fell forward, hiding my face, and my teeth chattered. "Come, move a little closer and I'll hold you," I whispered. Angela whispered. And very slowly I felt her inching closer, her warm body touching mine through the flannel pajamas. And she started another story, while gently rocking.

Now, in the studio, she faced me in a way she never did in real life. Her dark eyes were wide open, confident and trusting at once. I had spent time getting the color absolutely right, but the expression was hers and hers alone. I lifted my hand, and my index finger followed the line of her upper lip on the canvas. I had painted the mouth barely open, with just the possibility of a smile. I took a small step backward and put my fingers to my own lips. I had wanted to paint her smiling. Confident. Brave. And happy. Beyond the face itself, there was nothing, just a gradually intensifying darkness that grew from the hairline, the ears, and the base of the throat. But the face itself radiated light.

After a while I took out a blank canvas. I placed it on the empty easel beside the portrait, picked up a piece of charcoal, and began to sketch another picture.

The image was clear in my mind, in my hands, and the lines on the canvas flowed quickly, with no hesitation. I had waited so long to make this portrait. A lifetime.

36

I never knew how to tell you.

If I had found the words, perhaps everything might have turned out different. But now, when so unexpectedly and so very undeservedly I have been given this opportunity, I will try to explain. No, that is not the word. There are no explanations. But I will try to talk. Try to break the silence.

When you come, I will try to find the words.

You were the first person I ever brought here, to the island. Did you know that? No, how could you? How could you understand the significance of that invitation?

You see, the island was always my father's. Not the whole physical island, of course, but for me it was as if it were. It came to me from him, and my first memories there are all connected with him. Even now, sometimes when I stand down by the landing untangling the nets, I imagine wafts of tobacco mixing with the putrid smell of the drying scales and seaweed. He always had his pipe in the corner of his mouth, lit or not. And he always hummed. He played the old organ in the living room or listened to the radio. There was always sound then. Now I love the island for its silence.

It was such a short time, and so long ago. Yet those first few summers shimmer in eternal light. In spite of the darkness that followed.

To me this island was my father's, and it was impossible to

accept the subsequent intrusions. I felt that it should be visited by invitation only, and there were none. It was as if it should have been locked and abandoned when he died. Allowed to become caretaker of the beautiful memories in undisturbed silence. I wanted it to be exclusively his. In my mind, the memories of my father and this place had merged and become one.

The first summer without him, I remember refusing to leave the boat when we arrived. I could hear my mother impatiently calling my name as I sat looking out over the railing into the dark water where the seaweed slowly swayed. That was the first time Angela took the initiative. The first time I was aware of her. It felt like a part of me separated and acted independently, while I watched, as if another me jumped ashore, turned and looked at me, her arm outstretched and inviting me to grasp it and follow.

She was the one who brought me back to all the special places, made me visit them again. She made it possible. And slowly it took on another kind of life, my island. A kind of shadow life in which I had to tread carefully so as not to disturb its fragile existence. Never again would it be as it had when my father was there. No longer ours, my father's and mine. Now it was my own. Mine and Angela's.

And it lived again, summer after summer, a sort of cautious, different life where the colors were subdued and dangers loomed in the shadows.

Until that summer. I was almost ten. When I walked down to swim on the first day, the cliff seemed to have shrunk and the ledge was barely wide enough for me to sit comfortably. The water was cold that summer, but I swam every day. I would dive in, do a few quick strokes, and then heave myself up again, panting. Then Angela would glide back into the water. She swam properly, farther and farther. She could dive in, her slim white body barely rippling the water, and continue with steady strokes until she vanished around the point. Later my heart would pound as I sat on the ledge, still a little out of breath from the shock of the cold water. I'd spread my palms on the sun-warm surface of the rock, filled with a strange mix of excitement and fear. It would be a moment before I could breathe calmly once more. I licked my lips, and they were salty. And I could feel Angela beside me, her skin already warm from the sun. And then I was warm, too. We'd sit together, in silence, while my skin slowly dried. And we were one.

In the evening, after dinner, I would go and sit in the wicker chair in the garden. My mother would call from inside the kitchen, urging me to close the front door to keep the mosquitoes out. They didn't bother me, though I could hear them around my head and see them land on my arms. I stayed in the chair, my feet pulled up while the air gradually cooled. Then Angela would slowly rise, and I would follow. Upstairs in my room, I would change into my pajamas, averting my eyes from the mirror while I pulled off my clothes. Then I would quickly slide under the covers. I'd be still, my body eventually warming under the weight of the blanket. I'd twist the soft rag between my fingers and lift it to my face. And I'd think of Angela's thin, little-girl's body. I'd keep my eyes firmly shut, but tears trickled from the corners into the rag.

In the light summer night, and with the mosquitoes

droning just outside the screen that covered the window, I'd listen to my voice as Angela began a new story.

For me. For us.

So that the day would disappear and only the night remain.

"Come on, we're going fishing," he had said.

I closed my eyes tightly and saw the words bounce against the walls in the kitchen—bright white flashes trapped inside the small space. The light and the sound were unbearable, and I waited for Mother to react. To catch the words and make them disappear.

But when I opened my eyes and looked at Mother where she was half sitting, half lying on the wooden kitchen sofa, her legs crossed, a magazine on her lap, I knew she hadn't heard. The sound that filled the room and the blinding light—somehow none of it had reached her at all. Her cigarette sat between her fingers, which absentmindedly flicked the glossy pages while a pillar of ash was waiting to fall onto her lap.

He walked up to the sofa, stood behind Mother, and gently tousled her hair. "You're not coming, are you?" he said, more a statement than a question. I knew that his eyes were searching for mine, but I kept them fixed on the kitchen table, where I could see every crack in the blue oilcloth, every bread crumb left from breakfast, a fly sitting on a drop of orange marmalade. Then I raised my eyes and watched Mother lean her head back, laying bare her throat, eyes closed. I held my breath, waiting for her to speak. Hoping.

"Darling, no. Not in the middle of the day. I'll stay here. You go. You're so good. To make the effort."

She laughed her guttural laugh and raised one hand to hold his wrist for a moment.

"You're so sweet, darling. Just like a real father. Better than her father ever was."

She dropped her hand again and picked up the magazine.

The fishing rods were kept in the boat shed. The bamboo was dry and gray and the tips broken. The nylon lines were opaque, rough to the touch and knotted, the hooks rusted. There was no bait. He climbed on board clumsily and nodded to me to untie the stern line, then stretched out a hand to help me on board. But I ducked and slid onto the prow of the boat, where I sat down, holding my shins, my head bowed. He untied the stern line and then revved the motor. The boat bumped against the edge of the landing, reversing off, and the motor screeched as he changed gear. We took off with a jolt. I stayed where I was, holding on to the railing.

It was a clear day, late summer, with just a week left of the summer holiday. I leaned over the side of the boat, watching the water race by. It sprayed my face, and I closed my eyes. The boat tilted, but the motor wasn't strong enough for it to lift and ride over the waves, so it traveled bumpily and awkwardly, neither in the water nor above it. Too fast yet not fast enough. I looked up into the empty sky. It was absolutely clear, not the slightest hint of a cloud, no birds. We soon left the scattered islets behind, traveling farther out to where there were only the smooth gray rocks, barely breaking the surface of the water. They looked like the backs of giant submerged creatures. I could see no other boats. The sea lay empty before us, all the way to the horizon.

I scratched at an old mosquito bite on my arm and watched

the drop of blood trickle over my suntanned skin. I bent and licked it, and the metallic taste filled my mouth. I pressed my eyes shut.

I could hear the motor slow, and I knew exactly where we were. The usual place: the last small island with protection from the wind before the open sea. I knew that it was time to stand and make my way to the stern, but my limbs were frozen. Angela pulled me up, and we walked across, lifted the backseat, and hauled out the anchor. I stood with my feet firmly planted on the deck and threw it overboard, watching the coil of rope untangle. I tied the anchor line, balanced back along the cabin to the prow, and stood ready with the line as the boat glided toward land. Just when it was about to bump into the rock, I jumped ashore, my bare feet landing soundlessly. I yanked on the rope, and the boat drifted closer. Then he jumped off, landing with a heavy thud and almost losing his balance. He looked around for something to tie the line to, and his eyes eventually set on a large piece of granite. I stared out over the sea as he walked over and lifted the heavy rock. He panted loudly as he carried it up from the edge of the water and wedged it into a crack in the rock and tied the rope around it. I wanted the moment to last forever. But then he stood and looked at me.

"Right. Back on board."

He bent down and pulled on the line. I could see how his tight navy swimming trunks tugged into the flesh at his waist and thighs.

When the boat was close enough, I leaped back on board. But as I did, Angela told me I didn't need to do it. "Run!" she whispered. "Run over the cliffs to the other side of the island.

You can sit there, and you can keep your eyes on the vast sea that never ends. It is possible!"

So I did. In my mind I wasn't inside the hot cabin: Angela was. I was sitting by the edge of the water with the wide sky above me, not the dull white plastic roof. My eyes were on the water by my feet. That was all I saw, and the gentle lapping of the water was the only sound I heard. I never heard him speak. Just the water lapping.

"No fish today again," he said, shaking his head and smiling. He stood balanced on deck, feet wide apart and hands on hips, while the boat rocked under his weight. Drops of perspiration glittered on his back, trailing down the deep recess along his spine. He stood staring out over the empty sea for a moment. Then he turned and looked down at me.

"We're not fishing, are we, eh?" he said. "We have better things to do, don't we?" He climbed into the cabin, and for a second I could feel the smell of his skin as he sat next to me.

Then I took a deep breath, and I could smell the sea. Nothing but the sea.

I tried hard to stay where Angela told me to be, by the sea, on the other side. I really tried, but eventually I was back on board. Afterward. When he was already outside.

I sucked the mosquito bite on my arm. The gasoline-saturated air under the canvas top was hot. I sat very still and tried to hold my breath as I filled my mouth with the taste of my blood. I breathed through my mouth in quick shallow inhalations and tried to hold back the vomit that kept welling up into it.

"Get the motor started," he said, and jumped ashore, landing clumsily in his blue flip-flops. I walked over to the pilot's seat and sat down on the hot plastic cover. I opened the gas switch, put the gear into neutral, gave the choke a light touch, and pressed the ignition button. The motor started first time. He had untied the rope and stood with one foot on it as he lifted the large rock he'd used as mooring. He smiled broadly as he held it over his head with both hands and threw it in a wide arc toward the water, groaning loudly.

And that was the point where the images stopped forever. That split second when the rock left his hands and his foot was still on the coils of rope. I never again saw him lose his balance, the foot on the rope lift as the other foot slid down the smooth rock. I never again saw the rope run like a snake and slide into the water. I never again heard the dull thud as his back landed on rock. And I never again heard the sharp crack as his head hit stone.

All I ever heard afterward was the splash as the rock hit the surface of the water, sending a spray of cold water over me. That was all. Just the water.

The boat drifted slowly away from land, the line trailing behind in the water. His body slid down the steep rock, through the billowing bright green seaweed and into the water. It sank momentarily, then bobbed back to the surface, followed by first one, then a second blue flip-flop. A thin veil of bright red spread around from his head, dissipating quickly in the water. I could see the back of his head, the shoulders and the arms outstretched, as if he were trying to embrace the depths below. The rest of his body was underwater.

I sat absolutely still, sucking the mosquito bite and gripping the railing with my other hand. Suddenly the boat began to rock—it had drifted away from land and was no longer protected from the wind by the jutting rocks. I stared at the body, and it seemed as if that were what was moving, not the boat—as if he were swimming slowly away from me.

Just then Angela rose and went to the stern, bent over the railing, and began to pull the rope out of the water. My Angela.

When she was finished, she nodded silently.

I sat down on the hot plastic seat again and pulled the gear into drive. I gripped the steering wheel and turned the boat around. When I had it pointing away from the island, I stood for a moment to look back. I squinted and stared at the body, a slight elevation on the surface.

But I didn't see the hand stretch through the waves, the splashing of the arms. And I heard nothing other than the sound of the motor and the wind. I pulled the throttle.

Angela came and sat with me, and she told me what to do.

After I had moored back home, collected the fishing gear and secured the canvas hood, I stood on the landing.

"It wasn't my fault, was it? It wasn't my fault." I kept whispering the words over and over between chattering teeth.

"No, it wasn't your fault," she said. "It was an accident, Cecilia." I kept whispering the words as I crossed my arms over my chest and held on to my shoulders. I closed my eyes, and the images faded until there was nothing to see.

She held me. I held her. We were one.

38

I lay in bed listening to the muted sounds from down below.

"Shhhhh," I whispered, and wrapped my arms around myself. "Shhhh, I'll tell you a story." But I shook my head, a short whimpering sound escaping my lips. Angela's cold little hand reached out and closed my mouth. "Shhhh," she said. And she held me hard for a long time, while the curtains softly rippled in the night breeze.

"She doesn't talk," my mother said.

Angela was with me when we returned to school. I could feel the warmth of her body. It felt as if she walked a little ahead of me. Always.

"She just won't talk. Ever since the accident, she hasn't said a word."

And my mother took me to the nurse, who sent us to a therapist, who sent me to another one, who sent me to the doctor, who sent me to other doctors at the hospital. Wherever I went, Angela came, too. Mother also came with me, but her presence was always fleeting and vague, and often her gaze would land on me and take on an expression of surprise, as if she had suddenly become aware of my existence. Then her face would change, and just before she averted her eyes, there would be an expression of . . . what? Embarrassment? Dismay? Or, more frightening than anything, guilt?

I had nothing to say to any of the therapists or doctors, as

Mother sat clutching her patent-leather handbag, which contained the cigarettes she so badly needed. I said nothing.

In the end I was allowed to stay inside the silence. And wherever I went, Angela went, too, my constant companion in an intolerable world. There were no more stories, only the silence. Or perhaps the stories were told in another way. I would sit at the table in my room drawing, and Angela would be with me. The stories would weave from one piece of paper to the next, from mine to Angela's and back again. And whenever I looked up, I knew she could read my thoughts, as I could read hers. Now the stories were mine as much as hers. The two became indistinguishable. There was no separation, and the stories were without beginning or end.

39

I had been living on the island for three years, and I'd never seen the snow arrive so early.

It had covered the island the last week of November, a thin layer of grainy crystals, and had built up over the span of a few weeks until it was about four inches deep. After that, very little new snow had fallen, and the cover had stayed more or less intact. It remained throughout the winter, aging like old skin. Animals left their tracks on its surface—birds, mice, the lone fox that had visited from the mainland. Sun and wind had chipped away at the snow's hard crust, dulling the bright white to a soft, pale gray. There was a smooth, narrow path from the front door down to the main landing, another one down to the smaller landing on the eastern side of the island. And a zigzagging path up the rock to the lookout.

This time I walked ahead, but I knew she was with me, her steps falling into mine. I could sense her body hidden underneath the bulky sheepskin jacket, the red scarf flapping in the gusty easterly wind. The soles of my boots slipped on the worn path. I looked up into the white sky, and the emptiness made me want to cry out, "Stop! Let's leave it for another day. Let's turn back. Please, let's go back home. Together."

But I continued.

I arrived at the edge of the snow-covered landing. In front of us, the world was a seamless whole—the land, the sea, and the sky all merged into a dull, white infinity. The horizon was impossible to discern. I jumped down onto the ice. Here, near the landing, it was completely covered in snow, but farther out it lay bare. Some years the ice never sets at all; other years it freezes, then breaks up again, only to freeze once more. But this year it had set swiftly and early. What little snow had fallen since had been swept up by the wind and lay collected in long white strips traversing the black ice. The surface was uneven, as if the waves had petrified in an instant. The crisp top layer of ice crackled under my soles.

As soon as I left behind the inner bay and walked across the wide stretch of ice, I could hear it speak. The dark, distant voice of the ice reached me from below, a movement as much as a sound. Sudden dull bangs, like thunder echoing from infinitely remote depths, followed by slow rumblings. I had my eyes fixed on the white distance. My hands clutched the ice prods that I kept in my pockets.

I walked for a long time. The wind made the right side of my face numb, and I pulled my knitted hat farther down to cover my forehead. My steps fell on the uneven surface in a slow, steady rhythm and I never stopped to rest, or look behind me.

When I left behind the last small islands, blurred elevated shapes in the constant whiteness, and reached the open sea, the wind picked up harder. It lifted the snow and swirled it in the air. I pulled my hands from my pockets and held them against my face in a futile attempt at warming my cheeks and my nose.

I didn't see the barrier until I was almost upon it. The wide chasm of open water that divided the ice—a shipping lane—lay at my feet. A knee-high berm of crushed ice bordered the stretch of black water, which was sprinkled with matte patches where new ice was forming. I stood still, puffs of white vapor leaving my nostrils. I could feel the inside of my nose catch with each breath of the cold air.

I returned my hands to my pockets and squeezed the ice prods while my eyes measured the width of the channel. Wide enough to allow a large icebreaker through, I thought. Ten yards? Twenty? Thirty? Perhaps it wasn't that wide. But the other side seemed distant. And in between lay the icy black water.

She was right beside me. Still with me.

Then she took a quick step onto the barrier of ice. For a second that lasted an eternity, we balanced perilously, together. My eyes were on the black water below. The ice rumbled, as if activated by our presence. Or perhaps cautioning us.

I looked out over the wide expanse ahead, beyond the open water beneath our feet. There were no landmarks, nothing to separate ice and sky, and the only sounds were the stifled rolls of thunder from below and the dry whisper of the wind. I listened, and I had a vision of invisible giant creatures calling each other in the black depths, their slow-moving bodies occasionally rising to brush against the ceiling, causing the ice to respond with muted cracks and bangs.

Never trust the ice. It can break at any moment, however safe it looks.

The one time we had visited the island in early spring, just as the ice was breaking up, I stood with my father on the landing where the rented hydrocopter had dropped us off, looking out over the sea.

People die on the ice every year.

I had been small, small enough to have to reach up to hold my father's hand. And I could remember the absolute security of the hold on his warm hand. I had looked out over the smooth whiteness ahead. It had seemed endless. Still and cold. And it could kill. The deceptively soft surface farther away was revealed just beyond our feet. Jagged welts of ice, hard crystallized snow, and the deep, muted sounds of things breaking apart below. I squeezed my father's hand, and he looked down at me with a smile.

How about we go up to the house and make ourselves some hot chocolate?

We turned our backs to the ice and walked along the narrow path in the snow toward the house, my father first, I following in his steps.

Many years later, after I moved here, I often walked on the ice, but never this far. I had never stood by the open channel that cut through the solid ice. I had never been so close to that divide between land and eternity. And I knew I never would be again.

I nodded quietly, and my eyes stung.

And then I let her go.

I closed my eyes. There were no sounds other than the ice and wind, but I knew. I inhaled deeply. The cold air filled my lungs, burning.

And as I exhaled, it was over.

The instinctive awareness of someone close, of another body by my side, was gone. When finally I opened my eyes and stared down into the channel again, where the thin crust of new ice lay unbroken, I was alone.

I turned and stepped back from the barrier, sliding on the

ice and stumbling before I caught my balance. I lifted my eyes and looked at the thin trail of steps stretching across the ice in front of me, back toward the island. The wind had swept over it, and it was partly erased. But it was there. I tied the red scarf over my mouth and the tip of my nose and started retracing my steps.

I was alone. Alive.

40

In the house all was silent.

But it was a different kind of silence, Adam. Not like before. I'm not sure how to explain the difference. It felt like the silence of something new. Not the sort of silence that holds the unspeakable but a soothing, fresh silence, waiting to be filled.

And I began to talk. I listened to my own words. It was hard at first, but in time the words flowed more and more easily. As that winter slowly became spring and then summer, I did all the talking that I should have done years earlier. That I should have been helped to do.

I came to understand the difference between the words inside my head and the released, spoken ones. They have no likeness to each other. It wasn't until I opened my mouth and actually said the words that their meanings became clear to me. I realized that thoughts are not at all like words. The moment I had spoken a word, it became visible, and the effect was surprising. While it still lived inside my head, it seemed bigger, darker. A mass of matter without shape and form and frightening in its elusiveness.

You can make yourself believe that someone can look into your eyes and read your mind. You can wish for it, or dread it. There is no cause for either. As long as you carry your words inside, they are safe. You are the sole keeper. But sometimes that is a terrible curse, Adam. Those unformed words take on an enormous weight. Sometimes the burden of them becomes more than you can carry. For me it did. I simply had to share it. And Angela came to me.

I never understood that the burden we carried made everything else impossible. It was as if we both had to apply ourselves totally to the one task. If either of us took a hand off or averted our eyes, even for the slightest moment, then it would all collapse. Our burden, heavy as lead and fragile as glass, absorbed us completely.

I think I became an artist because in my art I was able to express what I could never say. It did not compromise my silence.

Then I met you. And everything changed.

Through the years I have gone over and over that day when I gave you up. As I think perhaps you have, too. But for you it must have been so different. I gave you nothing. No explanation. No words. No real words—no words that could have helped you. Or helped me. It was the awful silence, all that I left unsaid that destroyed us, Adam. I watched your face as I asked you to choose, and I knew absolutely that you never had a choice. And how it was to make the impossible decision.

I used to think that you walked away with life, though. In every sense of the word.

Here, on the island, afterward, I had only the history. I could play that scene, all the scenes, again and again, and they never changed. They were static. I always thought that for you they were alive. That you lived in the future. With our child. I imagined every stage. But it was never real. I saw our daughter only as she was in my arms before I gave her away. Her perfect little body, smelling like mine. Her soft black hair.

And more than anything else, her eyes. Black also. They say that newborn babies have no real eyesight. I don't believe that for one minute. My baby looked straight at me, and I thought she understood. And that she forgave me.

A folly, of course. I made myself see what I needed to see. But I held her in my arms and I truly sensed that she agreed—that we did what was best.

Do you remember when I put her in your arms? How she seemed to settle in so very comfortably? In an instant she was no longer mine. And when you looked up at me, you were no longer mine either. She had taken the space I used to inhabit.

I gave you the choice out of love, Adam. Between us, there could never be any secrets. There was a child and I could not take it from you. I knew how you would choose. It wasn't in you to make another decision. I knew you would choose life for our child. And a kind of death for me. And I allowed it. Because I loved you so, I allowed it.

I think that anything in your life you choose yourself, you can live with. It goes without saying, I suppose. However hard, you live with it. It's the things that are imposed on us that are so difficult to reconcile.

Did you ever know what I wanted that first night? How I longed for you to lift your arms and embrace me? I never told you to. And you never did.

And that day in the boat shed.

That day has haunted me. I suspect it has been with you also. But perhaps I am wrong. Perhaps it has stayed only with me. Appropriate, since it was all my doing. I accept that.

But even now, when I have accepted so much else, looked my life in the eye, I am struggling with that day. The awareness of what it meant. I do accept the responsibility for the grief I caused. But I would like you to know that the grief, the pain, was mine at least as much as yours.

When you come, I will tell you.

And I will listen.

V

Mig tyckes natten bära
ditt namn i svag music . . .

To me, it is as if the night carries
your name in soft music . . .

—from VILHELM EKELUND,
"Mot Alla Stjärnor Spanar"

41

I saw you the second the boat made the turn into the narrow canal that leads to the marina. You stood there, a solitary dark figure on the empty quay, and it seemed as if your eyes were fixed on the very spot where I appeared. As if our eyes met the moment it was physically possible. There was nobody else around; the few boats in the water were moored, the tackle swinging lightly in the breeze and tapping against the masts. You didn't wave, made no gesture, but kept your hands in the pockets of your long coat. As I slowly maneuvered the boat closer, I could finally see your face. I knew you must have changed—nineteen years must have left their mark on it. But what I saw was not that but the very essence of a face I now realized I had kept alive all this time. It felt as if I had lived with it, allowed it to age and develop in my mind. And as I took in its features, they were all familiar. In a way your face felt more familiar than my own.

When I pulled up alongside the landing and you reached out for the line and tied it with swift movements, I noticed that your hands were tanned, and this surprised me. Even that hot summer, you had seemed so pale, as if untouched by the constant sun. Your hands so white against my tanned skin.

I looked up into your face—the wide brow, the high cheekbones, the long nose. The generous mouth where a hesitant, thin smile lingered. The chin. I could sculpt it with my eyes closed. Except for the lightly tanned skin, it was all as I remembered it. Your hair was cut very short, and it was white now. The ears looked vulnerable in the chill air.

"Welcome back," I said without moving. The words sounded wrong the moment they left my lips. I stood with my feet planted firmly on the boards, my arms by my sides, rocking with the movement of the boat. In the silence I could hear the water lapping against the side and a couple of terns crying overhead. You didn't reply, and the smile left your lips as you turned to fetch your luggage. I watched your back and wished you had said something.

You had been shopping: there were four supermarket bags beside your small suitcase and the tattered old violin case. I took them one by one, placing them underneath the partly folded canvas hood. When finally you untied the line and stepped into the boat, you made no attempt to embrace me, just held my upper arm gently for a moment. I bent down and collected a life jacket and held it out for you before slowly reversing away from the landing.

We stood gazing at the sea over the blue canvas, I with my right hand on the steering wheel. The water stretched before us, its leaden surface rippling in the light breeze. The gray granite rocks rose through the waves, indistinguishable from the sea itself, and the larger islands lay dark and still.

"Thank you," you said.

Surprised, I turned my head and looked at you briefly before focusing again on the water ahead. You lifted your hands and held them over your ears.

"Here, take this," I said, bending and pulling out a knitted hat from the shelf in front of the driver's seat. "You'll need it when we reach the open sea."

You pulled it down over your ears and resumed your place beside me. As the boat picked up speed, the sound of the motor made words impossible.

If I don't speak, if I just stay like this, still and quiet, then I can allow myself to rest in this moment, I thought. If I keep my eyes on the sea and let my body rather than my brain acknowledge that you are standing beside me, so close I can feel the warmth of your body through my coat, then I can make it last. If I can let my hand sit here on the blue canvas beside yours, but not touching. If I try hard enough, there will be no beginning and no end to this moment.

But we crossed the open sea and reached the island, traveled along the eastern coast, past the familiar rock formations, and then finally we turned and I slowed the motor. It was over. We had arrived.

"There is no time here," you said as you stood on the smooth rock, waiting for me to fasten the wing nuts on the canvas hood. "Everything is the same. Time has stood still."

I jumped off the boat and landed softly beside you.

"Is that how it seems to you?" I said. "I can't tell. What you live with day in, day out, may seem ever the same. But then when you look back, you are reminded of things and people that have been lost, new growth, fundamental changes."

I pulled out the small bicycle cart that I use for transporting goods up to the house from its space beside the old boat shed.

"Nothing ever stays the same," I said as I watched you lift your luggage into the cart. I nodded at the bulging supermarket bags and asked, "What did you bring?"

"Just a few things I thought you might not get out here,"

you replied, smiling. "I thought I might ask you to let me cook for you." You took the handle of the cart, and we began our walk up the path to the house.

You cooked for me then, too. You didn't look like a man who enjoyed food. Then, as now, you were slim. Not unhealthily so—you just looked like a man who would keep his weight unchanged throughout his life. But you cooked with love, and you ate with focus and attention, as if you treasured the experience. Eating with you had been a joy, a new discovery.

It was such a hot, dry summer, and we had to be mindful of the freshwater supply. In the morning we wandered down to the sea for a swim instead of taking a shower. You always walked ahead, the borrowed bathrobe flapping behind you. I loved watching you from behind.

"He is here because he loves me," I used to tell myself. "It's because he loves me that he has made the breakfast that sits in the basket he is carrying." Later I lay on the warm, smooth rock, which seemed to absorb and accumulate the heat day by day, and watched you take off the bathrobe and walk to the edge of the water. I kept watching through half-closed eyes. The shape of your wide shoulders, the curve of the spine that divided your back, the roundness of your firm buttocks. Your legs were covered in dark hair, and there was a small triangle of hair at the base of your spine. I could sense how your skin felt under my hands. You moved with such grace, yet everything you did seemed to flow from an undercurrent of urgency. An intensity that you didn't acknowledge. I didn't know if you were aware of it, or if it was an unconscious aspect of your personality. To me it seemed that even your most trivial act was purposeful. You took a couple of steps into the water, then dived. When you appeared again, you turned on your back, gently backstroking. I lay with my legs outstretched, resting on my elbows, the rock warming me from underneath and the sun from above. But just then, in the fresh stillness of morning, I felt it all drain away. The warmth, the love. I was no longer able to hold on to it. And I had struggled to resist an urge to cry.

Now here you were again, walking ahead on the narrow path, pulling the cart behind you. As before, there was precision and grace in every small movement, every step. But the urgency was gone. It was a shock when I realized that the intensity that had once defined you had been replaced with a sense of calm persistence. You pulled the cart with one hand, the other moving rhythmically as your feet landed on the path. There were bright green tips peering through the web of last year's grass, I noticed. I thought I caught a whiff of your aftershave. Strangely, it upset me that I didn't recognize it. I looked at your neck, overcome with a desire to reach out and touch it.

I wondered what you expected from me. And I thought that if I were only allowed to put my palm on your skin, I would know. I lifted my eyes to the sky, where white clouds were stretched like cheesecloth over the pale blue base. I don't need to see you, I thought. Knowing is enough. Hearing the soft sound as your foot hits the grass and my own lands in the same spot. If you don't turn around, then I will always be here, a few steps behind, my feet treading the grass where yours have just been.

You slowed your pace and transferred the cart to the other hand. When we reached the point where the small path joined the slightly wider grassy road, you increased your speed again, and I stayed behind.

I glanced around, and though it was early spring, everything looked exactly as it had that summer. Nothing seemed to have changed. I caught sight of the house, surrounded by unkempt old lilacs that were still just tousled nests of bare branches. The mossy fruit trees in the small orchard along the road seemed no taller, and the fence still had the resigned look of something that expects no care, no attention. I saw it all with your eyes, as if I had lived here these many years without ever noticing. And suddenly I knew you were right. Time had stood still.

We came to the front lawn, and finally you had to turn around. Across the cart your eyes met mine, and for the first time you seemed to openly scrutinize my face. It was as if you were comparing it with something. Like me, perhaps you compared the person in front of you with memories stored in your brain. Memories of me? Or of our daughter?

In the unforgiving sharp light, we gazed at each other. Your bodily presence swelled my memory with new blood. I felt dormant nerves connecting, blood pumping through my body, and the tips of my fingers prickling. It wasn't sexual. Or it wasn't *just* sexual. It was as if my entire self had been reconnected to a source of power after a long break.

You are sixty years old, and I have known you for only one of those years. Yet you live in my every cell, I thought. I met your calm brown eyes, those kind eyes that always seemed to keep something hidden. Even in the most intimate moments, there had been something you wouldn't share. But when I looked into your eyes now, there was no longer any reserve. They locked with mine, and they hid nothing.

There were fine lines at the corners of your eyes and two vertical lines from the eyebrows above the base of the nose. The lines deepened, and you smiled a little. The eyes didn't waver but remained locked with mine. I felt as if you were waiting for me to end the silence, and I searched my mind for the right words. In the end I was the one who turned my eyes away. I walked over to the kitchen window and pulled out the key, which was stuck in its usual place underneath the windowsill. I unlocked the door and held it open for you as you came in loaded with shopping bags.

"Let's not talk. Not yet," I said. You nodded, and perhaps you felt as I did. That if we kept it at bay, we could draw out this moment that seemed to sit between the past and the present, perilously balancing between memory and hope.

We unpacked the food on the kitchen table and put it away. You had bought things I hadn't eaten since that long-ago summer. Delicacies I had never bothered to search for after you left. I wondered how you could have remembered, but as I held the packages and jars in my hands, I remembered, too. My favorite blueberry jam, black Finnish rye bread. The finest coffee. Bottles of vintage wine. Cheeses. Even a little box of delicate fresh figs. And a bag of handmade chocolates from that small shop in Östermalm. I weighed the packages in my hands as I slowly removed them from the bags. And I knew they were gifts of love.

"Let's walk down to the sea," you said when we had finished.

This time I walked ahead, and I felt self-conscious with your eyes on my back. My old jersey was worn and somewhat paint-splattered, my hair had come loose from its clasp in the wind, and I could hear my rubber boots making strange sucking sounds with every step. In an odd way, and despite the long period of anticipation, I felt like I'd been abruptly awakened from a deep sleep and hadn't quite had time to prepare myself properly. I walked briskly, but the familiar path I'd always taken for granted suddenly came alive, too. I noticed its twists and turns. The bare tangles of wild rosebushes, the dry dead grass.

"Can we climb up to the lookout first?" I heard you say to my back.

I stopped in my tracks, nodded but kept my back to you, and began climbing the steep rock to the left.

Here the first signs of life were visible in the crevices, where even minute amounts of soil were enough to attract the seeds of wild violets. In a few weeks, the flowers would open, followed by a few weeks of extravagant blossoms. I wondered if you remembered.

We arrived at the peak short of breath and stood looking over the sea. There were no signs of life, either on land or at sea, but a long streak of migrating eider ducks undulated across the white sky. It was hard to believe that in a month or so this dormant landscape would be alive with boats of all kinds, darting about on water glittering in the sun, with people sunbathing and diving from the cliffs. Children with fishing rods. There would be leaves on the trees, and the granite would be framed by fresh grass and wildflowers. Birds would hatch their eggs on every little islet. Life would return.

I ran my hand down your sleeve. You didn't respond; I didn't know whether you were aware of it. After a moment I turned and began the descent toward the sea. The smooth rocks, so inviting in the summer, looked cold. I walked to the edge of the water and bent down to dip my hand into it. Then I stood and put my palm on your cheek.

"Here, feel how cold it is. No swimming for you this time, Adam," I said with a little smile. I lifted my arms, and I was astonished to register that they wanted to embrace you. Instead I let them fall again and sat down on the rock, resting my arms on my knees. I looked up and smiled, but you didn't react.

"Let's sit here for a while," I said. You sat down beside me, and I could feel your eyes on my face as you studied my profile. I thought maybe you were hoping I would speak first. But then you turned your eyes to the sea again.

"I live on an island, too," you said. "Like you, I have made my home in a place where the winters are solitary. But not like this. Not this quiet. Not this lonely. Life never quite lets up where I live. The seasons are interwoven, and even winter has a streak of summer in it. Nature never takes a rest. There is often a wild wind, and the sea is unpredictable. Perilous."

I followed your gaze out over the calm, dark water.

"There are colors where I live. Bright colors. But they are not mine. I think that I chose the life around me there, the very colors, so that I wouldn't have to make them myself. They have been a substitute for real color. Real life. There are many like me in the new world. Escapees from the old one. But we bring it with us. There is no escape. And sometimes it becomes the opposite of what you were hoping for. The distance accentuates the memory of what you were hoping to leave behind."

I placed my hand on your arm for a moment. "Always so honest, Adam," I said. "You don't have to justify your every decision. There is no need to explain. Not to me, not to any-body."

I put my hand back on the cold rock.

"Oh, but there is, Cecilia, there is. It is absolutely essential. We may not be able to explain, but we must try. We may not understand, but we must try. We may not be able to forgive, but we must try."

You prepared to stand, and when you were upright, you looked down at me. Your face was painfully naked.

I nodded slowly and accepted your outstretched hand to help me rise. When I stood in front of you, you took both my hands in yours.

"I think you know it, too," you said slowly. "That we need to try to make ourselves understood. And we need to ask the questions that will help us understand others. It may hurt, but we really must try. My mother taught me not to expect explanations and not to give any. To accept even the un-acceptable without question. 'There is no comfort to be had. Truth can be too hurtful. Impractical,' she used to say. I know now that she was wrong. I was wrong."

We walked slowly, in silence. As we passed over the peak and wandered down toward the house again, I could see that the sun had broken through the sheer white gauze.

42

"If you sit here by the table, I'll do the cooking."

We had returned in the late afternoon, the sky not so much darkening as imperceptibly adjusting its shade to another kind of white for the night. The chill from the cold sea slowly drew in overland as the sun set, and before removing my jersey I stoked the fire in the old stove in the kitchen.

"You don't have to do anything, just sit here," you said, and pulled out one of the chairs. "I'll open a bottle of wine, and you can have a glass while I cook." You took off your coat, hung it over the back of a chair, and went to the sink to wash your hands.

"I was hoping you would take me out to lay nets for perch tonight. After dinner," you said without turning around. I looked at your back, wondering what you were thinking. We had trod cautiously thus far.

"I have never forgotten the taste of fried perch." You dried your hands and walked across to the pantry. "But tonight we'll have meat." I sat with my feet resting on the stretcher of the old wooden chair, my hands clasped on the table in front of me. I watched as you returned with your arms full of packages and bags. It seemed like an offering, I thought, as you placed them all on the table in front of me.

"I walked along the aisles at Östermalmshallen and thought about what to buy, what to bring. The game, the fish, the breads, and the fruits and vegetables—all so beautifully displayed. There are no places quite like that where I live," you said. "You can buy the freshest produce—vegetables, fish, meat. But it's different. It's . . ." You seemed to search for the right words. "It's innocent. Without history. And you have to invest more of yourself to make it into tasty food. Here it feels like everything comes already destined for specific dishes. With a concept attached." You smiled that same embarrassed smile. A little guiltily, I thought.

"Perhaps that's why I like the market there so much. It's like every counter, every product speaks to me of its history, its purpose. The smells and the textures are alive. They conjure up an entire cultural heritage. And somehow I feel as if I belong."

You kept working while you talked, peeling, cutting, whisking.

"It looks just the same, the market, perhaps a bit more elegant. As if it has had a subtle facelift, very professionally done, leaving the personality unscathed." You opened one of the bags and pulled out a package that looked as if it contained meat.

"I bought some wild duck." You glanced up at me, smiling a little, as if you wondered whether perhaps you were trying too hard. I smiled back. And I realized that my smile was genuine, warming me in a way I had not been warmed for a very long time.

"I bought celeriac, fancy lettuce, frozen red currants for the gravy. And dried wild mushrooms."

I looked at you, and for a moment I thought there was an expression of guilt on your face. As if you were ashamed of your obvious delight in offering me this treat. It passed quickly, and I thought I might have misread you.

"There were no fresh ones this time of year," you continued after a brief pause. And then, as if you had just remembered, "Oh, and here is a pot of bleak roe. I thought we could
have that while I cook. Do you have a toaster?" I stood and
retrieved the toaster from where it sat behind the cutting boards
on the shelf. You went to the fridge and took out a bottle of
wine.

"This will go well with the roe," you said, and set the chilled
bottle on the table.

I sat down again and watched as you began preparing the
duck, peeling the celeriac. And I remembered the night we
last laid nets for perch. That night when you were still happy.
The last night of happiness I allowed you.

"I'll do the rowing. You just sit over there opposite me," I
had said. You were so obviously out of your depth but keen, so
eager to show that you could function in my world. It was late,
close to midnight, yet still warm, as if the intense heat of the
day lingered in the dark water. It was August, and a full moon
sat high in the black sky. You looked at me while I adjusted
the oars, as if everything I did were worth admiring.

"You look so wonderfully at ease here, Cecilia," you said.
"So at home." You sat with your feet wide apart, leaning forward, your hands resting on your knees and your eyes fixed
on me. And I think you were absolutely happy. I averted my
own eyes and looked down at my feet.

"You are beautiful, Cecilia," you said slowly. I raised my
gaze and looked at you. In the dim light, your pale face shone
brighter than the moon. I held the oars above the surface of
the water and allowed the moment to stretch for as long as I
could. Then I let the oars dip into the dark water, rippling
softly. As we reached the islet, I paused with the oars in the

water while you stood, unsteadily, and lifted the net. I told you to make your way to the prow and up onto the front thwart, and as you climbed over the oar, you steadied yourself with a hand on my shoulder. The boat rocked gently until you were finally in position, with the net partly in the water. You nodded over your shoulder, with more confidence than I thought you had, and I slowly started to row.

"You have to spit on the float three times before you throw it in," I said as you reached the end of the net. "For luck." You turned your head and grinned.

"I have all the luck I need," you said, then spit three times on the float. You stood there, unsteady and awkward, gazing down at me, and you looked terribly happy. I longed to return your smile, to ask you to come and sit beside me, to hold me. To tell me that we could make this moment last forever. Instead I told you to sit, and I rowed back to the landing.

When we arrived, you jumped ashore a little clumsily, tied the line very clumsily, then stretched out your hand to help me out of the boat. I took it, though we both knew I didn't need it. I took it firmly in my hand and jumped ashore, and as I stood beside you, you pulled me toward you and put your arms around me.

"I love you, Cecilia," you whispered into my hair. I pressed my face against your chest and closed my eyes. I could smell the events of the day on your skin. The morning swim, the breakfast on the warm rock, making love with the sun above us, the lazy hours reading, the walk down to get the mail, the afternoon swim, diving from the rock, the dinner in the gently slanted sunlight, the late-evening walk down to the boat through grass where the dew had already settled. I withdrew a

little and looked at you. You held my shoulders, looking back
at me.

"Cecilia," you said. "Just at this precise moment, I am the
happiest I have ever been. I have never been alive like this. I
have never known how it feels to be fully alive." And you
pulled me toward you again. I closed my burning eyes and
swallowed.

In the morning, before breakfast, we went down to take
up the net and found eleven good-size perch in it. And side
by side, by the boathouse, with the morning sun on our backs,
we untangled the net. I showed you how to clean the fish,
and you smiled at the result of your first attempt. But you
caught on quickly, and when we finished, you had cleaned five
to my six.

You insisted on doing the cooking, and I sat watching
while you fried the breaded fish and steamed the new pota-
toes. In between your work, you kept looking up at me. I noticed that although you hadn't tanned, your skin had a golden
tinge to it. Slowly, day by day, there had been an imperceptible
change of hue. Now your skin set off your dark hair beautifully. Your nails shone white when your hands moved. As you
put the serving plate on the table, your arm brushed against
mine, and I lifted my hand and touched it, let the fingers run
down to yours. We both smiled.

But it was in the pale light of the night that the difference
was most remarkable. When I thought you were asleep, I
would support myself on my elbow and my eyes would run
over your body where it lay beside me in the narrow bed. And
my hand would follow, only just not touching the skin. You
slept on your stomach, your back exposed and vulnerable. I

would shift my own body closer and watch my tanned skin contrast with yours, which seemed to radiate light. And I would struggle to resist an urge to press my body against yours, to wake you again. Instead, with my fingers, I'd paint your image in the still air of the bedroom.

"Yes," I said. "I do remember the perch." I lifted my glass and swirled the straw-colored wine, absentmindedly watching. "And yes, let's lay the net tonight." I took a sip of the wine. "After dinner. If you like."

43

We had finished the duck and sat with empty plates in front of us, sipping the soft red wine. I felt you looking at my face, and I could feel my cheeks blushing. I placed my glass on the table. What were you thinking? You'd said little during dinner. I kept searching your face, just as I could feel you searching mine as soon as I averted my gaze. What were you looking for? I could see the subtle signs of aging on your face, and I became self-conscious about mine. My fortieth birthday was in a few months' time. It was impossible to imagine how I appeared to you, and I found no clues to your thoughts in your expression. You sat leaning back, turning the glass in your one hand, the other flat on the table beside the plate. Then I felt your hand cover mine, and I allowed it to sit there.

"Thank you for letting me come," you said.

I felt like smiling, but the impulse never reached my lips. Instead I raised my glass. "Thank you for the dinner," I said. "It's been a long time since I've had anything like this." We let our glasses touch before drinking. "If ever," I said as I put the glass down.

We started to clear the table.

"Still feel like laying the net?" I asked when we had finished the dishes.

"Yes, I do," you said, turning to look at me. "Absolutely."

"Okay, let's go."

As we stepped outside from the cozy kitchen, the air felt raw and cold. We walked briskly and quickly adjusted to the temperature. There was no wind, but as we got into the small rowboat, it felt like a chill was coming off the water. You sat at the stern, watching me intently as I slowly rowed across the bay toward the islet. The net sat in a pile on the floor between us. There were stars and a new moon, but the sky was not yet dark enough to provide contrast, and they shone with a weak, pale light.

We reached the islet, and I dipped the oars into the water to stop the boat while you collected the net and cautiously stepped past me to the prow. I thought you looked far more confident this time, and I wondered if life on your island had given you opportunities to fish. I suddenly longed to know. You dropped the net over the railing, and I began to row with soft, gentle strokes of the oars into the black water. You stood with your eyes on the net as it sank and disappeared from view. When the entire length of the net was in the water, I stopped the drift of the boat and you tied the float. You looked briefly at me and then spit on it three times before throwing it into the water. I couldn't help smiling.

As we walked toward the house, the warm light from the kitchen glowed in the otherwise dark and dormant world. I wondered if you were as curious about my life here as I was about yours on the other side of the earth. You had lived inside me all these years, but I had carried the essence of you, with no concept of your real existence. There had been light around you. The space where you lived had been the only light.

Did you wonder how I live here during the long, black winters? In this world where the only light is the one you make yourself?

Once back inside, I carried firewood into the living room and rekindled the fire in the old tiled stove. You brought a bottle of whiskey and two glasses, and we sat down in the two armchairs in front of the fire.

"You haven't asked me any questions," you said.

I started and turned to look at you. Your cheeks were flushed from the abrupt change from cold to warm. I said nothing and looked into the fire. I could feel you looking at me. And eventually I had to meet your gaze.

When I first met you, you were twice my age. We are closer in age now. But age always seemed irrelevant. I don't think I ever thought about it. In the glow from the fire, I thought your face looked altered, yet the same as before. I knew how it would feel under my fingers. I could follow every line, every curve, and they would be familiar. Yet I could see that your hair was white. I knew that nineteen years of life separated the image that I carried in my memory from the real man in front of me, but somehow they felt unimportant. I longed to touch you. My hands would know. I would be able to feel, and there would be no need for you to tell me anything.

I looked at you and felt younger than I had nineteen years ago. It was as if those years had given me the time I needed to reverse some kind of premature aging. Yet at the same time, I was acutely aware of the reality of my physical aging, and I wondered how I matched your memories.

We sat in silence, holding our glasses, watching the fire.

"No questions," I said. "That was the promise. No questions, ever." I watched you swallow, and I took a sip, too, feeling the alcohol burn a hot trail down my throat. I listened to my own words, and they burned as well.

"I am keeping my promise," you said. "But I would like to release you from yours."

I put down my glass and busied myself with poking the fire and blowing softly into the hesitant flames. "It's the same, Adam," I said. "You can't do that. My promise is only the other side of yours."

"Tell me something, then," you said. "Tell me something about your life."

I didn't answer. You bent forward and rested your elbows on your knees and looked into the fire.

"Are you happy, Cecilia?" you asked without looking at me.

"That is a question, Adam," I said. "The key question."

I took another sip of whiskey, and after a moment I stood. "I think I will go to bed. It's been a long day. And now we have time. We have time to be silent together. And we have time to talk." I walked toward the kitchen, though on the threshold I stopped and turned. I looked at the man by the fire. But I saw the other person who had been with us all day. In every breath, every look, yet never once mentioned. Our child. And I knew that I had to leave you and go upstairs. I knew I needed more time.

"I have made your bed in the master bedroom upstairs. I'll check on the fire in the stove." And then, as I turned to leave the room, I added quietly, "I am glad you're here. Good night."

But once I was in bed, sleep eluded me. I lay looking out the window, where I could see the moon. Small now, and high in the sky, but shining with a clear white light. I couldn't hear any sounds. But the awareness that you were there made all the difference. It was as if the whole house were going through a metamorphosis. It was alive. Just because of your body in the bed in the other room. I lay still, listening to the night.

I woke to silence, but I knew that sounds had interrupted my sleep. I sat up and listened, then stood and wrapped the blanket around me. I opened the door and stepped out onto the landing. The moon had crossed the sky and was shining through the window. The music started again, and when I slowly opened the door, it flooded toward me, fragile yet utterly intense. I watched your back where you stood outlined against the window and the pale moonlight. I could see the muscles flex underneath the skin on your back as your arms moved with the music. I didn't need to see your face to feel your tears.

I stepped over the threshold and sank down on the rug in front of the stove. The tiles still exuded heat, though the fire was only glowing embers. I pulled the blanket around me.

When you stopped playing, the silence seemed to hold the notes. You remained by the window, still with your back to me.

"I called her Mimi," you said. "But her name was Miriam. She—" I could hear your voice break as you placed the violin and the bow on the table.

"Shhh," I said. "Come here. Come here and sit beside me."

You crossed the floor, and I opened my arms. You sat, and I wrapped the blanket around both of us and held you in my arms as we lay down.

Much later, as the moon became visible through the bedroom window and your body lay still against mine, you began to tell me.

We had all night, and all the following nights.

We had all the time in the world.

VI

I was unprepared for how the old woman had changed.

The one time we had met, less than a year ago, she had surprised me with her vigor, her proud posture and strong voice. Now I was equally surprised by how fragile she looked. She lay in the anonymous hospital bed as light as a feather. Her head on the pillow seemed to have been placed there as an object on display. I stood by her bed, uncertain whether she was aware of my presence. But then, without opening her eyes, she spoke.

"Czy to ty, Adasiu?"

Her voice was just a whisper, and I wasn't sure what she meant or how to respond.

"Is that you, my dear Adam?" she continued after a moment's silence.

I pulled the bedside chair toward me and sat down.

"Yes, it is me, Adam," I said slowly.

A smile spread over her pale face.

"I have waited for so long," she whispered, her lips dry and cracked. She paused, as if the few words had exhausted her.

"But now, now it seems like no time at all. No time at all."

I searched my mind for something to say, but before I opened my mouth, she spoke first.

"You don't need to say anything. You must be tired. Such a long journey," she said. "Here, just take my hand." She lifted her hand from the sheet that was folded over her chest. I took it in mine. It felt like a wizened leaf against my palm, weightless and dry.

"It doesn't matter that it has taken so long. Strange—it doesn't matter at all now," she said as our clasped hands sank and rested on the sheet. I could feel her chest lift and fall with each labored breath.

"You will play for me again now, won't you, Adam?"

I nodded.

"The Bach partita—you will play that, yes? And I will listen. It will be just as before, yes?"

I felt her squeeze my hand before loosening her grip and running her fingers over mine, as she had when I met her the first time. And again she stopped when she reached the little finger.

"And I will come to your concerts, just as before. In the first row, so I can see your hands." She paused for a moment, and I felt her fingers caressing mine. "I think the Mendelssohn. That one first." She smiled thinly. "Just as it was meant to be."

"Yes," I said. "The Mendelssohn first. That one first."

"You have found what you were searching for, my Adam?" she whispered, a statement more than a question. "We have both found what we were searching for."

Again I nodded.

"We have searched for such a very long time, you and I. But that is all behind us now. Now that we have found each other again. Everything is over. We are together. And we will have music again. No more silence."

She closed her hand around mine and squeezed with unexpected force, but she said nothing for a while.

"I have found my home," I said slowly.

She nodded and smiled, her eyes still closed.

"And when I return, you will come with me, Clara," I said. "We will all be together. And every Thursday, Szymon comes to play chess. We talk and we listen to music. No more silence."

A brief smile drifted across the old woman's face. I bent forward and brushed my lips against her cheek.

"And Marta is there," I whispered into her ear. "She is safe, Clara. Marta is with me, too. And Moishe. They are all there. All our loved ones."

For a second the old woman's eyelids fluttered and her lips twitched. Then her hand lost its grip on my hand.

I bent forward and took her hand again and lifted it to my cheek, before placing it on top of her other hand on the starched sheet.

The room was silent and peaceful.

I walked over to the window and looked out over the parking lot below. It was a sunny day, and I could see a small child running across the almost-empty space.

I lifted my hand and tried the handle of the narrow window. Sound drifted in as I pushed it open. The droning of cars somewhere in the distance. But from below I could clearly hear the sound of the little boy laughing, and I saw a woman chasing him, teasingly. They were both laughing, I could see. But it was the boy's pealing laughter that lifted through the air and reached me.

ACKNOWLEDGMENTS

When Adam Anker first appeared in my thoughts, I knew virtually nothing about him. This proved to be fortunate, I think. If I had known more about the challenges involved, I might not have followed him on his journey.

So many have contributed material that I required. Early on Mrs. Tamara Green agreed to meet me in Wellington. With patience and kindness she accompanied me on my first steps on the way to Poland and Kraków. Curiously, on the coffee table in her living room there was the silver box that I had already given Adam!

Michail and Zina Tablis introduced me to friends in Melbourne, Jack and Carol Bloustein, who in turn brought me to the Holocaust Centre, where Willy Lermer welcomed me and generously shared contacts and knowledge. Among those who agreed to talk to me, Dr. and Mrs. Paul Hall hold a special place.

Destiny placed Maria Myhrman in my way just as I was despairing in my search for the holder of the rights to the two poems by Tadeusz Rozewicz. I owe Mr. Rozewicz immense gratitude for the kind permission to quote them, and I owe Maria gratitude for arranging it. Also, she came to play an instrumental role in giving me insight into Poland and matters Polish. Sometimes chance provides just what you need!

It wasn't just Adam's geographical and historical background that provided challenges, but also his profession. My knowledge of music is very limited and I needed help to understand and to describe my main character. Again, Michail Tablis came to my help and patiently talked to me about music in general and about the structure of a sonata in particular. In Stockholm, Peter Schéle at the Stockholm Konserthus gave me the most enthusiastic support. He and his colleague Lars Karlsson provided me with archival material that helped me picture the music life in Stockholm in the '70s and '80s.

Later, Bret Werber at the Holocaust Memorial Museum in Washington generously helped me find the sheet music for "The Passacaille" by Szymon Laks, which enabled me to finally get to hear the music that would so move the main character in the novel.

Again I owe my editor, Rachel Scott, enormous gratitude. Having my manuscript back after her editing is like having a raw stone magically turned into a polished gem.

To my indefatigable agent, Kathleen Anderson, provider of professional miracles, but also comfort and support on the road, my sincere gratitude.

Love and gratitude to my family, always. I have dedicated this book to my three sons, hoping that they will read and possibly learn a thing or two that I have not been able to teach them before.

The working title for this novel was *The Consequence of Silence*. I am pleased that it will now be published as *Sonata for Miriam*. From silence to sonata.

Linda Olsson, Stockholm, July 2008

A PENGUIN READERS GUIDE TO

SONATA FOR MIRIAM

Linda Olsson

An Introduction to
Sonata for Miriam

Linda Olsson's breathtaking debut novel *Astrid & Veronika*
captivated readers and critics alike, establishing her as a lyrical,
intelligent writer with an amazing talent for plumbing the depths
of human emotion. Now, in her latest novel, *Sonata for Miriam*,
Olsson confirms her reputation as a nuanced writer with a style
that is both poetic and precise. With her unerring sense of detail,
Olsson spins an elaborate web of love and sacrifice, grief and
deceit, all set in motion by a single chance encounter.

Transfixed by a photo of a young Jewish man lost during
World War II, violinist Adam Anker makes a shocking discovery: the man in the photo bears his name. Certain that there is a
connection, he begins a conversation with the man's surviving
sister, and soon disappears into a labyrinth of memories and
mysterious photographs, changed names and letters never
received. Light is shed not only on the secrets of Adam's family
but also on his personal life, as his former lover Cecilia shares
with him the truth of her own painful childhood, illuminating
the joys of their romance as well as its heart-wrenching
dissolution. Further, as he tracks down his family's history—and
his mysterious namesake—he develops meaningful relationships
with the lovers and siblings of the very people he is trying to
find. As Adam sifts through the recollections of his new found
friends, he is drawn into his own reminiscences, returning again
and again to the memory of his daughter, Miriam, and the day
that she died.

Weaving together interior monologue, letters, and
conversation, Olsson's writing is perfectly matched to the
ephemeral world of memories and secrets that Adam must

navigate. Following his journey, Olsson takes the reader to Vienna, Kraków, and Stockholm, all haunted by the secrets of love and loss in Adam's past. It is in Kraków, as witness to the public and private horrors of the Second World War, that Adam finally discovers the upheavals that occurred, and the long-lasting effects of momentous decisions made at a moment in time.

Wherever he visits, Adam finds voices long buried—"the elusive voices," he believes, "whose absence had been at the center of my existence." With the help of these voices, Adam begins to create the music that will fill the painful silence of his life and ultimately pay tribute to his lost daughter. In guiding him through this, Olsson avoids sentimentality and easy moral judgments, and instead explores how we balance the choices we make against the choices that are thrust upon us; how we behave in times of love, in times of grief, and in the times when we are caught between the two. In doing so, Olsson presents a rich multi-generational tale, as Adam moves forward and backward through time, each movement bringing him closer to understanding his own life.

About Linda Olsson

Linda Olsson has a law degree from the University of Sweden, as well as a B.A. in English and German literature. After pursuing a career in finance, Olsson published her highly celebrated novel *Astrid & Veronika* in numerous countries around the world. Olsson was born in Sweden and has lived in Kenya, Singapore, Britain, and Japan. She currently resides in Auckland, New Zealand.

A Conversation with
Linda Olsson

You introduce three sections in your novel with poems by Tadeusz Różewicz and Tymoteusz Karpowicz. Could you tell your readers a little more about these poets and what their work means to you? How does poetry inform your writing?

When I first realized where this story wanted to go—to Poland—I was gripped by something I can only describe as panic. I had never been to Poland before; I knew very little about the country and the people. For me, listening to music takes me wherever I want to, so I began by listening to Polish music. I then turned to the literature that comes closest to music—poetry. I don't speak Polish, so I had to rely on translations. They were the finest, though, by eminent Nobel Prize laureate Czesław Miłosz. And I was totally enchanted by the new world of literature that opened. I hope that for my readers the poetry will guide their reading, as it guided and inspired my writing.

During the war, Wanda makes an enormous sacrifice for Adam; this is not only emotionally affecting but historically accurate, as many families were faced with similarly difficult decisions during World War II. Was this story inspired by the experience of anyone you know? Did you do a lot of historical research before writing Sonata for Miriam?

Yes, I did a lot of research. I read history, of course, and I traveled three times to Poland. I also went to Melbourne to meet Polish Holocaust survivors. They received me with warmth and generosity and their stories gave me a basis for my writing. But no single real experience is replicated in my novel.

You convey Adam's intensely intimate perspective without ever suffocating your reader with too much information. In terms of detail, how do you decide what is necessary to further the plot or create atmosphere, and what can be left to the reader's imagination?

Perhaps because I *see* my stories rather than hear them, I expect my readers to see them, too. And if they can, not everything will need to be spelled out in the text. Or so I hope. I would like to think that they will get to know my characters just as I have, and that this will enable them to follow the story without everything being explicitly told on the page. A bit like when you are talking with someone you know well and you can just indicate something and know that the other person will follow your line of thought. It feels a little like what my character Cecilia says when she talks about her art in the novel: "It's like ripping open your chest. Or letting somebody—everybody, anybody—into your soul. Of course not everyone is able to interpret what is put in front of them. Or cares to. And that is a terrible risk too."

Your previous book, Astrid & Veronika, *centered on the friendship and experiences of two women. With* Sonata for Miriam, *you're writing mostly from a male perspective. Did you have any difficulties inhabiting that voice? What differences, if any, did you find in writing Adam's story, as opposed to those of Astrid and Veronika?*

Initially, it was terrifying. I worried endlessly, but for some reason he just wouldn't go away. And as soon as I began to write, it felt more and more natural. I listened to his story and I tried to write it down as it sounded to me. I came to like him very much, of course, and I hope that my readers—female and male—will be able to relate to his voice and that they will find it genuine.

Initially, Cecilia is somewhat of a cipher; we know she is a lover, perhaps a muse, but we don't know the details of her life. Adam gradually reveals elements of their time together, but then the novel shifts to Cecilia's perspective and we learn so much more. Why did you decide it was necessary to let her tell her own story?

I struggled with the technical form for a long time. In the end I felt that she had to be allowed to speak for herself. She is such a private person, an enigma to those who touch her world. Nobody else could possibly tell her story. When I had a first reaction from a [male] reader I was absolutely thrilled, and very relieved, to hear him say that Cecilia's part of the book moved him the most.

Your descriptions of the various locations in the novel are incredibly evocative. Do cities have particular personalities? Do they inspire specific moods in their visitors or inhabitants? How did you choose your locations for the novel?

Absolutely. The old cities of Europe are like old people to me. Friends. At the same time they are shaped by the people who inhabit them, of course. Under constant development, though often the changes are too gradual to be noticed during a human lifetime. Just like my character Adam, the city of Kraków came to me in a dreamlike fashion. I don't know why. But once I realized the city would come to play such an important part in the novel, I went there. I was unprepared for what it would be like. But just like Adam I walked the streets with an eerie sense of belonging. And I fell hopelessly in love with the city.

What is your least favorite aspect of the writing process? How have you developed as a writer since your first novel? In your work, what are you most proud of?

I like all aspects of writing. It's the *not* writing that is so hard. Days with no work done. Endless procrastination. I am proud of both my novels: proud that I have managed to finish what I started—and proud that I started. I think that I have possibly become a more conscious writer, and I am not sure that this is an entirely positive development.

Describe your ideal reader. What kind of reader are you?

I touched on this above. It makes me very happy when readers tell me that they cried when they read my book. My ideal reader responds emotionally to the text, takes it on board and makes it his or her own. This is also how I like to read. Sadly, I am finding it increasingly difficult to read without noticing language or structure. But when it happens, when the text finds its way straight into my heart, then it's a miracle.

Music is a prominent feature in your writing. In what ways, if any, do you find writing and music to be sympathetic arts? Do you listen to music as you write? If so, are there any particular artists or works you find yourself returning to?

I listen to music all the time, and most certainly when I write. I think that music evokes emotions better than any other art form. A piece of music has the inherent ability to transport you in time or geographically in an instant. With Chopin or Szymon Laks's music in my ears my study in Auckland became Kraków and Stockholm effortlessly.

What are you currently working on? How much preparation do you require before writing your novels?

Nothing. Writing and releasing this second novel was probably more of challenge for me than I realized while it was still in my hands. Now, I wander around in a state of bewilderment, not sure what to with myself. But sometimes during my daily morning walk the odd idea emerges . . . .

My second novel required a lot of research and reading, while the first novel drew mostly on material that was familiar to me. I have no idea where my next project might take me. Perhaps I should hope for a new challenge, being forced to enter unknown territory in some way.

Questions for Discussion

1. Olsson begins *Sonata for Miriam* with an epigraph by Szymon Laks, which reads, "But words must be found, for besides words there is almost nothing" (p. vii). What does this mean? How does it connect to the events of the novel?

2. In the beginning of the book, both Adam and Cecilia live on islands. How does the idea of an island work as a metaphor for their personalities? With that in mind, why is it significant that Adam eventually moves to Kraków?

3. In a very vivid way, Moishe embodies the truth that we all experience: our lives are filled with the ghosts of those we loved and lost. What was your reaction to the way he lives and how he honors the memories of Marta and others?

4. Wanda's decision to take Adam as her own certainly saved his life, but what effect did it have on her life? What did she gain from this choice? In particular, look at what she says to Adam on her deathbed. What does this tell us about her feelings?

5. Adam is presented with the impossible task of choosing between Cecilia and Miriam. Did he make the right decision? Why?

6. Like Adam, have you ever been prompted to action in pursuit of a family secret or unsolved mystery—to satisfy a question, seek out a person, or return to a place? What was the result?

7. Both Adam and Cecilia find emotional nourishment in their respective arts, yet Adam temporarily abandons his while Cecilia pursues hers to the exclusion of all else. Can art serve as an emotional refuge? Between Adam and Cecilia, whose approach do you believe is healthier?

8. What is the effect of hearing Cecilia tell her own life's story instead of having Adam tell it? Did it shed light on her decisions earlier in the novel? Do you blame her, sympathize with her, or both?

9. "Memories are unreliable," says Adam. "I carry memories that are now so worn I can't possibly tell if they are accurate. I'm sure they have been shaped by my handling" (p. 6). How does this statement affect your reading of a novel that is so rooted in memory? Do you have a similar experience with your own memories? Is it necessary for memories to be accurate, or does the act of remembering serve a deeper emotional purpose?

10. How do the poems at the beginning of sections I, II, and III connect to the themes of those sections? Express in your own words what you believe each poem says.

For more information about or to order other Penguin Readers Guides, please e-mail the Penguin Marketing Department at reading@us.penguingroup.com or write to us at:

Penguin Books Marketing Dept.
Readers Guides
375 Hudson Street
New York, NY 10014-3657

Please allow 4–6 weeks for delivery.
To access Penguin Readers Guides online, visit the Penguin Group (USA) Inc. Web site at www.penguin.com, or

www.vpbookclub.com.